For my dad, Patrick Boyd, who understood and believed.

*And for all the Wills, Chrises, Marks, Zachs, Jocks and
Tims who have touched my life.*

Thank you.

Copyright © 2006 by Maria Boyd
All rights reserved. Published in the United States by Alfred A. Knopf, an imprint of Random House Children's Books, a division of Random House, Inc., New York. Originally published in Australia by Random House Australia in 2006.

Knopf, Borzoi Books, and the colophon are registered trademarks of Random House, Inc.

Visit us on the Web! www.randomhouse.com/teens
Educators and librarians, for a variety of teaching tools, visit us at www.randomhouse.com/teachers

Library of Congress Cataloging-in-Publication Data
Boyd, Maria.
Will / Maria Boyd. — 1st American ed.
p. cm.
Summary: Seventeen-year-old Will's behavior has been getting him in trouble at his all-boys school in Sydney, Australia, but his latest punishment, playing in the band for a musical production, gives him new insights into his fellow students and helps him cope with an incident he has tried to forget.
ISBN 978-0-375-86209-0 (trade) — ISBN 978-0-375-96209-7 (lib. bdg.) —
ISBN 978-0-375-89404-6 (e-book)
[1. Conduct of life—Fiction. 2. Schools—Fiction. 3. Musicals—Fiction. 4. Theater—Fiction. 5. Homosexuality—Fiction. 6. Sydney (N.S.W.)—Fiction. 7. Australia—Fiction.] I. Title.
PZ7.B69245Wil 2010
[Fic]—dc22
2009039888

The text of this book is set in 10.5-point Goudy.

Printed in the United States of America
July 2010
10 9 8 7 6 5 4 3 2 1

First American Edition

WiL

Maria Boyd

Alfred A. Knopf
New York

Friday afternoon

Fight! Fight! Fight! Fight!

The words reverberated around the playground of St. Andrew's like the backbeat of drums at a live gig. The bell for the end of the day had echoed half as loudly fifteen seconds before and with it hundreds of boys had bolted out of homerooms, toilets, offices, corridors and bike sheds, sniffing the taste of freedom for another week.

Fight! Fight! Fight! Fight!

With each round of the chant more and more boys diverted from their quest for freedom and converged on the top oval. Everything was in place for the undertaking of one of the most revered rituals in an all-boys school: it was a Friday afternoon, the wind was blowing, there were no teachers around and two skinny Year 9 boys had been conned into believing that the other had said something about his mum.

I wasn't really into the mob fight thing, and I felt sorry for the two kids who by now probably wanted to bawl their eyes out and run home, but it didn't stop me loving the chaos it created.

Fight! Fight! Fight! Fight!

Right on cue the staffroom door swung wide open and out came security. Normally the PE blokes were the first to make it out, maybe because they were fit or maybe because they didn't want to miss out on the action. This time the charge was led by Waddlehead, aka Waverton, the deputy principal; he was old, but when he was wound up he could move. He powered across the oval flanked by a collection of year coordinators, and the rest of the teachers who hadn't already bolted to the pub for Friday-afternoon drinks. The door to Mr. No-Show Kennedy, the principal's office, remained shut, as usual.

The two skinny Year 9 kids, who had just managed to grab each other's shirt collars and kind of swing each other around, had absolutely no idea the posse, led by Deputy Waddlehead, had arrived. On instinct, most of the mob legged it upon their arrival. Unfortunately the two heroes took the mass exodus as a sign they were off the hook, and let go of each other's shirts, grinning stupidly at one another, completely unaware that they were seconds away from impending doom. Still grinning, they turned around to see where everyone had buggered off to. It was then that their eyes fell on the procession. Fear froze on their faces. Waddlehead deliberately slowed down on approach. Like startled animals they remained glued to the spot, mesmerized. No one did anything. Then, with the slightest lift of his chin and a razor-sharp point and curl of his index finger, Waddlehead seized his prey. The two prisoners turned back toward the school and made the long, slow walk across the oval.

No, it wasn't going to be a good weekend for those two buggers, no matter how much they swore to their mums that they were only sticking up for them.

The bus stop

The pack moved restlessly to the bus stop. They were unsettled, hanging around, waiting for something else to happen. They'd been left unsatisfied and were revved to the max. Because of the delay, most of us had missed our usual school buses. That meant there were even more of us squashed into a minuscule patch of grass just inside the school gates. We weren't allowed outside the gates because some moron had managed to get himself flattened by a souped-up Torana three years ago. The kid was fine now, but Waddlehead has never got over it.

I don't know why we had to suffer because some idiot forgot to follow his road rules. But that was the way things went at St. Andrew's College Lakeside. Lakeside was the name of the fake suburb where the school was built and, like most things at St. Andrew's, the idea of it being near any kind of water, let alone a lake, was bullshit.

I made my way over to where the boys were. Jock was causing havoc, as usual, running around trying to give any unsuspecting junior a wedgie. Tim, who was always up for anything, was Jock's accomplice. They'd worked out this routine: they'd cash in on their rugby-hero status and their size, single out a kid, make him feel really important, and then one of them, normally Jock, would move in behind and give the poor unsuspecting bastard a wedgie. The other kids would fall about cracking up, leaving the victim not knowing whether to join in or throw a complete hissy fit. The funniest thing was, though, once they'd readjusted themselves, most of them looked like they thought it was the best joke ever. Some even asked, sometimes begged, for Jock and Tim to do it to them next. Sad.

Jock looked up above his midget fan club and waved me over.

I shook my head and dropped my bag in our regular patch of grass. I noticed that one of the midgets had set up camp nearby with a music case half his size. He was definitely loving the Tim and Jock show—but only from a very safe distance. I was about to point out that he had to wait another four years before he'd earned the right to step on senior ground when I made eye contact. There was no way I could have told those eyes to get lost, they were too . . . trusting. Anyway, he wasn't hurting anyone and if he went over there and became the next victim, I wasn't going to protect him. I left the big-brother stuff to Jock and Tim.

If I thought about it, Tim and Jock were my closest mates, except for Chris. Chris was my best mate, but because he lived across the road from the school he'd never been a part of the bus bonding. This was something that had killed him in Years 7 and 8 but now, when we were whingeing about bad body odor on thirty-degree days, he just smiled and told us he'd be home relaxing after a cool shower in two minutes' time.

Jock, Tim and me had gone through the same routine since we'd begged our mums in Year 7 not to drop us at the school gates and kiss us in front of our mates. And even worse, be at the bus stop when we got home! Back then catching the bus was considered a rite of passage. But now, four years down the track, it was a pain in the arse. The anticipation of our own set of keys to a car, any car, teased all of us. One more year before we could be masters of our own destinies and do as many burnouts as we wanted.

At least this year was different. We had finally crawled our way up the bus chain and graduated to the top of the pyramid. The bus law of St. Andrew's may not have been written in the student diary but every St. Andrew's kid knew it. After five years we had earned the right to total bus control and power. We got on the bus first, the backseat was ours, and if anyone was going to peg something at someone it either came from us or was cleared by us. Only the Year 12 boys could pull rank. It was part of the unwritten student code, the one that teachers know nothing about.

The moon

I sussed the crowd. In the last ten minutes the rowdiness had grown to fever pitch. The fact that the buses were late increased that by a trillion.

On cue I heard the familiar rumble of the Lakeside Girls school bus. It was sitting at the lights about to begin the daily ritual of passing our stop. Just like us, the girls had their own bus law and their own code of behavior. They stared from the buses giggling, giving the finger or rolling their eyes in bored condescension. All three reactions were dependent on status and age, and were as predicable as ours. The main offenders were the Year 9s. This may have had something to do with them having reached puberty and being about ready to self-destruct if they didn't utter those romantic words, "Oi, you scrag!" or even better, "Get stuffed!"

The restless pack sniffed the air. Girls! The gate tilted under the pressure of the boys trying to get prime position to give the girls some hassle. Everyone was ready to take their part when the hugest, loudest blowout, like the farts of thirty giants, came from the back of the bus. The girls screamed and the boys pissed themselves laughing. This continued until it dawned on everyone that in fact the bus was stuck and, even worse, that they would all have to actually look at one another.

This was a clear breach of bus law, and everyone was a little unsure of how to act. Never one to let the boys down, I felt it was my opportunity—no, in fact my duty—to step in and save the day. I went over to Jock and whispered to him.

No way, Willo!

I smiled, extending my hand. **Wanna make a bet?**

Casually I moved to the curb. I strategically placed myself so no other member of the public could see—we did have the good name of the college to keep up. I faced the entrance gates, looking directly into the stony frown of the school's founder. The back half of my body was in full view of the stationary bus. Slowly, surreptitiously, I unbuckled my belt and grabbed the top of my school pants and boxers. I threw my head around ninety degrees on each side looking for the enemy, winked at the statue and dropped my pants. The first moon in full public view and in front of girls in St. Andrew's history. Or so I was told afterward.

It was over in a flash, pardon the pun. The impact of such a deed is such that too long means too much. As I rebuckled my pants, I looked up to see Tim nearly wetting his and Jock shaking his head shouting, **Good on you, mate,** as he reached into his pocket ready to square the bet. Admiration exuded from their every pore. There was noisy cheering from all the St. Andrew's boys. However, that was nothing in comparison to the Lakeside girls.

The bus looked like it had been invaded. Nearly the entire occupants had rushed to the St. Andrew's side. Those who weren't hanging out the windows screaming were bashing up against the glass. By this time the boys had bolted through the gate, others were climbing the fence yelling and bashing back. The bus driver could no longer be seen. He was surrounded by twenty teenage girls demanding their release.

Those girls who couldn't make it to the windows or doors were in the aisles, giggling, waving and then falling all over themselves when a St. Andrew's boy gave them a response. It was only along the back couple of seats that there was no movement. The domain of seniors. Some stuck their fingers up; those who were bothered called out **Loser!** and the rest ignored me completely. I wasn't worried. I was basking in the afterglow of the moon and loving every minute of it. I bowed to my fans on both sides. No doubt I did look like a major loser, but it's not every day you find yourself at the center of such adoration, even if it was more about hyper hormone levels rather than me.

As I looked up, I made direct eye contact with a girl sitting three-quarters of the way down the bus. I continued grinning, thinking the moon might be helpful in furthering Will Armstrong and Lakeside Girls relationships. A death stare that would have sliced concrete slammed that idea. And just in case I didn't get it, she rolled her eyes and flicked her head away so hard she nearly collected the girl next to her with her ponytail and green ribbon as she made her way to the front. What was her problem!

She must have been some sort of prefect or house assistant or something—that type of thing was big at Lakeside—because she was trying to get everyone to shut up and get back in their seats. And it wasn't working. Sucked in, serves her right for being such a brownnose and for having zero sense of humor.

It was right about then that another girl who actually was having a laugh started pointing, serious over-the-top pointing, at the school entrance. I just kept grinning and waving back. On the third attempt she gave up and stuck her head out the window.

The bus driver, you idiot! He's on the _phone_. . . .

It took me three seconds to get past the idiot comment and actually figure out what she was saying. Bus driver on phone. Bus driver not on the phone to his mates. Bus driver on the phone to dob in some loser senior who thought it would be a laugh to drop his pants at the Lakeside Girls school bus.

Instinctively I turned to face the principal's office and at that exact moment Waddlehead and Mr. Danielli, the Year 11 coordinator, left the staffroom and began heading directly toward us.

Willo, run! Willo! Get out of here!

It was Tim, thirty seconds behind as usual. But there was no point in running. It was too late and, besides, it wasn't my style.

The bus stilled instantly. The girl had obviously given the word. An occasional giggle escaped, silenced by a loud **Shhh.** The St. Andrew's mob needed no such warning. Each boy was programmed to recognize Waddlehead's walk from twenty meters away. Each boy also knew what it meant.

It became deadly quiet. The boys parted, creating a guard of honor delivering me to my fate. No way around it.

Busted. Busted bad.

Walk with me immediately, Mr. Armstrong.

Danielli's office

I watched Waddlehead and Danielli from behind as I followed them back into the school. Waddlehead was pointing to his watch and shaking his head, Danielli was doing a lot of nodding. They shook hands and turned in my direction. Waddlehead made laser-like contact, zapped me with one of the best teacher death stares of all time and hissed, **Monday!**

Instantly Monday was no longer a day of the week but the launch day of an attack.

I followed Danielli through the senior quad over to his office. This was not going to be good.

It's not that I like being in trouble. I mean, what difference does it make if your shirt's not tucked in or you have gel in your hair? It's not exactly helping the pursuit of world peace, is it? But the past few months had been different. I had well and truly moved on from "minor misdemeanors" and was heading for the expulsion end of the scale. The afterglow of the moon was fading fast.

William, come in, please.

The air instantly cooled in Danielli's office. The more trouble you were in the colder it was. I don't know how he did it, but it got me every time. Right at that moment, the mercury was around one degree and falling.

Danielli stood there silently, running his hand through his hair.

He was taking big breaths and letting them out really slowly. I figured it was best if I didn't look in his direction just yet.

The Danielli domain was more like an old library than an office. It was jam-packed with folders, books and magazines all about the same thing: ancient Greece. And if that wasn't enough, every single bit of wall space was plastered with pictures of old Greek guys. Not old guys like some Greek kid's grandfather, I mean really old famous guys who came from ancient Greece. I didn't know exactly who they were, but every time I was in Danielli's office I would read the same quotes about democracy and everybody having rights. Which was pretty funny considering every time I was in there I was trying to defend my own rights. Apparently they didn't count.

There was one particular guy who sat on top of Danielli's filing cabinet. He was made of cement and had no arms. The story goes that six or seven years ago one of the Year 12 boys stole it during muck-up day. Then, every day after that, Danielli received ransom notes and photographs warning that if he didn't meet the demands, the Greek guy was going to be smashed to pieces and poured into some Greek family's entertainment area somewhere in Marrickville. Everyone thought it was pretty funny. The statue even had his own Web site—until Waddlehead got involved, that is. It turned out that Danielli had been awarded the statue from a uni in Greece for some type of special study. Waddlehead said it was the "despicable action of an ignoramus who had forfeited his right to attend the college." Before one of Waddlehead's famous inquisitions fired up, the kid turned himself in. He was Danielli's top Ancient History Extension student, who anyone with half a brain could have seen was just having a laugh. Waddlehead, however, was all for expelling him before he could sit his Higher School Certificate. Parents were up in arms and kids were talking about protesting. Somehow Danielli calmed everyone down. No one had touched the statue since. But I got the impression that this time around no matter what Danielli said to Waddlehead, he wasn't going to be able to save me.

I heard a noise coming from the other side of the desk. I knew that was my signal to look up. I attempted to make eye contact, but all I could do was stare across the desk at the photo of Danielli, his wife and their three kids.

Danielli began to speak, shaking his head as he flicked through my ever-expanding file.

I'm going to have to ring your mother, Will. You leave me no choice. I spoke with her just last week to comment on some small improvements you were making. She is going to be so disappointed. . . .

Forget disappointed, Mum will be majorly, majorly mad.

Sit down, Will.

I began to list in my head the stuff I'd been involved in over the past couple of months. Busted for smoking in the toilets. But the point was I wasn't smoking. I know that's what everyone says but this time it was true. I mean, I had tried it a couple of times but I worried too much about my fitness level for soccer to smoke seriously. That time in the toilets I was truly the innocent bystander, catching up on the latest weekend "who did what" when Deputy Waddlehead walked in. Guilt by association. They were doing a crackdown and I copped a suspension with the real smokers. Mum eventually believed me, but only after she threatened to do what her mum did to her and make me smoke three cigarettes in a row. I pointed out that they had laws against that these days. She told me to be quiet and I was grounded for a month.

What else was there? They'd busted me for jigging but I don't reckon that was fully my fault either. One of the Year 12 guys who drove was able to leave after recess and he offered me a lift, so I took him up on it. I honestly didn't think anyone would notice. I got home, watched some telly and then spent most of my time on the guitar. My argument: it wasn't as if I was out terrorizing nanas or anything. So in the scheme of things it shouldn't have been that big a deal, although at the time Mum and Danielli didn't agree. Then there was the usual wrong haircut, no blazer, no tie stuff. But nothing that I thought was a really big deal. There was something else, though . . . I know there was something else . . . what was it?

How many times have you been called to this office in the past six months?

I shrugged. That's what I was trying to figure out.

I'll tell you. Six times in the past six months and this makes the seventh. Smoking . . .

But, sir . . .

Listen! Smoking, truancy, failure to meet deadlines in Modern History, underachievement in mathematics, repeated uniform and hair offenses, including that outrageous hair color, water-bombing the girls at the bus stop . . .

That's the one I forgot about, the water bombs! Even though that was definitely my fault, Jock and Tim were in it as well, it was just that they didn't get busted.

I know things haven't been easy for you over the past six months, and we have tried to make concessions, but you have pushed it too far this time. Really, Will, indecent exposure! Mrs. Young said the phones haven't stopped ringing with anxious members of the public alerting the school to a flasher on school grounds!

I bit the insides of my cheeks, trying so hard not to crack up. I couldn't help it.

Danielli's chair bounced off the wall as he stood.

You think this is funny?

I looked away. **No, sir.**

You very nearly single-handedly created a riot. Did you stop to think what would have happened if anyone had been seriously hurt?

But they weren't.

No, sir.

He picked up my file and waved it in the air.

And as for your academic performance, you continue to underachieve. This is Year Eleven, it's time to consolidate and move out from the rest of the pack. You want to secure a good University Admissions Index, don't you?

I shrugged again.

Well, don't you, Will?

Yes, sir.

The truth was I didn't have any idea what I wanted to do, let alone whether I needed a UAI.

Do you care?

I stared straight back at Danielli's family photograph.

Will? Look at me, please. Do you care? Honestly?

I thought about how I should answer. He said honestly, but the problem is they never want to hear honestly. I looked up at him.

Honestly, sir?

Of course honestly, Will.

Not really, sir.

Mr. Danielli shifted his gaze to the papers on his desk and didn't speak. He looked disappointed more than annoyed. See, they're the ones who can't handle the truth. Why did he ask in the first place if he didn't want to hear it?

Well, you know there will be severe consequences for your actions today.

Yes, sir.

OK, Will. He released a sigh that filled the entire office. **An interview has been scheduled for you at three-thirty Monday afternoon with myself and Mr. Waverton. Given her present circumstances, we will not require your mother to attend; however, I will be speaking to her by phone. If Mr. Waverton decides on the most severe form of punishment, she will of course need to be called in.**

He looked up from his papers. **I'll leave it up to you whether you tell her over the weekend.**

I hate it when teachers do that. Forty-eight hours of sick-in-your-gut guilt trip and they bloody well know it!

You do know that this latest escapade, combined with the other serious incidents you have been involved with, could mean permanent exclusion from the college?

I said nothing.

It is a very real and serious consideration.

Again nothing. He eyeballed me directly.

Do you have any idea how serious this actually is, Will?

Yes, sir.

He continued to stare and then his face crumpled into a frown. He sighed and his voice softened.

Will, you are better than this, and the real shame of it is that you have such leadership potential. You're well liked among the

rest of the boys, especially the ones who get a hard time. I know you've always been a bit of a larrikin, but you used to know when to stop. Now . . .

What the hell was I meant to say to that? Isn't a guy allowed to have one bad year?

He sighed again, disappointed there was no reply. **You've let a lot of people down, William.**

I was sorry I'd let him down; I felt even worse about Mum. All around I was feeling like crap. But I didn't know what else to say so I relied on the old standby.

Sorry, sir.

Yes, Will, so am I.

Planting the seed . . .
or not?

I had resigned myself to spending the whole weekend hanging out at home. The only other real option was the Holden House of Chaos, but Chris and the Holdo boys had gone away on one of their father and sons camping love-ins. I had scored an invite—I always did, and I usually went. Due to a lack of siblings, I liked being a Holden ring-in, especially when it meant I had a legitimate right to beat up the twins, but this was the first one since . . . well . . . this year and I didn't feel like it.

Will, are you ready?

Mum was at my door; faded purple overalls, bad paisley gardening hat, two pairs of gloves, mud-covered boots and one of the happiest faces I'd seen on her in a long time.

Come on, the soil is just about damp enough.

I tried hard to look enthusiastic. But being enthusiastic about having to put down your guitar and get off your bed to go and work in the garden with your mother on a Saturday afternoon is a very big call.

I grabbed the bad granddad type fishing hat Chris and I had bought as a joke in some ancient servo we'd rolled into on a previous Holden road trip, and followed Mum out the back door. The backyard was a decent size, decent enough for a pool, something I'd reminded Mum and Dad of every day of the summer holidays since

I first made it into Tadpoles at the local pool. They were dead against it. Said it was a *needless extravagance* when it only took us thirty minutes to drive to the beach. That didn't mean, however, that the backyard escaped being an Armstrong Family Project.

Ever since I could remember there had always been a big stretch of untouched grass right along the back fence. Mum and Dad always went on about how perfect it would be for a veggie patch. In seventeen years they'd never got around to it. That was until one day earlier this year when Mum came out dressed in exactly the same gear she had on today. That time she didn't stop at my door to ask for help; she walked straight out to the back shed, grabbed a spade and a scary-looking pitchfork and got started. Mum's not that big, and even though she's a yoga-head and looks pretty young for forty-seven, she's not exactly a teenager, but none of that counted because, man, she made a huge mess. Normally she would have been really careful about cutting up the turf and stuff, but that time she didn't care. She just kept hacking. Whenever I offered to help she smiled, shook her head and took another swing. She kept going every afternoon for three weeks, until there was no green anywhere in sight. It was just brown dirt turned over and over, like it had been ripped apart by mini explosives.

I had thought that was going to be the first Patricia Armstrong Solo Project but I was wrong. One night Mum came and sat on my bed and talked about launching the first Armstrong Mother and Son Project. All that digging must have done something good because it was the first time in a long time her eyes had come alive. There was no way I could refuse.

After the hacking came the fertilizing. This is where I got to be involved. We put in a whole pile of manure that smelled worse than anything Jock and Tim combined could produce, which was saying something, and waited until it didn't stink so much. Then last night Mum finally announced we'd made it to the planting stage and if I didn't have anything on, tomorrow would be the perfect day to get started. So here we were, just me, Mum and a whole lot of cow shit.

How has your week been?

It was no surprise that as soon as we got down to work Mum started firing questions. That's how she operates. It's all about sharing quality time together, and quality time in Mum's world means she asks the questions and I answer.

Um . . . Yeah, good.

My gut constricted. If I didn't play this right my hands weren't going to be the only part of me to be in shit this weekend. It could have been the perfect time to spill it all but I figured, why spoil the weekend when the next hundred were going to be hell? Then again, maybe it was better to tell her myself before Waddlehead had a go. Knowing Mum, she'd rate the fact I'd fessed up before someone else had to do it for me. But that would mean I'd have to spend the next thirty-something hours watching Mum look like crap again.

Bloody Danielli, he knew that giving me the *you can tell her before we do* option was going to mess with my head all weekend.

I watched Mum as she dug a small hole in the soil. She extended her hand, indicating for me to pass the tomato plant. She then gently shook off any excess dirt and carefully placed the seedling in the ground, making sure all the roots were where they should be. She'd swung into a gentle, soothing rhythm.

Mum . . .

Hmmm . . .

My gut constricted again. I couldn't. I wanted to but I couldn't.

Here. I shoved another plant in her direction.

She'd been edging along the ground like a crab. At this point she looked up, smiling, trying to blow away the hair that had fallen into her eyes without using a muddy glove.

So?

So! What did she mean, so? So I could be chucked out of St. Andrew's forever, and here's another tomato plant. So had Danielli changed the rules and secretly rung Mum and they were both waiting to see if I would confess?

I turned and pretended to look for another plant, feeling my face redden with every second.

So?

Her eyes were lasering holes into my back.

What was good about it?

The week, that's what she was asking about! Idiot! I could feel my guilty blush, something that had given me grief since the time I learned how to lie, wash away with relief.

I don't know. The same as usual, I suppose.

She looked at me for a long moment, spade in one hand and baby tomato plant in the other, then sighed.

Are you going out tonight? she asked after she'd planted the next seedling.

I'll probably head over to Tim's later. . . . The boys are planning a big night.

A Lakeside girl was meant to be having a party, some girl Tim was convinced was into him because she happened to say sorry when she stuck her artwork into his backside on the bus. I pointed out that her response was called everyday politeness. Tim, however, was certain that she wanted him, especially his backside.

Oh. Mum nodded. **OK then.** And she returned to the digging, shaking, planting, patting.

She stopped suddenly and looked at me again, her face a strange combination of a frown and a tight-lipped smile.

What?

How big a night?

I grinned back. **Relax, Mum, you can trust me.** She rolled her eyes and returned to her plants. We had both found our place again and for the moment everything was as it should be.

The weekend of guilt

It turned out I didn't go over to Tim's place after all. No real reason, but I figured I'd seen Jock and Tim make idiots of themselves plenty of times before so I wasn't missing out on much. Hanging out at home was pretty usual for me these days, so Mum didn't pick anything up on her maternal radar as she usually would have when there was drama in the air. Anyway, I reckon she liked having me kicking around the house.

Mum looked pretty happy with herself after our quality time in the veggie patch. She always loved a project, especially anything to do with the house. That was her thing, the house. Well, if I was really honest, it wasn't just her thing, it was her and Dad's thing. You couldn't separate the three of them. It was like the house was another member of the family.

They bought this place the same year I was born, and it definitely needed a lot of love. It was a dump! But that's what they wanted. They were into DIY way before it was on telly every night of the week. They wouldn't go anywhere near IKEA or Freedom, though, like normal people did. Oh no, the Armstrong family had to get up at the crack of dawn every weekend and go to garage sales, junkyards, smelly old nana stores and freaky run-down warehouses. They would spend hundreds of hours happily trawling through crap, dirty crap, and get really excited when they found something that no one in their right mind would even touch. Then they'd spend what was left of the weekend and every weekend after that getting whatever piece of junk they'd found back to how it was originally. It seemed like a huge waste of time to me. So I'd point out that we were in the twenty-first century in case they'd missed it and they'd both smile as if *I* was the idiot and keep sandpapering the latest 1850s table they'd scored from somebody's skip.

Stuff was different now, though, weekends were different. There was no junk in the backyard, and no Armstrong projects. Except for the veggie patch.

Which was how Mum spent most of Sunday morning, staring at the veggie patch over her pot of tea. Then she flicked through the weekend papers. That was weird. Before, she'd never allow them through the front door. She'd carry on that they were a journalistic disgrace and full of trash. Dad reckoned that was exactly the reason why you should buy them. They would sit at opposite ends of the kitchen table and throw smart-arse comments back and forth at one another that I had to dodge every time I went to the fridge. Now Mum'd actually go and buy the papers, sit down at the table in the same position and mutter as she flicked through them. I told her she sounded like a madwoman and she told me to get used to it because it was going to get worse with age.

Sunday nights always make you feel sick in the gut. It's that time when you remember all the crap for school that you haven't done over the weekend and are too tired to do now, which means you know you're going to get in trouble for it tomorrow. Or in my case, the fact that I had had all weekend to tell Mum everything before it hit the fan, but I hadn't.

But that's how the *you can decide whether you tell your parents* thing works. The whole time it sits in your belly reminding you that there's something you have to do. Then you go and catch up with the boys, kick the soccer ball around, hang out in your room messing with chords on the guitar, and you forget. But then you hear your mum singing in the kitchen, happy after working in the garden all day, or you watch her settle back with a glass of wine and a chick flick and that's when it hits. It comes up from your gut and sits in your mouth like you want to vomit it all out. Then you see that she's dressed in her home trackies she'd never be caught dead in anywhere else, lying on the couch laughing at the telly, and you know you can't. You just can't. So you walk back to your room and decide that, like most things lately, it's better to swallow and pretend that it's gone away.

Monday

Even though I knew it was all going to hit the fan with Waddlehead and Danielli this afternoon, I was more than happy to be entering the grounds of St. Andrew's. This was a Mum-Free Zone, which translated into a guilt-free, end-of-guts-churning zone. No, I knew it wasn't going to be pretty tonight, but at least for the moment I had escaped.

I walked past the bloke I winked at on Friday afternoon. He was the main man of the brothers, that's why his statue was stuck right where everyone could see it. The front of the school looked old, like one of those posh English boarding schools. Lots of sandstone and gardens, with a bell tower on the main building that made sure everyone in the area knew how important the place was. But it was the only building like that. The rest of the school was brick and concrete, and then farther back, so no one could see them, they stuck the demountable schoolrooms. That's exactly what St. Andrew's was like. It thought it was a cut above the rest, but when you really got down to it, it was just the same as any other school except that it was majorly strict, and the gates that kept us in were fancy gates.

I could hear the senior quad before I got within thirty meters of it. If someone came up with a way to take the sound from boys schools and make it into fuel, they would be a trillionaire and everyone could stop freaking out about the world's energy crisis.

I walked past the canteen and swung into the quad to find a full-scale handball competition in progress between Years 11 and 12. No doubt the brainchild of Tim and Jock, who have not yet come to terms with the fact that with the passing of every year they are moving away from childhood. They spend most of their energy trying to keep themselves at twelve.

No way that was out, man! I'm not going anywhere!

See.

Jock looked around for someone to acknowledge his cries of injustice and found me.

Willo! My hero! At which point he knelt down in his square, careful not to lose his position, and bowed.

Get up, you wanker. This is all your fault.

No way, mate, don't you go blaming me. I only offered five bucks. I didn't think even _you_'d be that cheap.

At this point the other boys joined in.

Whooo!

Nice arse, Will! How about you and me make a date for the toilets at lunchtime?

That was Tim—he always made it his job to push things too far. The other boys followed.

You'd want to be careful the boys on Oxford Street don't track you down.

Well, it wasn't as if the Lakeside girls were exactly throwing their phone numbers out the window.

Yeah, but I heard they were throwing up!

At this point they were falling into one another they were laughing so hard. I walked away to dump my bag to the sound of their triumphant hand-slapping, shaking my head as I went.

This was exactly how it had been for the past four years. The usual piss-taking and shaking of hands that greeted every morning. This was what I knew. This was where I belonged.

I came over and took my place on the line. Jock was still refusing to get out and no amount of yelling from the other blokes was going to shift him. Eventually the game started again. The St. Andrew's boys were a mixed crew, the seniors even more so because we had blow-ins from other schools for Years 11 and 12. It was one of the selling points in the glossy brochure the school tried to flog every year: *St. Andrew's, a college that celebrates diversity* or some such crap. And it was crap because most of the time all they ever went on about was making sure we all looked and acted the same.

Over near Danielli's office was where the wogs hung out. The wogs—a title they proudly gave themselves, even though Danielli always told them off about it, and he was one himself—were made up of mainly Italians and Greeks, with a spattering of Croatians. The skips—the Aussies, another title Danielli didn't like—hung out on the seats outside the senior classrooms. They were a combination of footy-heads, a few skaters (though normally the skaters would be with the druggies) and some classic yobs. The Asians took up what was left of the seats next to the skips. Danielli didn't get too worked up about the Asian label but he was always very careful about acknowledging their different nationalities. This was something Jock didn't figure out until last year, when St. Andrew's was running its own version of the Soccer World Cup. He couldn't understand why they didn't just have an Asian team and why they had to split into Korea, China and Japan. Then there were the Lebs—Danielli did get really worked up about that one. They hung out with the wogs and the skips, but mainly the skips, maybe because most of them played league, not soccer, who knows?

The goths and the druggies hid under the stairs of Harrigan

block. There weren't very many of them and they weren't exactly hard-core. The extent of most of their gothdom was their dyed black hair, although the talk around the quad was that one of the Year 12 guys actually wore white makeup and black lipstick on the weekends. And the druggies, well, they were pretty harmless and didn't do much more than smoke the occasional spliff.

That left the rejects, the kids who'd been backpackers all their school life, moving from group to group, not quite sure of where they fit in. Some of those guys ended up in the library, and others found each other and spent their senior years hanging out together anywhere they could find a clear space.

Us? We took up three long seats underneath the walkway from the quad to the library. We were mongrels, a hybrid of all the groups: a couple of footy-heads, soccer players, good students and musos, assorted Filipinos, Lebs, wogs and skips. We were the easygoing crowd. We did well enough at school, which meant we had to fight hard not to end up in the nerd category. At various times in our school careers we had all engaged in several incidents which guaranteed our *we may be smart but we are certainly not geeks* reputation.

Me, I was a soccer-playing skip, an honorary wog, though I'd pulled out this season. I just wasn't interested. Something else Danielli had given me a hard time about. I thought about what he had said about me being different from last year. I didn't know what to think about that. Danielli and the others reckoned I was going through a difficult time. No doubt they'd collect the moon incident as further evidence to support this finding.

I just wish they'd get over it. So I've changed, who cares! But I wasn't going to think about that until 3:30 p.m.

Period five

All right, boys, let's make a start.

Mr. Andrews, Advanced English. Cool dude even though he did have the same name as the school he worked in, a fact one intelligent individual or another reminded him of every day.

Andrews looked in my direction. He raised an eyebrow at me and said, **So I hear you have added more legend to the folklore of St. Andrew's College, Mr. Armstrong.**

That's one way of looking at it, sir.

I grinned at him, encouraged by the laughs around the classroom.

You only serve to demean yourself and others around you by engaging in such acts.

Instantly the laughing stopped. Dead silence.

Don't you think that young men get enough bad press without you adding to it?

Feeling more and more like a loser with each second, I gave it another go.

Come on, sir, it was just for laughs. It's not a big deal. I thought you'd at least get a kick out of it.

No, Will, I didn't. It appears that I happen to think far more of you than you obviously do of yourself.

Slammmmmmed!

Man, that came from left field. Normally Andrews was really

cool about everything. You could mention all the teacher taboos around him—girls, the fact that you haven't done your homework (for other subjects, that is), and parts of what you did on Saturday night—and you would only get a raised eyebrow. But not today. Well, he needed to go back home and have a look around for his sense of humor, because he sounded just like every other boring teacher.

So, gentlemen, if we can draw our attention away from Mr. Armstrong's amazing feat, we need, ironically, to get back to the idea of looking at the male stereotype and in particular the *young* male stereotype.

He was always on about that type of stuff, about the evils of pre-judging and typecasting, and insisting that we be critical learners. He reckoned young blokes got a bad rap in society, especially on those lame current affairs TV shows. I didn't know what he was so uptight about. It wasn't as if I was a walking stereotype who was going to go on some sleazy guy's bullshit TV show. He needed to lighten up. I'd tell him where he could put his irony . . .

Mr. Armstrong, do you intend to do any work this lesson?

Just not right now.

Yes, sir.

3:30 p.m.—
The punishment

Danielli and I had been waiting outside Waddlehead's office for over fifteen minutes. Every five minutes Danielli would stand up, walk three steps, stop, check his watch and sit down again.

I was spending my time staring at Waverton's name on his door, trying to remember when we first started calling him Waddlehead. I think it was back in Year 7. It was definitely Jock who made it up. He'd seen an old Batman movie and he thought that the Penguin was exactly like Waverton. Except he forgot that he was called Penguin and called him Waddlehead instead. Even though the name was wrong, the walk was spot-on.

The door opened. Instantly Danielli and I straightened to attention. Waddlehead stood with his back to us, facing the window. We walked in silently. Danielli pulled a chair toward the left side and melted into the background, leaving me to face the attack alone.

Sit down, William.

Waddlehead turned around and stared right at me. As he stared he clicked his mouth, like he was trying to get a candy out of his back teeth. Except I couldn't imagine Waddlehead having candy. It would be more like one of those really bad mints your grandfather offers you as if it was *some* sort of treat. The room was silent except for Waddlehead's *click . . . click . . . click. . . .*

Mr. Kennedy, Mr. Danielli and myself have been thinking

long and hard about the appropriate punishment for such a foolish and reckless act, William. However, it has become clear that we cannot view this latest incident, although quite spectacular in its severity, in isolation.

He waved my file in the air.

You, my young man, have been summoned to this office due to a long list of equally serious misdemeanors of which this latest degrading escapade is the final straw.

At this point he stopped the clicking and began to circle me.

Mr. Armstrong, you have come to the end. You will no longer run roughshod over our rules, our school name, our hundred-year-old traditions. It is time for you to step up and accept the consequences for such blatant disregard for St. Andrew's standards.

I broke into a sweat. My head filled with pictures of Mum's face.

Long pause. Expulsion is something that was considered very seriously.

I broke into a sweat of a different kind. OK, so no expulsion . . .

Very seriously. In fact I remain unconvinced that it is not the best course of action for everyone involved. Including you, William.

He slammed my file back onto his desk and it exploded on impact.

However, it appears you are a well-thought-of young man. A number of people wish to see you succeed and make something of yourself—Mr. Danielli being one of them. He has spoken very highly of your past academic performance, your popularity with the boys and your flair on the soccer field. He seems to believe that you can pull yourself back on track.

I tried to look over my shoulder at Danielli but Waddlehead had me trapped.

Is this confidence misplaced, William?

No, sir.

Your mother agrees with Mr. Danielli. It is one of the things she assured me of during our rather lengthy conversation this afternoon.

I really hated it when they brought Mum into it.

She is worried about you, William. She said you seem aimless and distracted. I suggested the school counselor but she said you were very reluctant to go. Quite frankly, it appears you have reached the stage where you need someone to step in and set very firm boundaries for you, as you clearly can no longer decide what is good for you and what is not.

Now, we are well aware you find yourself in a difficult phase at present. But you cannot use what has happened as some sort of excuse. God knows, life will always throw difficult things our way, but it is how we choose to deal with them that shows the real character of a man. However, we will not have it said that St. Andrew's deserts its troubled students. We have always prided ourselves on having an educational institution that caters to the whole child. As such, we see last week's act as a clear cry for help.

What the . . . ? All of a sudden I could see myself being carted off to some sort of loony bin.

We have decided to proceed in a somewhat unconventional manner. Actually, you have Mr. Andrews to thank for this suggestion. Yet another member of staff who has gone in to bat for you, William.

I knew Andrews was acting strange in English.

He tells us you're quite a gifted musician.

What?

William?

Traitor!

Is this true?

I couldn't tell where the hell this was going and it worried me.

I wouldn't say gifted, sir. Not like the next Jimi Hendrix, maybe more like . . .

He started clicking again. I quickly shut up.

As you are no doubt aware, William, the annual combined musical with Lakeside Girls is coming up and there is always a desperate need for volunteers. It is one of the highlights of St. Andrew's school calendar and an excellent public relations exercise. You, Mr. Armstrong, are to offer your services over the coming months as musician and general dogsbody . . . whatever role is deemed necessary. But not only that, young man, you will present yourself as an exemplary role model for the junior boys who, unlike you seniors, take the musical very seriously indeed.

He paused and rubbed his chin. Eyeballing me the whole time.

Make sure you thank Mr. Andrews for such a creative solution. This means you can give back to the college in a positive and productive manner—very progressive, very progressive.

A creepy grin filled his face. It was pretty clear that Waddlehead was very pleased with himself.

Well, what do you say?

NOOOOOOOOOOOOOOOOOOO!!!!!!!!!!!!!!!!!!!!! Years of cultivating my ranking at St. Andrew's instantly shattered. The school musical was always on the fringes of geeksville, but to be involved with the band was the lowest. At least when you were acting in the musical you got to hang out with the girls. The band was full of losers.

He continued to look at me. What did he think, that I was going to bend over and kiss his bloody feet? Mr. Andrews was going to die!

Yes, sir.

Yes sir what, Mr. Armstrong?

Yes, sir, I'll do it, sir.

Of course you will do it. You have no choice. It is now up to you, William. Do not let us down.

He put his face right into mine and spoke really, really quietly.

Be assured, my boy, if you do there will be no second chances.

Forget the fact that he had just stuck his head in my face, something he would have suspended any kid in the playground for. What bothered me the most was that Waddlehead really needed to suck on one of my grandfather's mints.

Yes, sir.

I looked over at Mr. Danielli and waited for my cue to get the hell out of there. He thanked Waddlehead for his time, shook his hand and left, looking as relieved as I did to be released. I didn't know what his problem was. I was the one who had just been signed up for two months' service in a sheltered workshop.

Home

Mum was waiting for me in the lounge room. This threw me completely off guard. Normally all Armstrong business was conducted at the kitchen table: holiday discussions, school reports, conflict resolution, the handing down of punishments, what you wanted from Santa Claus. I could hear the sounds of Joni Mitchell, one of Mum's sad but serious CDs, coming from the stereo and knew it wasn't going to be pretty. I stood in the doorway and tried to prepare myself.

It was quiet except for Joni's voice, quiet and dark. Mum had lit all the candles and she was sitting right in the corner of the sofa, surrounded by cushions, with her feet up, holding a glass of wine. She was staring, looking at nothing, with her head resting on her knees. She looked really, really small and I felt really, really bad.

I knew what was coming. Sometimes I wish Mum would just lose it and yell and scream, but she has to talk about everything. She'd been extra vigilant since January. It made me think of Mad-Eye Moody in those Harry Potter books. But instead of looking for the evil bloke Voldemort, she was looking out for any sign of me losing my grip.

The *he who can't be named* in our house was Dad. Actually, that was not strictly true; I think Mum really wanted to talk about Dad but I wouldn't. I didn't see the point. It made her upset and it made me feel like an idiot. Clearly not an enjoyable experience for anyone involved.

Anyway, Dad was not the topic of conversation this evening; the fact that I had exposed my backside to the world was.

Why, Will?

She hadn't moved. I shifted from the doorway and made my way to the other end of the sofa.

Why, Will? she asked again.

What do you say to your mum when she asks you why you dropped your pants in front of a hundred adolescents in full view of the general public?

I don't know, Mum. I didn't think about it. The bus was stuck, everyone was looking around waiting for something to happen, it was Friday afternoon, Jock dared me, and it seemed like a funny thing to do at the time. Millions of reasons. No real reason.

She hung her head for a few moments and then put down the wineglass.

Mum, it doesn't mean I'm a dirty pervert. It doesn't mean you have to put me in therapy. It doesn't mean anything. I just did it, that's all. I promise you it will never happen again.

She looked so sad and tired. By this time my feeling like a complete loser had multiplied by infinity.

But it's not just what happened on Friday, Will, can't you see that? The past six months have been full of moments when you do something stupid or dangerous and then you say you're sorry but in another few days you go and do something stupid again. And whatever we . . . I . . . try to do doesn't seem to have any effect.

She turned and looked straight into my eyes.

Do you have any idea how close you came to being expelled today?

My gut started its second workout for the day.

Do you? It was only because the other teachers spoke on your

behalf that you weren't. I tried to tell them that maybe I could have been more supportive or—

No way, Mum, it's not your fault. . . .

I'm worried about you, Will. Really worried, and I'm not sure that—

This was way out of control! She had nothing to do with it.

Don't be worried about me! I know Waverton reckons I need to be in a loony bin, but I honestly just did it for a laugh.

But you seem so—

I cut her off. No poor William session, not tonight.

Honest, Mum, I'm fine. I know I'm seventeen years of age and too old to be doing such stupid things. But it's going to stop from now on, I promise.

I just kept plowing through, trying to mop up her hurt with my words.

Look, they've given me my punishment and that's going to make sure I don't have a life, so you don't have to worry about me getting into trouble ever again. Really!

She cut me a look that said that if I ever did anything that stupid again, she would pack me off to my grandparents' house, the land of nana smells, bed by eight o'clock and side-part comb-overs—and that's just my grandmother.

I knew from past experience that her silence meant I was finally winning some ground.

You should see what I have to do over the next two months! Operation Musical will be a death sentence for my social life. Every friend I ever had will disown me for fear of being infected.

The eyes lifted.

So you see, Mum, when you think about it, this might have been the best thing that could've happened to me.

The eyes flashed.

If you think for one minute that I am going to buy that rub-bish, then you have clearly underestimated my intelligence.

Mum . . . I don't know what else to say. I don't know why I did it and I am really sorry. And I am really, really sorry you're so upset.

And I meant it, I really did. She's the first in my top three of things I'm most sure of: my mum, my guitar and my mates.

I know I've been in a bit . . .

Her eyebrows jumped nearly to her hairline.

. . . a lot of trouble lately, but . . .

She interjected. **I'd stop now if I were you.**

But I knew she finally believed me, and a tiny half-smile flick-ered on her face.

Serves you right, William. I hope you're condemned to being a social reject for the rest of your teenage life and you have to spend every Saturday night looking after your mother.

That's not very motherly of you, Mum.

You're bloody right it's not.

And about three seconds later a pillow landed square in my face.

Elective music

There were very few things about school that were cool, but without a doubt you would have to rate the music rooms and the music-room dwellers in the cool category. I don't mean full-on geeks who only played in the school band. I mean those of us who were in bands and made our own music. Now that was where the cool factor could be found.

Take the school music room: there were virtually no desks or chairs; electric organs, speakers and leads covered the few that were lying around. It didn't matter if you only knew three chords, you could just turn up the amp and blast yourself into a different hemisphere. And the best part about senior music was the fact that the teachers basically left you alone to do your own thing, so as not to stifle your creativity or something.

Music: it's all good.

I made my way over to plug in my amp. Chris was already there. He and I had started hanging out together in preschool. I was put there so my liberated social worker mother could go off to crusade for the needy, Chris because he was the first of five and his mum needed a break. We've hung out ever since. He's the closest thing I've got to a brother. And he's a good bloke, the kind of bloke that people look up to and leave alone. Ray Casey had been running a book from the beginning of Year 11 working out the odds for who was going to get school captain next year; Chris had been a consistent favorite. And he can play the drums like a demon.

He looked up from his drum kit. **Mate! St. Andrew's hero!**

Shut up. I've already had enough of that hero crap from Jock.

But you are! The twins didn't shut up about you when they got home. You're rating higher than *The Footy Show* in our house.

You're a day late, Chris. I heard all of this yesterday. Where the hell have you been anyway? Your best mate is about to be kicked out of the school and you're Mr. No-Show.

Cut me some slack, a guy's allowed to be sick, isn't he? Dad made his famous Holden Camping Goulash and it had me squatting behind a bloody bush all night. Everyone else was fine but, man, I was lethal! Mum reckoned I should stay at home, but if I'd known that I was going to miss out on the Willo and Waddlehead show, I would have made a real effort and let everyone else suffer.

Thanks for your support, I said sarcastically as I strapped on my guitar.

No problem. So what did they give you? Saturday detention until you finish Year Twelve? Cleaning out the toilets with a toothbrush? Or my personal favorite, the gum-scraping, graffiticleaning happy participant of the St. Andrew's cleanup day?

I shook my head. It was pretty obvious Chris had never been in real trouble his whole school life.

Worse. Waddlehead got me right in the gonads. He's making me be part of the school musical. Can you believe that? Some sort of bloody experiment for disturbed students. If he has his way I'll be director, star performer, on the box office, selling lime cordial and striking the set on the last night. And he reckons that's getting off lightly!

By this time I had plugged into the amp, which meant I had limited room to move. But the more I got wound up the more I walked around like a madman. I was like one of those Energizer bunnies trapped in a shoebox.

Imagine having to spend the next two months hanging out with those jerks. The bloody band, Chris! You know it's going to be made up of Brother Patrick's Year Seven brass-playing try-hards. And the performers will be worse! No Year Twelves do it because they have to study. So that cuts out guys who'd do it for a laugh. I don't know anyone in Year Eleven who's trying out for any of the guys' parts and they are probably all puncey anyway. And let's not even think about the hundreds of screaming Year Seven girls. They'll be wetting their pants with excitement just being in the chorus, deluded into thinking it will be their chance to be spotted by the producers of *Australian Idol* or some other really sad reality-TV show.

I was on a roll now and wasn't stopping.

And you know what's even worse? It was Andrews's idea. Do you believe that? Andrews betrayed me big-time. Bastard.

Chris was looking at me calmly, a slight smile on his face.

Oh, I don't know, according to some of the boys there are some rather fine babes who get involved in the musical. If I had more time and wasn't such a coward I'd volunteer my services.

That was an angle I had not considered.

Come on, Chris! I begged with no shame. That would be so cool. At least then I wouldn't have to suffer alone.

Chris picked up the drumsticks.

Nah, mate, you're on your own this time. Besides, even if I did, I wouldn't be doing it to hold your hand. He threw the drumsticks up in the air and caught them. I'd be doing it so I could have the chance of holding the hand of someone far prettier than you.

I ducked the drumstick he pegged my way and threw it back at him.

Shut up, you wanker, and play.

A very different kind of Friday afternoon

Even for St. Andrew's, news of my punishment had sped around the school in *Guinness Book of World Records* time. The fact that I was condemned to a life of geeksville for the next couple of months proved to be a constant source of amusement for everyone in the senior quad. And they seized every opportunity to remind me of my sentence.

It was another Friday afternoon and the quad was filled with anticipation of the weekend: football matches, barbecues, parties, drinks and girls, not necessarily in that order. Boys moved among the groups, hearing who was going where and what the best offer was. There's nothing like that Friday-afternoon feel, except when your mother's grounded you and your English teacher has condemned you to *death by musical*.

Hey, Willo, are you going to Dion's brother's party? Should be a big one.

I shook my head. Mum had made it pretty clear that I wasn't going anywhere for a very long time.

No, mate, can't. All part of the St. Andrew's payback.

At least he had the decency to look sorry for me.

I turned around and saw Tim running toward me. This was going to be a completely different story. You could see he was already buzzing with the thought of the weekend.

Hey, Willo! He jumped over my bag and landed right in front of me. **There's a new guy from Melbourne who's just made it on to the footy team, Mark someone, top footballer . . . big bloke . . .**

I looked at Tim blankly, waiting for him to get to the point.

Anyway, he's invited the footy boys to watch the game at his place tonight. We asked if we could bring some ring-ins, soft soccer heads like yourself.

Great, so the new guy's been here for two seconds and he has more of a life than I do.

He's a good bloke, you'll like him. It'll be a pretty quiet one, though, because we'll be saving it up for Saturday night.

Right. Dion's brother's eighteenth. I bet your new man got an invite to that as well.

It's all about the keg and the girls, Willo, all about the keg and the girls. He nearly broke his face he was grinning so hard. **The Jockmeister's putting on the recovery on Sunday.** He slapped me on the shoulder. **Man, everything about this weekend is good. We are going to *parrrteee!***

This was obviously a rev-up. I waited, saying nothing.

What?

His face was like a five-year-old's who's been accused of doing something he didn't do.

How can you have given me shit all week and forgotten now?

What, Will? I don't know what you're talking about!

Hey, Willo, Timmy boy, what's up?

Whereas Jock, on the other hand . . .

Willo's giving me grief for telling him about the weekend.

He even said it like a whingeing five-year-old.

Jock looked at me and grinned. He put his arm over my shoulder and spoke to Tim.

Mate . . . mate, you know what this means?

Tim shook his head.

This means young William here gets to hang out all weekend with the geek freak show. That would be *sooooo* much fun. Don't you wish we had to do it too?

By this time Tim was finally getting it. He burst out laughing and high-fived Jock.

Ohh. Right. Yeah mate, we'll miss you. But don't worry, we'll be thinking of you when we're out pulling chicks and having beers. Don't you worry, mate. Two *loooooooong* months will pass in no time.

They high-fived each other again, slapped me on the back and laughed all the way to the bus stop, waving as they went.

I left them to it and decided to head over to Chris's, the only place I was allowed to go apart from school and home, and even then only in half-hour intervals. I could still hear Jock and Tim carrying on at the bus stop. If it were either of them in trouble, I'd give them heaps too. It wasn't not being able to go out that bothered me so much. Since the accident I'd been happy to come to school, see the boys, go home, play the guitar. Considering I had been up for anything last year, I suppose it was a pretty big change, but the boys accepted it. They'd throw an invite my way and then leave me alone.

That's what got me most about the Save Will Armstrong campaign. I was happy with the way things were. I'd been making a real effort to do nothing and the musical screwed with all of that.

The end of freedom

It was Saturday morning. Early. Too early, but the time for the crime had already begun in Mum's book.

Come on, Will, it's time to go.

She stood in my bedroom doorway dressed in jeans and a T-shirt. At least I could be grateful that she wasn't wearing that kooky gardening outfit. I was still in my boxers, mucking around with a new tune that had been hanging around in my head.

No it's not. The auditions don't start till nine.

Her hands were already on her hips: no chance for negotiation.

I don't care. You're going to get there early and you are going to offer any assistance that you can to the teachers, especially Mr. Andrews.

That man was going to die.

Mum, I don't need to get there this early!

I negotiated my way around her and made it to the bathroom. She followed close behind.

I *don't care*. Will. You're going whether you like it or not. And more to the point, this is the last time I will be dropping you at school. You can ride your bike in future.

Great. Most people were beginning to beg their way into taking their parents' cars out and I had to ride my bike. Dad's car sat in the garage waiting for someone to make it useful. But even if I could drive it I probably wouldn't.

All right, Mum!

I closed the bathroom door and started to brush my teeth. A sense of dread filled my gut in anticipation of the day's events. I tried to concentrate on the girl factor. I mean, what girl wouldn't be interested in a sensitive, guitar-playing guy like me? I love to throw words around, and that's what girls are meant to like, isn't it, the fact that a bloke can talk to them? I can talk and play music . . . and I'm all right at football and soccer.

I'm not ugly either. I mean, I don't look in the mirror and think, *Man, you should lock yourself up you are so damn ugly.* I reckon I'm pretty average. Lots of brown happening: brown hair, brown eyes, brown skin. I've had the really bad growth spurt that most blokes go through, all legs and arms and not much else. That really is when you're ugly. When you can barely coordinate your feet with your legs, your arms with your torso, your head with your chin. No, I've definitely moved from the *my nose doesn't fit my face* stage. Suppose I'm fairly tall, tall but not huge. Mum reckons I've got big dreamy brown eyes, but that's what mums are like.

William!

Her voice came loud and clear through the wooden door.

You have exactly five minutes to get out of that bathroom, get changed and get yourself in the car!

I looked into the mirror. Who was I kidding? My mother was driving me to school on a Saturday morning so I could play music with a bunch of socially retarded geeks.

I may as well have *loser* printed on my T-shirt 'cause no girl was going to rate a guy like that.

The freak

Mum lightened up during the car ride to school. She was going off to have her hair cut in what she called a *funky* hairdressers and have lunch with "the girls." She made the *you may actually enjoy it* speech, as anticipated, and drove off before I could deliver my comeback.

Which of course meant it went round and round my head as I made my way around from the school's side entrance. Andrews had made a big deal of saying they would be the only gates open and if we didn't make it on time we'd be locked out. Fine by me!

I walked up through the Years 8 and 9 yard, picked my way over the squashed banana and oranges that had probably been used as ammunition in some *You're not the boss of me, wanker!* battle and made my way to the hall. St. Andrew's Hall was like some kind of museum, full of old stuff and old smells. The walls were covered with ancient dusty photos and wooden boards that showed the names of school captains, sporting captains and guys who had fought and died in wars. The best thing about the photographs was the really bad haircuts and the size of the footy shorts.

Underneath the boards were rows of cabinets full of old trophies. Above the stage there was a giant banner proclaiming ST. ANDREW'S COLLEGE: RICH IN TRADITION FOR ONE HUNDRED YEARS. It was meant to inspire us, or that's what Waddlehead told us at assemblies. I didn't get what the big deal was. So the school'd been around for one hundred years. It was old, that was all it meant; old, old-fashioned and dead boring.

There was the definite sound of strangled cats and elephants' farts coming from the guts of the hall. I wasn't the only one who'd arrived early, except this lot had probably begged their parents to get them here at this hour. I tried to think positively. Chris was right. I just had to concentrate on the girl factor. I moved into the hall to do a recce . . .

Oh no! Seriously bad! Seriously, seriously bad. There were no girls anywhere.

I was completely surrounded by blokes! And not just any blokes but the singing, performing, dancing kind who were willing to give up their weekends for the sake of their art. I scanned the room, wanting one glimmer, one spark of hope.

Where were the girls, the babes, the chicks, the hotties?

Nowhere!

Wall-to-wall blokes.

I looked over at the band. Yep, just as I had predicted. Year 7, 8 and 9 try-hard geeks. Even worse, junior try-hard geeks who didn't know they were responsible for the strangled cat and elephants' fart sounds I'd heard five minutes earlier.

I was two seconds away from making a really fast exit. I knew Mum would freak but I'd talk her around. There was no way I could survive this! Just as I was about to leave I saw some of the band nudging one another. Chris was right: all these younger guys seemed to recognize me. They'd probably heard about my punishment before I did. There was no way I could bolt after being seen. It would get back to Andrews and he'd be straight on the phone to Waddlehead or worse . . . my mother.

What can you do but try to act casual and make it clear you're pissed off with being there? That part wasn't hard.

Hey!

I turned my head ever so slightly, enough to acknowledge the little geek's existence, but nothing more than that.

Aren't you the guy who mooned the Lakeside bus last week?

I raised my eyebrow in response.

Everyone in Year 7 thinks you're so cool. Not that many of them talk to me, but even on Friday . . .

I turned to face motormouth straight on. A bit of hero worship was OK, but if I didn't find the off button soon I figured I'd blow the role model thing within two seconds of being in the hall. I located the sound at just above waist height. It was the geek from the bus stop. Staring at me with exactly the same eyes and exactly the same trusting expression. I checked out the rest of him. He could have been the poster boy for geek, minus the heavy brown glasses with milk-bottle lenses. He had a deadset bowl cut, what could only be Kmart jeans that fell to his ankles and school socks worn with ugly white sneakers. The kid was lost in a time zone all his own. No one would dress like that for real.

I turned away but he'd attached himself to my right elbow.

So you're going to be in the band then?

Looks like it.

That's great. There aren't a lot of seniors. Actually, there aren't any, apart from you.

I looked out beyond the orchestra pit and into the hall. Yep, the kid was right, I was surrounded.

It's mostly just Year Sevens, Eights and Nines in the band. But we sound good. Brother Pat always says so. He thinks we

sound as good as the band he plays in and he's been playing for years.

He drew his first breath in thirty seconds, then hit me with: **You can hang out with me if you don't know anyone else.**

The comment drew my head toward the kid like a magnet. I stared at him, looking for any trace of irony. There was none.

I think I'll be right, mate, thanks.

He stared straight back. There was definitely something about this kid's eyes . . . like they belonged to someone ancient. He wasn't going anywhere.

I play the trombone. What instrument do you play?

I lifted up the case I held in my left hand. **The guitar, mate.**

My dad plays the guitar. My dad's cool. He's really cool.

I felt my head go down instantly. Winded like one of those destructo balls had slammed me in the gut. This type of stuff just comes up sometimes and grabs you by the balls. You never know when it's going to happen and how to protect yourself. My silence must have had some sort of impact on the motormouth midget 'cause he actually shut up for three seconds. Just as the little guy was going to start up again I grabbed my guitar and looked around for Andrews. I knew I had to check in with him before he made a big deal of me being late.

I nodded in the little guy's direction and he moved into a huge wave in return. I hoped for his sake his father was as cool as he said he was, because the kid was definitely going to need some help.

Mr. Andrews of St. Andrew's

Well, well, Mr. Armstrong, I see you made it.

Andrews was grinning like he had won the lotto and the woman who presents it on telly. I was beginning to look at him in a very different light. He was enjoying every millisecond of this.

All right, sir, I'm here so let's not make a big deal of it.

On the contrary, Mr. Armstrong, it is a big deal. Here you are on a Saturday at our hallowed and revered school, reinforcing its good name as an educational institution that produces outstanding and accomplished young men such as yourself.

English teachers speak such crap!

Give it up, sir.

No, no, I think we should all give recognition where it is due and celebrate the fact that you are indeed here, regardless of the reason why.

Sarcastic bastard. I looked around to find we had an audience. The teachers were loving every minute. Even some of those little geeks were smiling, but my snarl quickly whipped the smirks off their faces. Fortunately I was saved by the unlikeliest of heroes, Brother Pat.

Brother Pat had been kicking around St. Andrew's since Chris's dad had gone there. Which was a long time ago. He'd been principal for years and was now retired. After he'd hung out in Ireland for a year, he came back to St. Andrew's to help out. Music was his thing. He was a bit like a musical Santa Claus: old, fat and great with kids. He could play any musical instrument he picked up and his singing practices were a St. Andrew's institution.

Hello, young Will. It is wonderful to see such enthusiasm from one of our most high-profile senior students. This will be an excellent example to the younger students.

Yes, he's good at setting examples, Brother Pat.

I threw Andrews a look, and turned to Brother Pat for more praise. Well, why not, it had been a little scarce over the past week.

You're an accomplished musician, so I have been hearing, William. Guitar, isn't it?

Yes, Brother.

A fine instrument. Perhaps not as well regarded in classical circles but still an excellent instrument. Fancy yourself the next Paul McCartney, eh?

Probably more of a Daniel Johns, Brother, offered Mr. Andrews.

Daniel Johns, Brother puzzled. **Isn't he a football player?**

Not this one, Brother.

Anyway, son, I'm proud of you. Giving up your time to be here on a Saturday so as to help with the auditions. You know, Will, I'm going to be relying on your help over the next couple of months. This is a great opportunity for you. We can't have your mate Christopher Holden thinking he's the only one with leadership ability.

First Danielli and now Brother Pat. What was it with this leadership crap? But he was wrong about Chris. He didn't rate himself. I reckon that was why all the rest of the boys did—because he didn't.

Right, well . . . Brother scanned the geeks. **We'll have you set up next to that young chap who plays the trombone.**

Yes, Brother.

I walked over and started to remove my one prized possession from its place of residence. At least I could still retreat into its world when it all became too much.

Cool, they've put you right next to me!

I looked up to see the geek grinning at me. I grimaced back. Could this possibly get any worse?

Andrews called us to attention.

All right, everybody, let's meet in five minutes to give a running order for the day. I'll then hand over to Brother Pat to announce the choice of musical for this year! There has been a great deal of debate and the final decision was quite contentious.

The teachers really needed to get a life!

Many of us thought we should be looking at more contemporary musicals, more up-to-date, but Brother Patrick was insistent that the oldies are always the best. And I have to say I think I agree with him.

Come on, sir, what's it called?

This came from one of the midgets with a clarinet hanging out of his mouth. The kid couldn't be serious!

Brother Pat and Andrews exchanged smiles. It was becoming pretty clear to me that everyone in the hall seriously wanted to know. Brother Pat moved forward.

All right then. He raised his hands and the hall stilled.

It's called *The Boy Friend*. It was written in 1954 and is set in 1920s France in a girls' finishing school. It is what we call in the business a pastiche. . . . But that will do for now.

What do you mean a girls' boarding school? Do we have to wear dresses?

This came from one of the guys in Year 10, who was cracking up like it was the joke of the century.

Andrews stood up, frowning. Brother Pat indicated for him to sit down.

Finishing school, not boarding school. And, if you wish to try out for one of the girls' parts, Paul, by all means do. The rest of the boys will be auditioning for the roles of the dashing young men who accompany the ladies.

The hall cracked up and gave Paul crap. He shrank a little in his seat. I was sitting stunned in mine.

The Boy Friend?

There was no way I was going to be part of a play set in the last century that was about boyfriends! They couldn't be serious.

It was official—even before Jock and Tim found out—my life was over.

The Boyfriend!

I didn't get it. Lakeside was meant to be full-on into *girls can do anything,* including producing Australia's first female prime minister, so why the hell were they doing a musical set in the 1920s written in the 1950s, set in a girls' finishing school, called *The Boy Friend?* And as for Andrews and all the stuff he carries on about in English, well, he's just a hypocrite.

Not that I gave a crap. I zoned out again, securing the ear plug of my iPod in my left ear. I drifted in and out, but you didn't need to be an extension 2 mathematics freak to figure out the plot. It was the usual boy meets girl, boy and girl can't get together because of parents, but boy and girl get it on anyway and everyone loves everyone by the end.

Will, get rid of that MP3 player or I will take it. Sit up and show the courtesy of listening.

Nobhead. It was an iPod, not an MP3 player. I pulled the plug out of my ear, shoved it in my pocket and glared at him.

Not in your pocket, in your bag. We don't want you to be tempted.

He couldn't be serious!

Come on, sir . . .

Now!

I shoved past the midget circus, thinking of ways I could humiliate him back. The wanker had managed to get everyone to focus on me. I threw them one of the filthiest looks I could and sat where I left my bag.

OK, Brother Pat got to do the fun part. It is up to me to spell out the reality of putting on a show in eight weeks.

What!!! I got the distinct impression I was the only person reacting because eight weeks was way too long.

Yes, eight weeks. It is not a long time, people, and it is going to mean a whole lot of hard work and dedication.

This guy must be on some serious drugs.

You will be required every Saturday for the entire day and when it comes closer to the performances, you will be expected to attend on both Saturday and Sunday.

The man's dreaming.

Every Wednesday afternoon until six o'clock you will be working in your specialized areas, which means leads, chorus, band, dancers, et cetera.

Thank you, God! Detention. It made the water-bombing even more worthwhile, and Waddlehead would never let me get out of it.

As for the actual performances, they will take place on Friday and Saturday night consecutively.

I put my head in my hands. This couldn't be happening! My life was ruined. I may as well just give up right now.

If there is anyone in this hall, and I mean anyone, who cannot meet these commitments, then I need you to stand up and walk out now.

The hall was full of silent noise, the type that comes from people shifting in their seats with their coats rubbing against the backs of the chairs. I felt Andrews and the other boys looking in my direction for the third time that day. But this time I wasn't going to give him the satisfaction.

58

Right, then. That means one hundred percent commitment from one hundred percent of you. Congratulations, you are all part of the musical team.

The hall sadly but predictably erupted into applause.

As for the girls . . . Silence. **Yes, I thought that might stop you. As you can see, the teachers from Lakeside have been here this morning. Their auditions will be happening tomorrow.**

So let's get started. Those wishing to audition for main parts over here with me, please. Chorus over to Ms. Sefton and the band with Brother Patrick, of course. We will be working right through until lunch. Good luck, everybody.

I watched everyone move to their areas. The hall was buzzing. The geeks circled Brother Pat, eagerly awaiting instructions.

Brother Pat pointed at me and waved me over. As I approached I heard him saying something about me being his *right-hand man*.

Isn't this right, Will?

Speechless, I nodded my reply.

Will, here is your score. The younger lads can work with photocopies.

Right at that moment, if someone had said stay on earth and be Brother Pat's right-hand man or be taken by aliens, stuck in an isolation chamber and piped with '80s power rock ballads for half a decade, I would have willingly and knowingly chosen the alien abduction.

Not funny

Andrews was tying up the first half of the day and looking very pleased with himself.

Lunch, gentlemen. Be back here by two-thirty sharp.

I walked over to the front of the orchestra pit where he'd been sitting watching and taking notes for the past three hours. His head was down and he was scribbling something next to the guy's name who had just sung really badly.

Sir?

Yes, Will?

How do teachers know who you are without looking up?

Why no girls?

He didn't look surprised in the slightest that I'd asked him this question.

I thought I explained this morning. He smiled at me. **Disappointed?**

I'll give him disappointed. Couldn't the idiot see that these auditions were a stupid waste of time? The whole idea was stupid.

It doesn't make any sense. Obviously these guys have got to be matched up with the girl characters, right?

He nodded. **In most cases, yes.**

Then why aren't they auditioning at the same time?

He turned around, hitched himself up onto the stage and put his feet on one of the chairs in the orchestra pit.

Truthfully, we thought it might be easier for all involved to audition in a setting that wasn't threatening, so we decided on single-sex auditions for the first phase. Don't you think you'd be even more nervous if you had to perform for the first time in front of a hall full of Lakeside girls? His tone changed. Or perhaps, considering your latest escapade, you may have experienced no difficulty whatsoever.

That's not funny, sir.

I saw just a hint of surprise on Andrews's face.

Come on, Will, it was a joke.

I decided to break my silence. Let him know he'd stuffed up my life.

You stitched me up, sir.

He smiled again. Was this bloke actually enjoying this?

I'm sorry you feel I betrayed you, Will. That wasn't my intention.

That was it? That was all he had to say? He was sorry if I felt I'd been betrayed? It had nothing to do with how I bloody felt and everything to do with what he had bloody done. If he hadn't opened his mouth, I probably would have only copped a term's worth of detentions. They wouldn't have thrown me out of the school, not this time anyway. I could feel my heart hammering against my chest, and I was clenching my teeth.

Come off it, sir, how was I meant to react? Because of you I've got the longest punishment in the history of Australian education. What did you expect me to do—come up and tell you what a great guy you are?

I could tell by his eyes that he was surprised at how pissed off I was at him. Andrews rarely lost his temper; it was one of the things the boys liked about him. But there was something inside me that wanted to push him till he lost it. That wasn't happening, though. He seemed to get more calm the angrier I got.

He said really softly, **I know it seems like I'm singling you out at the moment, Will, but I honestly think you're going to get a whole lot out of this experience.**

He paused for a moment and looked at me. He went to say something and then stopped. Then he started again.

Will, I didn't want you to lose everything you had built up for yourself over the past four years, and Mr. Waverton was seriously considering asking you to leave. Which is the last thing your mother needs at the moment and the last thing you need. I know it's been really hard for you. This was my way of trying to show you my support. Last year you were one of the best—

Every bloody time they always got back to this! I cut him off before he could get started. **That was last year, sir! Things are different now! Everything is different! I'm different!**

I turned and left him sitting on his pedestal.

The Dumpster

I walked out the door, right out of the playground and into the car park. It was only when I was at the gates that I started to slow down. I hadn't felt this wound up in a very long time. I *was* different from last year; so what! I wished people would just get over it.

There was no chance of me going back into that hall. I didn't give a shit what happened, it wasn't worth the grief. I couldn't open the gates because they had two big fat padlocks wrapped around them. The only escape route was out the driveway past the industrial estate.

I'd made it halfway when one of the skips I was passing began to spew up rubbish. I stood and stared. Maybe I really was cracking up. But it was like the bin had gorged itself with the entire contents of the tuckshop and was now upchucking the lot.

It was at this point that I heard the cries for help. I approached the skip and began to investigate.

I threw an **Oi.**

Help!

I walked closer.

It really stinks and I can't get out!

I definitely was not in the mood to be a hero, I just wanted out. What idiot gets himself stuck in a Dumpster anyway? He deserves to stay in there.

Help!

But what could I do, leave the kid in there and wait for the garbage truck to completely masticate his body and give the poor garbage men a heart attack?

All right, mate. Take it easy. I'll get you out.

Easier said than done. This took a little more strategic thought than dropping your daks at a bus. It wasn't that the Dumpster was so big, it was more that it was curved and the little guy couldn't get any leverage to haul himself out.

I scanned the area and found a bunch of milk crates surrounded by piles of cigarette butts. The not-so-secret teachers' smoko area. Waddlehead should have a go at them just like he does at us about all the crap in the playground. I grabbed a couple of crates and chucked them into the Dumpster, hoping it wouldn't cause the kid more injury.

See if you can put them on top of each other and then just hurl yourself up onto them.

I could hear his efforts and gathered that this kid had not had his ugly but useful growth spurt and was not used to hoisting himself out of anywhere. Just as I was thinking I was going to have to climb in there and give him a leg-up, which I really didn't want to do, I saw two hands grip the edge of the bin and then two eyes peer out over the top. I knew those eyes. They belonged to the freak I met earlier. It all began to make sense. Of course he would be the one that even the geeks would pick on. Every group has its pecking order. This kid had *Pick on Me* tattooed all over him.

By now he'd managed to throw his right leg over the edge and was holding on tight, not really sure how to proceed. You could tell the kid was scared brainless of falling out but just as scared of falling back in.

It's all right, mate. Just throw your other leg over and you'll drop to the ground. It really isn't that far.

The two eyes attempted to make contact again. This time they didn't seem so ancient, just plain frightened.

I'll come and stand underneath you and try to break your fall.

I think I heard a tiny whisper. **Thanks.**

I maneuvered myself underneath where I thought he would fall and braced myself as I would for a tackle. Within a second the kid dropped. We both fell to the ground. It wasn't a pretty sight, but neither of us had broken any bones.

He quickly got up and beamed at me.

I knew you and I were going to be friends.

Yeah, yeah. Let's not make a big a deal of it. I just happened to be passing by, that's all.

My dad reckons that things always happen for reasons, the kid replied, attempting to match my stride and having to skip a little as a result. **Synchronicity. Have you heard of it?**

Of course I've heard of it. I'm not in Advanced English for nothing, you know.

I didn't know what he was on about but I wasn't about to admit that to a Year 7 geek who had just escaped from a Dumpster.

Man, you stink real bad.

He ducked his head like I'd hit him square in the gut. But it also got his mouth moving again.

All the kids reckon I stink, that's why they put me in the bin in the first place, because they reckon that's where my home is. They reckon I get all my clothes from a bin too.

He took a breath.

No, mate, that's not what I meant. I mean you stink from being in the bin.

He lifted his head up.

Come on, I don't know you well enough to hang crap on you.

That doesn't stop the other boys.

Yeah, well, I'm more mature than those little dropkicks. If only Andrews could hear me now. Listen, mate, you can't go back to rehearsals smelling like that. If you do, your life at St. Andrew's will be over. You'd better go home and change, or at least give someone a ring to come and pick you up.

He was shaking his head as soon as the words were out of my mouth. He seemed more uptight about this than actually being thrown in the skip.

No, I live ages away and I can't ring Dad 'cause he's gone out for the day. Can't I come with you?

No way, I'm out of here!

His eyes nearly popped out of his head.

But haven't you got to stay after lunch too? Brother Pat will be expecting you.

I'd forgotten about the Brother Pat factor. He'd be pretty let down if I bailed, especially after all that role-model stuff he'd gone on with this morning. The last thing I wanted was to encourage the kid, but I couldn't let him go back inside like that. The teachers would get involved and make a real thing of it. This would only ensure his life would be hell for the next couple of months.

Listen, my mate Chris has got three little brothers, he'll have some clothes you can borrow.

Chris who?

Chris Holden.

He cut me off before I could say anything else.

I know him! He's the guy who always speaks at assemblies

and stuff. You're mates with Chris Holden! Cool! OK, let's go. This is so cool.

All right, settle down. It's no big deal.

But apparently to the little guy jumping around beside me it was.

Getting chucked in that bin was the best thing that has happened to me since I came to St. Andrew's!

This kid's life was definitely sad.

The Holdens

The little guy gave a running commentary as we made our way over to Chris's place.

In between nodding and throwing the occasional *yep, nope* in his direction, I tried to remember what Chris and I were like at his age. I'd forgotten how hard-going we found the first couple of months at St. Andrew's. That move from primary to high school is pretty big and I don't reckon many kids handle it half as well as they pretend to. At primary school you think you're kingpin; then you arrive at a place where you're nothing, a tiny, insignificant, lowly bit of nothing. You're bullied into standing down the front of the bus, harassed into lining up all of lunchtime to buy food for ten people you don't know and threatened into giving over your lunch money to some guy who's got his fist in your face.

In the beginning Chris and I just used to take off. It wasn't planned or anything, it was like we both knew. We'd get out at lunchtime, look around for the teacher on duty, who was normally yelling at some kid to pick up papers, and then, when no one was looking, we'd walk out the gate. Dead easy. We'd arrive at the Holdens' right in time for lunch. It was funny, it was only now that I wondered why we didn't get in more trouble considering they were always going on about legal permission to leave school grounds. Chris's mum never said anything. She'd just smile and ask us if we were hungry. Then she'd leave the room and make a phone call.

Yes, Helen, they are here. Can you pass that on? No, they'll be fine. I'll ring Patricia.

Helen was Mrs. Young, the school secretary; my mum said she was a saint, and she was for Chris and me because it must have been her who smoothed it over with the year coordinator. We would have done that at least once a week in the beginning and then we kind of stopped.

I reckon it was around then that I developed this thing about the Holdens' kitchen. It's one of the places I rate in my top ten. It's big and warm and cozy and filled with great smells, and there is always someone in there, guaranteed. Five males multiplied by hunger equals a lot of time spent in the kitchen. The Holdens definitely have an open-door policy—everyone is welcome. That's why I knew it would be all right to take the kid there.

I could see the screen door hanging open as always, like it was expecting company. Surrounding it was a runners' shop full of shoes. Once Mrs. Holden made the rule that you washed the floorboards, all of the floorboards, if you dirtied them, the boys figured it saved a lot of time and work if they left their shoes at the door. It worked for the floorboards, but it meant there was always a whiff of bad feet as soon as you came into the house.

I walked straight in with the kid hopping behind me. There was never any door-knocking at the Holdens'. Chris had obviously had a shower and then not bothered to do much more. His hair was sticking up all over the place; no shirt but he had his footy shorts and socks on. Typically he only looked mildly surprised.

Willo, mate! I thought you had detention duty at the St. Andrew's gaol. Did you stage a breakout?

I raised my eyebrow and indicated the kid behind me.

Oh great, so you've corrupted a juvenile as well.

Chris stepped forward and shook the little guy's hand.

Chris Holden.

The kid was barely able to contain himself.

Yeah, I know you. You're the guy who's going to be school captain next year.

Chris looked confused. **Right, well, you had better come into the kitchen then.**

I think you'll find the little guy here has had an accident. It might be better if he goes to the bathroom.

Bad wording on my part—it sounded like Chris had to go and grab one of Jess's nappies.

I mean he had an accident with a Dumpster.

Chris was watching the kid rather than me. He didn't know what I was on about but he could definitely see that the kid needed some assistance.

Sure. You're just lucky everyone's out doing the Saturday sports shuffle, otherwise you'd be surrounded. It's only Jess and me here.

Jess? the geek asked.

Yeah, replied Chris. **She's the number-one girl in my life.**

The freak obviously intended to get as much information about Chris Holden, St. Andrew's pin-up boy, as he could.

You mean your girlfriend?

I think Chris might have even blushed.

No, mate, she's my two-year-old sister. But don't you think I should be the one asking the questions?

The freak had no problem starting up.

It was lunchtime and the kids in the band asked me what I had for lunch so I told them and then they started to follow me, so

I ran down the driveway and that's when they got me and threw me into the Dumpster.

They what! I interrupted.

I'd spent all day with those little peewees and there was no way they could have picked up this kid and thrown him anywhere.

Well, that's not completely true. Dad always says to tell the whole truth because you always get found out.

So?

Well, they kind of backed me into the corner and told me to get into the Dumpster.

And you did? It was really hard not to put *you idiot* on the end of that question.

I thought they'd leave me alone.

Did it work?

Yeah it did. They ran as soon as I got in. I stayed in there for another five minutes to make sure they'd all gone and then I tried to get out but I couldn't.

And that was when yours truly came along, I told Chris. **I thought maybe our friend here could borrow some of James's clothes, you know, just for the weekend.**

The kid suddenly looked very uncomfortable. Clearly something was wrong. What could be worse than getting harassed by a bunch of geeks and thrown in a bin?

I don't want Dad to . . . His voice trailed off.

What could be worse? Your dad finding out.

He already worries about me. He's had to come up to school already. He keeps saying that if it happens again he's going to put me in a different school. But I like it at St. Andrew's.

This kid really was sad!

Chris looked him square in the eye.

Listen, you've got to tell someone about the kids hassling you. Your dad's right to be angry with the school. They should do something about it.

The kid began shaking his head.

They haven't done it for ages. It's just these band kids. They want to show off that they're tough.

I was ready to go and find the little jerks and lock all of them in the Dumpster for the next month. I bet this was the first time any of them had had a chance to pick on anyone. I bet they were always having the crap kicked out of them.

Well, if you hang out with Will here there won't be any more trouble. But you still have to do something about those clothes. What will the guy who's got to play next to you say?

That's me, I said, more enthusiastically than I'd intended.

Right, well, forget about that, Will stinks already so he wouldn't notice, but what about the other guys?

The freak's eyes grew in his head again and he shrugged.

We could throw your jeans and jacket in the wash and dryer and I'll drop them off on my way to footy?

The kid's whole body lit up with hero worship.

Yeah, and then I could get changed and Dad wouldn't have to know.

The kid took the clothes Chris gave him and went into the bathroom. I knew this meant I was going back to the hall to finish my sentence. Just knowing that Andrews was there wound me up again, but I figured I could ignore him.

So, Will, it looks like you've made your first new friend from the musical. Your mother will be so happy!

I chucked the geek's shirt at Chris and yelled out **Hurry up!**

The geek left Chris's place the way he'd arrived—talking.

You're the best, Will. I always knew Chris was a really nice guy. No wonder he's going to be school captain. And look at these clothes! These are the coolest clothes I've ever worn. Dad reckons I shouldn't worry about how I look. He reckons you have to stand on your own and be an individual. It's not that we're poor. That's what all the kids at school think. They think I dress the way I do because we don't have any money. We do. Dad's a university lecturer and we live in Balmain, looking over the water. It's nice. He paused, looked away and then continued. **Heaps nicer than around here. Apart from Chris's place. His place was cool.**

I had started to listen after he had finished with his Chris Holden Fan Club routine. This kid's parents had to catch up with the times. It was all right for them. They were safe in their hippie suburb living their hippie lives.

Listen, when we get back to the rehearsals, take it easy, act cool.

Yeah, Will. I get you.

We walked in silence but I could feel that he was gearing up for another question because he became all jumpy again.

Will?

Yeah?

My name is Zach. Zachariah Cohen.

I stopped walking and held out my hand.

Nice to meet you, Zachariah Cohen.

I cut his smile short.

Come on, Freak, we better bolt, otherwise Andrews will have my balls.

The smell of guilt

Good to see you made it back, Will. I was beginning to worry you had reneged on your responsibilities.

Andrews hadn't backed off since my outburst. But like I'd decided earlier, I wasn't giving him the satisfaction.

Come on, sir, as if I would do that.

I slowly eyeballed every one of the tiny geeks in front of me.

In fact I met Zachariah Cohen during the lunch break. He found himself in a bit of trouble and needed some help.

The geeks weren't old enough or skilled enough to hide their fear.

Andrews's face crumpled into a frown.

Was there a problem, Will?

Andrews became teacher serious, letting me know he would step in if I needed him to. But to dob these guys in would have meant playground death for the Freak. No. I just wanted them to live in fear of me putting them in it.

Nothing that I can't fix myself, sir.

The geeks' restlessness increased. They looked at their music, in their bags, at their instruments. One even put his head into his lunch box. Anywhere but in my direction.

Well, let me know if I can offer any assistance.

The smell of guilt escaped like silent deadly farts.

Don't worry, sir, I will.

And with that we got on with the rehearsals. I just managed to look over my shoulder and saw the Freak giving one of the guys the finger before he picked up his trombone. There was hope for him yet.

Still at auditions—
the new guy

Andrews and Ms. Simons, the teacher from Lakeside, had narrowed it down to a top ten for the male leads. Thank God for that! The band actually sounded pretty good considering they had just learned the songs this morning. I'll give the geeks that, most of them could play a tune.

We had exactly an hour to go and it was going to be a very long hour. I stretched out my arms as far as they could go, threw my head back and sighed. It must have been really loud because when I lifted my head, Brother Pat was staring right at me.

When you're ready, Mr. Armstrong.

Sorry, Brother.

We were up to the final four who were trying out for the lead role, some guy called Tony. One or two of them had been all right. But in my opinion not good enough to get up there and play the lead without causing themselves and every single person involved in the musical severe embarrassment. I settled on my guitar, ready to have my eardrums bleed again. Possible Tony number four. About five notes in it became pretty obvious this bloke was different from the other wannabes. Whoever he was, he could sing.

Every person in the hall stopped and stared. Not only could he sing, but he didn't look like he could sing. He was built. Not gym-junky built, but like an AFL player and nearly as tall. It didn't seem to fit. I had no idea who he was. He had to be a senior and, since I hadn't seen him in our year, he had to be in Year 12. But they'd been warned off the musical this year.

I watched Brother Pat and Mr. Andrews exchange looks.

Thank you, that was excellent. How about having a go at another of the tunes?

Brother Pat waited for all the geeks to scramble behind their music stands.

Ahh, William, would you mind preparing yourself.

The boom from his voice nearly blew me off my seat. I was definitely over being Brother Pat's right-hand man. We played the song through once and then the new guy joined in on the second go, taking it all in his stride. He mucked around when it got to the sappy parts about how much he loved this girl he'd met for two seconds and he was actually pretty funny.

Good! Good! I'd like to see you, young man, once this is over.

I kept my ears open trying to get the guy's name, but Andrews and Brother were tying everything up and finally seemed to be in a hurry to get out of there. No complaints from me.

Mr. Andrews stood on stage and called for silence.

All right, thanks, everybody. A big hand to those boys who got up and sang today, we know it's never an easy thing to do. And an extra big thank-you to the members of the band. It was a long wait between singers but you all did very well.

The geeks shone like their newly polished instruments.

Even you, Mr. Armstrong . . .

Wanker! I smiled a fake smile and bent down to start packing away my guitar. As I did a pair of jean-clad legs moved in and out of my vision and at various intervals jumped up and down in front of me. It could only be one person. I looked up slowly.

Do you think Chris has left the bag of clothes? You don't think he's forgotten, do you? If he's forgotten then Dad is going to find out and he'll contact the school and then it will be really bad. It's not that I'm not grateful, I am, it's just that . . .

I continued to stare, wondering how someone with such a small head and mouth could manufacture so many words in such a short amount of time.

I've got a great idea. How about you go out and have a look?

Zach stopped. Well, I was going to but I was waiting for you to come out too . . .

He trailed off and his eyes bulged like they had at Chris's place. This kid was waiting for a bodyguard and I was it.

All right, mate, just give me a little room to get the rest of this stuff away.

And with that he pogoed his way over to Brother Pat and offered to help with the cleanup. I shook my head. What chance had this kid got?

OK, Freak, let's go.

It was about then that Brother Pat moved into the frame.

It appears your young friend here has offered to pack away the music stands, Will.

The Freak nodded enthusiastically.

And I'm sure he'd love some assistance.

I gave Brother as much of a smile as I could and then threw a death stare at the Freak. Not only did I have to give up my Saturday but now I was cleaning up as well!

Hey, Willo.

It was Chris, dressed in full gear, ready to go and smash some heads.

Here's the little guy's stuff.

He smiled at the music stand in my hands. **Good to see you're helping out.**

Get stuffed.

Just at that moment the Freak bounded over.

Hey, Chris. Thanks heaps. I'll just go and get changed before Dad gets here. Will, I'd really like you to meet my dad. Do you reckon you could hang around until he comes?

I looked at him and then at Chris, who had a great big smile on his face.

Watch out, mate, you might have yourself a one-man fan club there.

At least he's not going to campaign for me to be school captain.

Can't hear you, mate, got to go.

Chris bolted out the door, his football studs echoing throughout the hall.

The Freak positively skipped out of the toilets. He looked around and then pointed over at the entrance to the hall.

Hey, there he is!

I could only assume that the *he* was his dad. One thing I knew was that I was definitely not meeting his father; it had been enough of a spin-out day without that.

Listen, mate, I've got to go. But I promise I'll meet him another time.

Disappointment flickered over his face for the briefest of moments and then evaporated.

It's all right, Will. There'll be plenty of time to meet him. Just think about it, we get to hang out for a whole two months.

Brilliant! Just bloody brilliant!

Wednesday-
afternoon detention

Waddlehead had made the fatal mistake of announcing to the whole
school that the first combined rehearsals for the musical would take
place this afternoon in the St. Andrew's hall. The school went into
a frenzy. It was one of the few occasions when boys actually hung
around after the bell and, just coincidentally, outside the entrance to
the hall.

The room for detention was diagonally opposite. It looked
like they would have to open two more classrooms, so many people
turned up. I figured I would have to spend enough of my time over
in the hall, so I wasn't exactly full of the same excitement. Jock,
however, who'd been nailed for taking an incident in the wood-
work room involving a jigsaw and a junior a little too far, was very
excited.

We were outside the H block waiting for the teacher to arrive.
Even Chris had decided to hang around before we were called into
sixty minutes of torture by lines and silence.

So, boys, who's on?

It was a Wednesday-afternoon regular, Dion.

Danielli, I think.

Shit!

I knew what he meant. Some detentions could be a laugh de-
pending on what teacher was on. Danielli meant this week was

definitely not going to be a laugh. Jock, however, was oblivious to everything except the girl factor.

Come on, mate, you must have seen them!

He hadn't stopped harassing me since the bell had gone for admin.

You've been involved from the start. What were they like?

Jock, I told you they weren't there.

Come on, Willo, you can't keep them all to yourself, that's being selfish. Were there any real hotties? You know, the dancing, wear their hair in a ponytail type.

The *what* type? The boys cracked up laughing.

I heard that the head of Green House is a real sort.

Who?

Jock ignored the question.

You know, man, when I first found out about your punishment I thought it was slack. I really felt sorry for you, man, but now, when I think about it, it's not even a punishment.

Yeah right, Jock.

No, think about it. This has the potential to be a major babe fest. The ratio of cool fellas to hot babes would have to be in your favor. You said yourself that the auditions were full of Year Seven geeks.

That was the band, you idiot!

Whatever! He pointed to the other group of St. Andrew's students who were staying behind on a Wednesday afternoon—except this lot were there voluntarily. **As if those nobheads are going to be in with a chance.**

Most of us just let Jock crap on; Chris, however, would always arrive at a point where he'd tell him to pull his head in.

Mate, don't you go to the movies? Don't you watch people get

paid millions for what they do on-screen? They would've been the types who were in school musicals.

No way, man. You can't tell me that Russell Crowe was ever in a puncey school musical.

Yeah, he was. He was in the Coffs Harbour production of *The Sound of Music*.

Incredulous, Jock scanned the group, looking for support. **No way! I don't believe you.** We nodded back at him with fake serious faces. **Have you seen him in** *Gladiator*? **A bloke like that could never . . .**

There was no way Chris knew whether Russell Crowe was ever in a school musical, but he was enjoying watching Jock's reaction as much as the rest of us.

Jock refused to change down a gear.

The point I was trying to make was that Willo here could turn the punishment from hell into pick-up palace. And when he does, I want him to spare a moment's thought for his mates . . .

What Jock didn't realize was that his mates were now firmly focused on the arrival of the Lakeside Girls bus, which was making a slow procession up the side entrance.

A nice sensitive guy like myself could get on really well with one of those dancer types. I don't want one of those arty types, though, they think too much. . . .

Jock was the only St. Andrew's student in the yard who had missed the bus come to a halt at the hall.

Jock!

No, Willo, you've got a—

Just shut up, mate, and have a look!

The bus doors opened. Silence filled the middle quad.

There she is! She's the one I was talking about, the head of Green House!

The entire occupancy of the quad, including the girls, turned and looked in our direction.

Shut up, mate!

You bloody idiot!

Don't point, you loser!

We stood captured in the spotlight, victims of the Jock factor. This time a moon was definitely not going to help the situation. I decided the best way to handle it was to turn around and pretend that I wasn't there.

At that point I heard a familiar *Wooooooooooooo!* fill the quad and the boys started slapping Jock on the back. I turned around to see the backs of the girls as they made their way through the doors of the hall, laughter trailing behind.

You missed it, Willo! Jock's in love. The head of Green House just blew him a kiss.

OK, boys, that's me out of here. Chris nodded at Danielli, who was making his way over from his office, detention folder in his hands. **Thanks for the show, Jock!**

Danielli looked over his extra-large coffee. **This must be the first time all year that everybody's here.**

He looked over at the hall and turned.

Any particular reason?

The boys put their heads down. Some grinned.

Well, it's all right, fellas, I'll make sure that you're out of here on the dot of four-thirty. I hear that's right about the time rehearsals finish up.

Danielli, he was all right really.

The special
assignment

It was Friday, the last period of the week. We were always restless in this lesson and seized any opportunity to get out of having to do any writing, or anything that resembled work.

I'd kind of gotten over being angry with Mr. Andrews. I was doing my time and there was nothing I could do about it. I was pretending to be listening to him but really I was watching the clock.

He was on one of his favorite topics.

So tell me, gentlemen, what is the stereotype of the footballer? Jock!!!

The class cracked up. Even if Jock had been there, he would have had no idea about the pun. Even Andrews had a grin on his face.

Let's steer away from names, please, especially when they aren't here to defend themselves. And we all know that a stereotype can't be just one person. Don't we?

I don't know about that. Jock was pretty much a walking, talking stereotypical footballer.

Chris, what do you think?

Strong, big thick neck, dumb, sexist, violent, drinks beer . . .

There was an outcry from the footy-heads in the room.

No, no, no way, sir! It's changed from that.

This was coming from the winger on the St. Andrew's winning side.

But we are talking about a "type," Dion. Chris plays football so he wouldn't be saying that about himself.

Groans and mutters from the class.

Yeah, but he's different! Let's get back to Jock again—he's heaps more entertaining.

And the class cracked up for the second time.

That's why stereotypes are so dangerous, sir, isn't it?

It was a deliberate windup and as expected the class turned on Chris again, yelling out, **Teacher's pet!** and **Brownnose!** Chris grinned, exactly the reaction he planned.

Do you think there is a positive image of the footballer, Dion?

If you're talking about real football, then yeah, there is.

Groans started up again,

Urr . . . soccer isn't real football!

Get over it!

Pull your head in!

Let him speak, please, gentlemen. Andrews silenced the group and looked in Dion's direction.

Yeah, I think you could say loyal—

Someone else interrupted.

That's rubbish, sir! No footballer in any code has loyalty anymore, it's all about the cash.

Mr. Andrews told everyone to shut up. Only he would never say shut up—he only had to hold his hand up and the boys stopped.

All right, Dion, continue . . .

Loyal, educated . . . More reactions from the class. **Umm . . . fit, quick.**

OK. What about if you start to compare different codes? Is the same true of league or rugby or AFL?

The whole class started up now, reigniting another of St. Andrew's long-standing traditions—football versus soccer rivalry.

No way, sir, soccer players are gentlemen in comparison to league players . . .

Yeah, that's because they're soft!

They are not soft, you idiot!

What would you know?

Loser!

I sat back and watched. At least this was making the lesson go more quickly. It was exactly the type of stuff Andrews loved to do in his classroom. Friday, period six, was about the only time he ever let us have a full-on discussion, though. Mostly he was too concerned with getting us through the syllabus. He was smart, though; it was these types of lessons and the fact that he let us have our say that kept everyone on side for the rest of the lessons. I think he did genuinely want to hear what we thought, but it wasn't only that. He was big on getting us to see the world, and the people in it, in different ways. I just wasn't sure it was going to work with some of the boys, especially the league players.

I only started to pay attention again when I heard the familiar groans from the class. It could only mean one thing—another assignment.

Your job over the next month is to collect images or representations of stereotypes and catalog them. What type of medium? Negative or positive? What messages are being given to the general public? How are these images deliberately manipulated by the media and to what purpose? I want you to create an extensive

portfolio and then write a 1,500-word reflection on what you have learned about the power of stereotyping.

Everyone moaned and carried on into their bags as they sifted through empty lunch-box wrappers, personal stereos and PE gear to find their diaries.

Just as I was lifting my head he started on me.

I see you are awake, Will. I have a special task for you.

Every head in the classroom stared in my direction.

I want you to explore the stereotypes that surround those students who involve themselves in the school musical. '

The class erupted into laughter mixed with **Sucked in!** and **Ahh, Willo's special!**

He couldn't be serious!

Come off it, sir, you can't do that! No one else has been given a special assignment. That's not fair.

Oh no, I think it is very fair, especially considering I am giving you the duration of the musical to complete the task, which means you have at least a month longer than the other boys.

Sir . . . I . . .

He walked out of the class, leaving me swearing at his fading back. What was his problem? As if I didn't have to give up enough of my precious time for that bloody thing already, let alone have to study it.

If he thought I was going to do it he was wrong.

A car ride into uncharted waters

I woke up on Saturday morning to the sound of rain ricocheting off the Armstrong entertainment area. Mum was in her trekking-in-Nepal gear attacking the veggie patch again. She came in dripping and spent half an hour in the shower. She emerged from her room and began to walk around the house mumbling to herself. There was definitely something up. I thought a morning with her plants was meant to make her feel better.

My mum radar said to keep right away, as far away as possible, which I did in my bedroom with my guitar. But considering any minute now she would be at my door telling me it was time to go and be king of the geeks, I thought for once I'd be prepared. If only to give her absolutely no opportunity to sit on my bed and have one of her talks.

Will, it's nine-thirty, haven't you got to be at school by ten?

She stood in my doorway, looking shocked and even a little disappointed.

You're ready?

What was going on with the woman? One minute I get the irresponsible, not meeting my commitments stuff and the next she looks like she's going to cry because I am actually ready on time.

Yeah, I'm ready. I'm just about to go and get the bike.

Oh for goodness' sake, Will, you can't ride in this weather. I'll drive you.

The radar system was ringing out its alarm. Car. Confined space with no way of escape.

No, Mum, I'll be right.

Will, stop procrastinating. You'll never be able to ride to school with your guitar in this weather.

I have before.

Oh, stop carrying on and get in the car.

But I wasn't the one carrying on. For one of the only times in her life Mum started to jabber. She likes to talk but she never jabbers. In fact she can't stand people who jabber.

The rain will be good for the veggie patch. It's coming along well, don't you think? Have you seen the little shoots of lettuce coming up? Another couple of months and we'll be having fresh veggies every night. I was thinking that we might drop some over to the Rohannas—they've been so kind lately . . .

I switched off and began to think about the fact that I was going to be stuck in the St. Andrew's College hall all day. I couldn't be bothered going, I couldn't be bothered playing and I certainly couldn't be bothered communicating with a Year 7 reject no matter how much he needed the attention. I just wanted to hang out at home. It was chucking down with rain, freezing cold, and all I wanted was a date with my bed, TV and guitar.

I suddenly noticed the jabbering had stopped. We'd pulled up at the lights and Mum was staring dead at me saying nothing.

OK, this was too weird. I eyed her nervously.

What's going on, Mum?

I'm allowed to look at you, aren't I? I am your mother.

She drove on in silence. That was about enough questions from me. Everything in my body told me to shut the hell up. The familiar wash cycle started in my gut.

Well, if you must know, I woke up thinking about your father. And when I was looking at you I was thinking of how much you remind me of him.

Silence.

But I didn't want to say it because I knew you would react exactly like you are now.

The water continued to slosh around in my gut.

Then I thought about what we would have done on a rainy Saturday if he were still here. That made me think we hadn't spent any time together lately.

Now that was where she was definitely lost. I had spent more time at home this year than I had since I'd reached puberty.

I know what you're going to say, Will, but that's different. You're home, but you aren't really there.

Mum was moving into uncharted waters and she knew it. She also knew that if she kept going I'd bail. I turned away from her and looked out the window. She pulled over to the side of the road. Her hand was on my shoulder and mine was on the door handle.

Will, I'm sorry. This is hard for me too, OK?

I released the handle and turned to look at her.

I just wanted to . . . There were tears in her eyes, hanging on the lids like big fat water bombs.

Well, I just wanted to make a connection, that's all.

The bombs never dropped. They retreated with the act of speaking.

It's all right, Mum. It's no big deal.

We drove to school in silence. The tension was gone, replaced by a weary sadness.

Will?

It's sweet, Mum, I said, grabbing my guitar. **Thanks for the lift.**

And then I did something I hadn't done since I was eleven. I reached over and gave her a kiss on the cheek. It was worth it. I hadn't seen the smile she gave me as she drove away for ages.

Mum had probably been sitting on that all week. Now that she'd had a little chat with me she'd be fine. That was what she was like: she had her say and then she was happy. Me, on the other hand, I was left feeling like crap. That was the problem in our house: she loved talking about Dad and I hated it.

Hey! Hey, Will, it's me. Zach.

That was all I needed.

Hey, Freak, how's it going?

We walked into the hall together, the Freak giving his running commentary. This time I didn't mind so much; the more he spoke the more the car ride and the conversation disappeared. And as he kept talking the washing machine continued to work through its cycle until finally it switched to off.

That girl!

Because Wednesday's rehearsals had taken place at both Lakeside and St. Andrew's, today was the first day the entire cast, band and crew had been together at the same time. The vibe was completely different from the auditions. It seemed like everyone had traded in their egos and were actually getting worked up about being involved. It had the same feel as when the boys and I were just about to go onto the soccer field. You weren't thinking about yourself, you were thinking about how you were going to win the game and annihilate the opposition. Except there wasn't any opposing team to the musi- cal, apart from me. And after the morning I'd had, I didn't have the energy to be a one-man opposition. I figured I'd try to sit today out on the bench.

There was another really good reason for the excitement and maybe this was the most honest one. We were in the presence of GIRLS! I reckon the musical thing is different for girls. They don't seem to find being involved in this type of stuff as wanky. It's a far cooler thing to be involved in the school musical if you are a girl from Lakeside rather than a boy from St. Andrew's.

As soon as I hit the newly polished floorboards that Mr. Jenson, the maintenance guy, always had a go at us about scratching, Brother Pat had me doing band stuff. We had to set up right down the back of the hall until recess, so the leads could run through their dialogue onstage without having to yell over us. This meant I had to get the geeks organized with music stands, musical instruments and whatever other stuff was essential in a junior band geek's life. After half an hour of setting up and making sure everyone had the right lunch box, we were finally ready to start. That was when Brother Pat stepped in, and he kept at it for the next two hours. Not one of the geeks complained. They just played nonstop, loving every second of it. The only thing I kept at was looking at my watch, counting down to the break. I was hanging out for the moment I could check out the girl factor. But as usual Andrews got in the way.

OK, everyone, I know you're ready for a break but I want to run through the opening before we stop. Complete with overture, so band to the pit, please.

The geeks moved in tornado-like time, leaving a similar trail of destruction. I took my time.

Right, thank you, everyone. Silence, please. Polly, entrance!

She entered from stage left, without her script. As soon as she came onstage the whole hall faded away, including Andrews. I felt strange. Removed. Disorientated. From that moment on I was gone. Completely and totally gone.

I remember in Year 9 when we did Shakespeare in English. We watched *Romeo and Juliet* with Leonardo DiCaprio and got to talk about love and sex and stuff, something Year 9 boys are obsessed with. There was this one scene with a fish tank in it, when Romeo and Juliet saw each other for the first time. I remembered our teacher said this was the moment they fell in love—well, I think she said lust actually—and we all thought she was an idiot. How could you fall in love after one look over a bloody fish tank? Right now I could safely say that we had quite clearly been talking out of our arses. You obviously knew nothing about anything in Year 9.

I was locked to the spot, paralyzed, but still managed to stay on my chair, just. My jaw felt as though it had dropped to the floor like in the cartoons. It was difficult to breathe, like suddenly I had to think about doing what my body had been doing on its own for the past seventeen years. And then I knew I was really in trouble because I could feel myself starting to come over a bright fire-engine red.

She was . . .

She was . . .

She was hot!

And I was behaving like a dickhead.

It wasn't that she was drop-dead gorgeous—you know, like on the front of *Ralph* magazine gorgeous—but she was just awesome! She had brown hair that was long, past her shoulders. She wasn't that tall but she wasn't short either. She fit together with all the right parts so that everything was in exactly the right spot and in exactly the right proportions. Not super skinny, just, I don't know, like she was meant to be how she was.

But it was her face that really blew me away. All I could see were these bright, deep brown eyes, like they were always ready to have some fun. And her mouth looked like it was molded into a permanent smile. I couldn't drag my eyes away. It wasn't only her looks, though they had a lot to do with it. I also had this feeling that I had definitely seen her somewhere before.

Will? Hey, Will?

The Freak was hitting me with his trombone.

Will!

Back off, man! You could do me some serious damage with that thing.

It was then I realized the whole band was waiting for me to play. No!!!! Had they noticed? Had they seen me just completely lose my head over this girl? I looked around slowly. The geeks were doing their own thing as usual and the other guys were happy to have a chance to goof off. The two up onstage were looking a little annoyed, especially her. But they didn't seem to know where the holdup was coming from.

Come on, Will, hurry up, the Freak whispered.

Andrews was grinning directly at me. Had he been watching? He would have been watching the stage, surely.

When you're ready, Mr. Armstrong?

Bastard. He never missed a thing!

A smooth exit

What's wrong with you?

I looked over my shoulder and saw the Freak bouncing up and down behind me. We were on a fifteen-minute break and I was keen to make a smooth exit to try to figure out what the hell had happened. The last thing I wanted was to be followed by the annoyance machine.

Listen, Freak, can you give me a minute? I've got to, got to . . . ahh . . . fart and I didn't want to do it in front of people.

Is that why you weren't ready to play? Because you had wind?

I stared at the kid, wondering how he was going to survive the next six years, six months, six seconds of his life. Wind! What self-respecting twelve-year-old refers to farts as wind without remotely cracking up?

My dad reckons that even though it's socially awkward it's always much better if you release the wind rather than hold onto it.

I continued to stare. It's not often I can't think of a comeback.

Yeah, right was the best I could do.

I walked away, shaking my head. The kid had no idea, absolutely no idea.

I found myself a decent wall and sat, making sure that the Freak, or anyone else for that matter, couldn't find me. What had just happened? This girl walks onto the stage and I'm left sitting there like an idiot. I'm interested in girls, that's not what I'm saying. I had one

serious girlfriend toward the end of last year and the usual bus relationships that last for a week or two before you're dropped. Sure, I
wasn't a stud or anything, but I wasn't a complete reject either. It was
just . . . It was just, well, I wasn't used to feeling stuff that strongly
anymore. It was like I'd stopped feeling.

I hadn't deliberately shut down, my body seemed to do it on its
own. I had no say in it. I hadn't always been like that. But since . . .
well, since early this year, I hadn't felt much of anything. I didn't
care and I didn't want to care.

Today was the first time Mum had really pushed it with me. I
mean, she had tried to get me to talk before, but when I wouldn't she
let me be. What was the point in opening it all up? It only left you
wide open for the destructo ball to come back and flatten you again,
and who was to say this time you were going to get back up? Nuh, life
was much easier with the Bubble Wrap left on.

Right, you lot, back inside now!

I watched everyone make their way back inside and my eyes fell
on her.

But, man, she was gorgeous!

Tony and Polly

It was the end of Act One. The girl wasn't needed but the guy who played opposite was. I'd been so blown away by the girl playing Polly—what a name, Polly!—I hadn't realized it was that bloke from the auditions. No surprise really. He was bound to get the Tony part. And he got to play opposite her. Lucky bastard.

Andrews obviously hadn't called them onto the stage so they were mucking about at the back of the hall. I took my guitar and sat down near to where they were. It was no big deal, all the band separated out to tune their instruments. It sounds desperate, but I wanted to know what the score was between them. If I happened to overhear their conversation while I was tuning my guitar, so what?

What are you going to do with the rest of the weekend?

She didn't answer him for a moment; it was like she was finishing off her lines in her head.

What do you mean, the rest of the weekend? There is no rest of it. I have to look after my brother tomorrow and finish my assignments, otherwise I'm in big trouble.

She's not the only one!

Me too. It sucks, doesn't it? I mean, you'd reckon they could cut us some slack for being involved in something for the school. But if I say anything to the parents they just tell me to drop out of rugby and that's not going to happen.

Right, you big football he-man . . . Did you play rugby in Melbourne? I thought it was meant to be all AFL down there.

He's new . . . and he plays rugby . . .

I went to a private school. But I used to play AFL when I was a kid.

He's an all-round sporting hero . . .

Is it really different to here?

Heaps. I went to a coed school for the last three years. I really miss the girls not being around.

I bet you do!

No, I mean it. The whole atmosphere changes and the guys act less like morons.

And he was on himself.

You mean like the other day when we came over for rehearsals? It was like they'd never seen girls before. One idiot pointed and yelled out at us as we got off the bus. It was so embarrassing!

Yeah, well, blowing him a kiss wasn't exactly showing him how much you hated it.

What was I meant to do, every guy in the yard was staring at us.

The Jock factor strikes again! Not only did he get the head of house bit wrong—she was definitely a junior, which meant she could only be an assistant head of house—he'd also managed to make us all look like idiots. Thank God I'd kept my back turned.

That's what I mean—that wouldn't happen in a coed school.

Well, at least you acknowledge who is the superior sex.

And *she's* not exactly shy.

Hey, I didn't say that, I just said it was a better atmosphere.

My parents would never let me go to a coed school.

Strict?

Worse than strict. Italian strict. I don't get it, though—Mum went through it all with her parents and she used to tell me stories about how she had to sneak out all the time. It's not that they don't let me out, they're just really big on *clear boundaries* and *making sure I achieve my full potential.*

Yeah? I'm the youngest, so my parents have lightened up. My brothers and sisters can't believe the stuff they let me do. But the thing is I actually do work—well, harder than any of them ever did. Maybe I'm just dumber than they were. But there is no way I am ever going to do this again!

Do what?

The HSC. Nuh, I want out of school and into uni so I can get on with things, and if that means I've got to be a social nerd who sleeps with his books, I'll live with it.

As soon as I saw you I knew you were a reject.

Assistant head of Green House was not only feisty, she was also not a very good liar. There was no way she thought rugby-playing Melbourne boy was anywhere near a reject.

So why get involved with the musical then?

He put on this fake voice.

'Cause I knew it was a way to get onto hot chicks in the area.

Shut up, you loser.

She launched into him with bad girl punches, laughing and flicking her hair.

It was settled. I wasn't a major expert, but there was definite flirting on both sides. I could feel some of the bubbles on the Bubble Wrap begin to burst.

Can we have Polly and Tony back onstage, please?

They ignored Andrews and kept talking.

That means you two, onstage immediately!

Oh, us? Sorry, sir, we're not used to the names.

Well, you had better get used to them.

It had been a long time since I was thankful for hearing Andrews's voice, especially lately, but this was definitely one of those times.

Romeo

Hey, what do you know about that new Mark bloke?

Chris was normally good for information. He had to do a whole lot of meet and greet with the new kids, and he's just one of those blokes—people meet him and in ten minutes they've spilled their guts. Especially girls.

Which new Mark bloke?

The one in Year Twelve. From Melbourne.

Oh yeah. The boys went over to his place the other Friday to watch the game. Seems all right. They were carrying on about him being the only forward with a brain.

Freak! This guy was sounding a little too perfect. Especially when you lined him up against a guitar-playing, pants-dropping underachiever like my good self.

What's with the questions? Are we going to have one of those *I've got something to tell you* moments?

I looked at him, wondering what he was on about.

You know, one of those *I'm questioning my sexuality*—

Shut up, you wanker!

Well, you know they told us in Pastoral Care last year, it's completely natural to question your sexuality and perhaps experiment . . .

No, you wanker, I mean I want to know if he's seeing that girl from the musical.

What girl from the musical?

The one Jock waved at the other day—you know, I think she's some sort of prefect.

You'd want to watch it, mate, cutting Jock's grass.

I'm serious, Chris! She's gorgeous!

Chris knew when to shut up.

I'll ask around.

Chris, don't say anything . . . Well, don't mention my name. I don't want anyone to think that I'm, you know . . .

. . . interested in Mark? Sure!

I bolted after him, but he'd taken off, bag and blazer flying out behind him, collecting Year 7s like bowling pins.

You're going to get it, mate, I shouted.

His right of reply was the raising of the middle finger of his left hand as he disappeared around the corner of the quad.

Hangman

Chris was sitting next to me in English giving me the lowdown.

As far as I can make out he's not seeing anyone. So you can go for it.

The joke's an old one, Chris.

Loosen up, mate. Miss Assistant Head of Green, do you know her name?

Not her first name, I think I heard him call her Miss Zefferelli.

Yeah, well, I do . . . full name and status.

Andrews looked up from his desk.

Chris, Will, be quiet.

We put our heads down.

Tell me her bloody name! I whispered.

You heard Sir. He said we had to get on with our work. I can't spoil my excellent reputation.

Actually he told us to shut up, not get on with our work. A major oversight on his behalf.

This time Andrews put down his pen and made direct eye contact with me.

William, talk again and you'll be moved.

Yes, sir.

Chris smirked at me. **See?** he mouthed.

I then resorted to what any resourceful student throughout the centuries would have done—I passed Chris a note.

So tell me her bloody name.

It's not that easy, my friend. Chris scrawled nine dashes. *I challenge you to a game of hangman. Work it out and her name shall be revealed.*

Finally we had a result. **E-l-i-z-a-b-e-t-h.**

Mr. Andrews had a very straight face as he spelled out the letters aloud but his eyes were belly laughing, I swear.

I can only conclude that as we are not currently studying *Pride and Prejudice,* this Elizabeth has nothing to do with English literature at all.

I had no idea how long he'd been standing there and it was too late to try to cover it up.

The class went mad. The usual chorus of **Woooooo** sounded from all corners of the room. I threw a pleading look at Chris, who could normally talk his way out of any tricky situation.

No, sir, you're wrong. I was just helping Will find a . . . ahh . . . find an appropriate name for one of the female characters in his narrative.

Hangman, quite a unique method, Mr. Holden. You must excuse me, I thought you were discussing another Elizabeth. If my memory serves me correctly, there is an Elizabeth who has one of the lead parts in our school musical. Isn't that right, Will?

He looked down at me. The room filled with hundreds of noises that translated to **Will Armstrong, loser.** I could feel that fire-engine red beginning to burn again. Only this time the alarms were ringing and the smoke was coming out my ears.

I was beaten and Andrews and I both knew it.

All right you lot, as interesting as Will's life is, let's get back to work.

I sat staring at my blank page. Humiliated. Someone was bound to know someone who knew someone who . . . And she was going to hear. That was how the rumor mill worked. I was a dead man.

Dead man

My humiliation in English got around the senior quad in a flash.

Hey, Willo. You grasscutter!

What?

You know, Head of Green. Her and me . . .

She's in Year Ten, you idiot, so she can only be assistant head of Green, which shows exactly how much you don't know about her!

Whatever! It doesn't matter, mate, she blew that kiss at me. It's the Jockmeister touch.

He shook his head and slapped me on the back.

You know, Will, I'm not worried, 'cause as soon as she meets me you don't stand a chance.

At that point I grabbed my doughnut and chocolate milk and retreated to the music room. The safest place in the school.

I was wondering when you'd slide your way in here, you coward.

Chris. The perpetrator.

Yeah, well, this is all your fault.

Take it easy, mate. Nothing like a little bit of public humiliation to make the school day more interesting.

Yeah, right! It would be different if it was you being hung out.

He stopped mucking around with the kit and looked at me.

It was a joke.

I know, I said, starting to relax a little. **It's not just the Elizabeth thing, it's Andrews. I don't know what his problem is.**

He's all right. He would have done that with any of the blokes in the class. Lighten up, mate!

Lighten up! The man's out to destroy me.

Chris shrugged and picked up his drumsticks. He was over the conversation and so was I. I strapped on the guitar and played loud. We fell into jamming with one another and then the music room began to work its magic. Andrews, the musical, everything faded away.

After a good ten minutes Chris looked up from the drum set and grinned.

What? I asked when I saw him looking over at me.

Have you finished freaking out? Because there is one more piece of information I did find out.

I grinned back at him. **Sorry.**

It's cool. So do you want to know?

Know what?

If she's seeing anyone.

Yeah?

Well, she's not.

How do you know?

One of the Year Ten reps knows her little brother.

How did you find that out?

I asked at the combined reps meeting.

You didn't!

Mate, don't freak out again! Since when did you turn into such a drama queen? I did it smoothly. I just asked if anyone knew any of the girl leads in the musical because we'll have to contact

them and do an interview for the next edition of *St. Andrew's Angles*. That's all.

Chris looked pretty pleased with himself.

So come on . . .

What?

He went to grab my chocolate milk and doughnut.

Payment.

I sidestepped him and shoved the doughnut in my mouth and attempted to speak.

No way, mate. I still hold you responsible for all the hassle. You should have heard bloody Jock. Wait until everyone else starts.

They'll get over it.

There was a crashing at the door. After three attempts at turning the lock the wrong way, Luke Chan made his way into the room. It was a comfort for those of us in the St. Andrew's world of piss-takes and rumors that Luke could always be depended upon. He was never quick enough to get a smart-arse comment together and he was always forty-eight hours behind Tim, who was always twenty-four hours behind everybody.

Hey, Willo, I hear you're mad for some girl in the musical.

OK. I am a dead, dead man.

The assignment

Andrews had insisted I see him at lunchtime to discuss the stereo-types assignment. I nearly didn't go but I figured that would have caused me more grief. I think he knew I had no intention of doing it and was trying to avoid a full-on confrontation in front of the class. But then again, maybe he wanted to apologize for humiliating me. Anyway, I was curious and he would have gone and whinged to Danielli if I hadn't turned up.

I'd always rated Andrews as a teacher, but lately it felt like he was always in my face. It was like the dropping of the pants incident signaled his appointment as my keeper. Like he was playing Big Brother, and I don't mean the TV show, I mean the George Orwell, *1984*, I'm-always-watching-you kind of Big Brother. It was bad enough with Mum watching me all the time, but that was her job. It wasn't his. I had enough bloody keepers, thanks.

He was sitting in a chair behind his desk, which seemed weird because in class he was always on it or around it but never behind it. I didn't bother knocking.

Hello, Will.

Sir.

I stood, ignoring the chair he'd put out.

I'm pleased you made the time to see me. I'm also pleased with the way you are meeting your responsibilities with the musical.

Praise now. An unexpected tack. Unless it was a windup.

This assignment, Will, what's the problem?

Sir, I don't think it's fair. How come I can't do what I want?

I can understand your frustration, Will, but the assignment stands. He stopped and indicated the seat. Please.

I sat down.

He pulled his chair around to the front of the desk and faced me.

When Mr. Waverton and Mr. Danielli agreed to your punishment, they also insisted you write a 3,000-word statement about the negative effect your misdemeanors have had on the college and your academic life.

They couldn't be serious!

I suggested that since you were involved with the musical, perhaps it would be better for you to journal your thoughts about the experience, which would be a far more positive focus.

Andrews paused. If he was waiting for me to thank him, we'd both end up being very hungry.

However, when I set the class assignment it occurred to me that you could use that instead. That way it would count for something rather than just ending up in your file.

He paused and sifted through some of his papers on his desk as if looking for something.

So I thought I was doing you a favor.

He looked right at me.

I know that you might find that hard to believe, Will, but it's true. Your reaction to the assignment, however, told me loud and clear that no one had informed you of your contractual obligations.

Sir, I don't know what you're talking about.

It's all in that behavior-management contract you signed after your meeting with Mr. Waverton.

I vaguely remembered signing something in Waddlehead's office. As if I would have read it.

Not much more I could say to that and Andrews knew it. It didn't mean I was going to shut up, though.

Yeah, well, what am I meant to write?

Come on, Will, you're smarter than that. This is a traditional boys' high school. How do you think the boys who try out for musicals, who are involved in things other than sport, are perceived?

I don't . . . I nearly said *I don't care, sir*, but figured he might add an extra five hundred words to the assignment. **I don't know, sir. I don't think it's that big a deal anymore.**

Why did you have such a big reaction to being involved then?

That's different, sir. It's just not my thing.

You're a musician, aren't you?

Yeah, but I'm not that type of musician.

What do you mean by that, Will?

Well, you know the type, that . . .

He gave me one of those looks that said he was just about to prove a point.

Well, you know what I mean, sir . . .

And what about that kid who keeps trying to hang out with you? Zachariah Cohen? Don't tell me you don't view him as some sort of type.

Well, maybe I do, but that doesn't—

That has everything to do with it, Will.

He turned away and started to pack up his things. That was it?

Sir?

You have to do the assignment, Will, no negotiation.

He stopped his packing and eyeballed me.

You could use this opportunity to demonstrate to the world just how capable you actually are, Will.

Here it was, the underachiever talk. They never leave it alone.

I'll do the assignment because I have to, I interrupted before he could get started. **Save the motivational talk for someone who cares.**

And with that I was gone. I knew I had stepped over the mark but I didn't give a crap.

Middle Eastern feast

That afternoon the veggie patch got a real workout. Andrews was such a wanker. He came over all friendly with the whole *I only did this to help you* bullshit and then the very next thing out of his mouth is how crap I am and how I could be so much better.

I threw the weeds I was ripping out at the back fence, imagining they were sections of Andrews's hair. How did he know? How did he know what I was and what I could be? And what the hell did that mean anyway? I was who I was, end of story.

I grabbed the fertilizer and piled it on, digging it in around the veggies that were just beginning to push their way to the top.

That's what the difference was: with these little buggers, if you piled shit on them they actually started to grow. If they kept piling shit on me, I was just going to keep living in it.

I looked up to find Mum staring at me. I had no idea how long she'd been standing there. I couldn't deal with another Patricia Armstrong heart-to-heart tonight.

Don't look at me like that, Will. I called to tell you dinner was ready three times.

Dinner I could manage.

I moved into the kitchen, half expecting to see the old fancy place mats and flowers. Mum and Dad always had this thing about eating together at the table, like it was some kind of big deal. TV was definitely barred. I hated it when I was a kid because it meant

I missed out on the TV shows they talked about at school. Later on I didn't mind. Dad would carry on telling us stories from work, and considering he was an engineer and always visiting building sites, they were pretty funny, sometimes so funny that Mum would tell him they weren't appropriate, but he'd just grin at her, say *Come on, darl,* and keep telling his story.

Since January we hadn't really sat at the table together. Mum would sometimes, but I'd go and watch TV or take dinner into my room and listen to music. Mum never made a big deal of it.

I thought we might eat in here tonight.

I followed Mum's voice to the lounge room. She was sitting on a cushion at the low table where she'd set out one of her Middle Eastern feasts she used to do on special occasions. She'd lit all the candles, put the screen in front of the TV and arranged floor cushions around the table.

I stood in the doorway. Instantly I could hear their voices carrying on at one another like they always did. The lounge room was yet another Armstrong Family Project, but it was also a constant windup for both of them. Dad wanted to have the big lounge and telly to match so he could relax and watch the Manchester United games on cable. Mum wanted no couch and no TV, only a decent stereo system and big cushions. Dad kept calling her a sad hippie and Mum kept calling him an Aussie yob. Eventually they came to a compromise. Mum dragged out the screen she had from when she was teaching English in Japan and put it in front of the TV. Dad got his big couch but Mum made sure she covered it and everywhere else with huge floor cushions. And that is exactly how they always did things. They'd keep at something until both of them were happy and then continue to give each other heaps about it while they were cuddling up together on the big couch with the big cushions. Watching the big TV.

Mum looked up at me expectantly. She was obviously thinking it was a good idea.

Come on, Will, this used to be one of your favorites.

What could I do? She was happy.

So what's the occasion?

I was just thinking it would be nice. . . . It kind of reminds me of good things and I thought maybe . . .

She looked at me.

Yeah, Mum, it's all good.

In fact, it was better than good. It was a feast! She'd prepared enough food for a Lebanese family, including cousins. I sat myself opposite her on the second-biggest floor cushion in the room and hooked in. Mum was obviously doing the same as I caught her putting three stuffed vine leaves in her mouth at the same time.

Hey! You go mad at me for shoveling food . . .

She stopped chewing for one second, and then laughed until she nearly choked. I shoved a vine leaf into my mouth, searching for something to talk about. As good as the feast was, if we were going to get through it I had to find something she could get a hold of or we'd end up exactly where I didn't want to go.

So Andrews has given me this assignment to do during the musical.

She beamed. The tactic had worked.

I've got to do some sort of stupid report about stereotypes.

Mum's brain had already started to work overtime. She loved this type of stuff.

Do you remember that time in Year Eight, Will, when you got in trouble for throwing a mandarin at someone's head?

Actually she was wrong, it was a banana and I only pegged it at somebody because they threw an apple at me first.

That was about a racial thing, wasn't it?

It was right at the peak of the Year 8 skip versus wog thing. The school did do something about it: we had to sit down and shut up at lunchtime for two weeks in a row. Mum was all for having a round-table conference about it. Dad fortunately settled her down.

Well, Will, in the world we live in, it's not such a bad idea to get your head around the effect of judging before you know anything about individuals, or countries for that matter. He's right, the more you exercise your critical thinking skills the more informed you'll be.

I gave her one of my looks.

OK, I understand that it's the last thing you want to be writing about. Just know you can run it by me anytime you'd like.

It was definitely time to change the subject.

So . . . the veggie patch is, ahh, looking good . . .

She looked back at me strangely and, fair enough, it was a pretty bad attempt at changing the subject.

. . . don't you think?

Mum's face broke into a huge grin and then she cracked up laughing so hard she had tears pouring down her face. I grabbed the rest of the vine leaves and ate three more falafel wraps. Once there was no more food on the table Mum broke out the ice cream. Both of us were so full we could barely move, so I got rid of the screen and for the first time in ages we watched telly together.

And it felt good.

The kiss

Andrews was calling for the actors to get their backsides onstage immediately. We were near the end of the rehearsal and he was definitely getting pissed off. He was using the same tone of voice he did in English when one of the boys had *stepped over the mark*. The whole cast was onstage and from what I could hear he was angry that some of the chorus members had forgotten where they were meant to stand. It wasn't normal for him to get so wound up. He was going on about how even though it was only the second week of full rehearsals we needed to block the final scenes today so that everybody had an idea of the shape of the show blah, blah, blah. It was good to know the bloke could get stressed as well as creating it for everyone else.

Mark and Elizabeth seemed to be getting tighter. I heard Andrews saying to Ms. Sefton that he was seeing them three afternoons a week to work on their scenes. That was a lot of time to be spending together. It was on the cards that they'd end up with one another for sure.

She was hanging in the background talking to him—as usual. It was hard not to stare. She looked great. She always wore jeans, the type of jeans that fit just right around the backside; actually, they fit just right everywhere. They sat on her hips like they were teasing anyone who looked that they were going to fall down lower but they never did. She always wore different T-shirts, mainly ones with weird, funky designs. Jock would be beside himself because Elizabeth wore her hair in a ponytail to most rehearsals.

One of the best things about her was the way she laughed. Man, she could laugh and crack up the whole room. She laughed a lot. She especially laughed with Mark.

I had to find some way of talking to her. I was starting to feel like one of those guys who *like to watch*.

OK, let's see what you've got. Curtain up—and action!

They ran through the song and arrived at the scene everyone was waiting for: the one where the guy who's from the wrong side of the tracks kisses the rich girl, except in this story they're at a costume ball, dressed in really bad clown costumes, pretending that no one knows who they are. I think it was even worse than the plot of every love story Mum hung out for at the video shop.

The hall fell suddenly silent. Silent and expectant. The chorus members had been gossiping about this since last rehearsal. The kissing scene. And let's face it, in a school musical that was the most action you were going to get. The entire cast had pulled up seats around the band to watch. Even the geeks got the idea something important was going to happen.

OK, everybody, Mark and Elizabeth may need your support in the following scene. As you are all aware—Andrews looked around at the body of expectant voyeurs—**this is the scene where our two lead characters, Polly and Tony, fall into each other's arms and kiss.**

Snickers from the geeks. I suppose you've got to cut them some slack considering their stunted development.

I have asked Mark and Elizabeth if they want the hall cleared,

for exactly that reason . . . Andrews frowned at the geeks. **But they have both said that they need to get used to it. So are we all clear with what is expected?**

Everybody nodded and a couple of *Sirs* came from the pit. So much for not making a big deal of it. I wish they had bloody cleared the hall, then I could've got the hell out of there. No one else in the hall was moving apart from Romeo and Juliet onstage. At that point I looked up. The silence had reached a deafening roar. I watched as their lips met, and then continued to meet. They didn't stop meeting.

Applause broke out all around me. Whistles, cheers and clapping were the backdrop as the two of them finally separated, looking just a little embarrassed.

That kiss was not acting. That kiss was for real. It was pretty obvious it wasn't just the sick losers watching who enjoyed it. Elizabeth and Mark were mad for each other.

A perfect note to close rehearsals, I heard Andrews offer. **Thanks, everyone. See you next week.**

I was throwing my guitar into its case as he spoke. I'd worked up a bit of speed by the time I'd made it to the doorway.

Will?

I hesitated for a second. That kid had a radar system you could sell to the Australian army.

Hey, Freak, I'm kind of in a hurry.

He half jumped and waved at the same time.

See you next week!

Yeah, next week.

I raised my hand to him and as I did I caught the bloody prom king and queen arm in arm going to talk to their adoring public.

Chris's place

It'd been a big week for someone who'd spent the last six months not being bothered, what with Andrews and the assignment, the mother-son bonding the other night and now the kiss. I needed some serious normality. I took the bike out of the shed, hooked the guitar under my arm and rode three minutes to Chris's place.

Weekend nights were always fix-it-yourself over there, and one more wasn't going to matter. I walked in to see the footy on the TV and the boys in various positions around the room, cheering on their teams and telling the ref to get stuffed in alternating intervals. I said g'day and, as usual, received barely a grunt. This was exactly the type of response I needed.

When I walked into the kitchen Mrs. Holden got up from the table and came over and kissed me just like she'd been doing for the past thirteen years. I shook Mr. Holden's hand and was moved into a huge bear hug. This was also expected. They were big about touchy-feely stuff in this family. Because they had four boys, five including me, they were really into making sure we were all in touch with our feelings and stuff. The boys were used to it. They just rolled their eyes and made really bad faces. I wondered how they'd work it with Jess. Everybody in the family, especially Chris, fell over themselves to give her kisses and hugs. She was only two but she pretty much ran the place. Pity the bloke who asked her out first. There'd be no touchy-feely bullshit from the Holden boys then, I bet.

Chris was in the bathroom, getting her ready for bed. I followed the splashing and squealing noises until I found him kneeling over the side of the bath squirting a rubber ducky at Jess.

I sat on the edge of the bath. Chris squirted water from the duck's backside straight into my face. He and Jess thought it was hysterical.

Get f—

Now, now, Will, not in front of the child.

I glared at him.

What's wrong with you, mate? It's not like you not to get revenge.

I shrugged. **They kissed.**

Who?

You know who.

Chris looked at me blankly. Then he got it.

You mean really kissed?

Yeah, I mean lips and mouths and stuff.

Tongues?

Shut up, Chris!

So?

So what?

How serious was it?

I don't know. They had to kiss for the show.

Chris looked at me and sighed.

Kissed for the show? That's a completely different story.

He took the face cloth Jessie had put on her head and spoke directly to her. **Uncle Will's such a loser!** She nodded her head in agreement.

Man, I haven't seen you this uptight about anything forever, Chris said, lifting Jess out of the bath and cocooning her bug-like into a big, fluffy towel.

I followed him into Jess's room and watched as he went through the pj routine.

Will, you're going to have to speak to the girl, otherwise you're going to turn into a major pain in the arse.

Yeah, but I don't know what to say.

Well, don't ask me. The only girl I get to spend any time with is Jessie here.

What do you mean? All the girls love talking to you.

Yeah, they may love talking to me but that's it. I'm the guy they love to talk to but don't want to date. Unlike you, my friend, I still cannot lay claim to ever having a proper girlfriend. Apart from Penelope Barry in Year Six, and that only lasted for a week after she held hands with Peter Sharkey at Tim's party.

I was so used to Chris having every corner covered in terms of the bloke most likely to succeed at absolutely everything, I hadn't thought about him and girlfriends. I knew he had plenty of girl friends, but when I thought about it, he'd never had a relationship girlfriend.

Do you want a girlfriend?

Yeah, I want a girlfriend, you idiot, but I can't exactly go out there and demand one, can I? No, mate, for the moment the closest thing I'll get to a relationship is hearing about you and this Elizabeth, so hurry up and do something about it so you can introduce me to some of her friends.

He bundled Jessie up in her pajamas and called out to his dad. Jessie work tended to be done in shifts: Mr. Holden was in charge of stories and bed. Chris flew her into the kitchen and rugby passed her to his dad.

Chris and I moved our way into the lounge room and sat right in front of the twins, blocking their direct line of vision. It was something we'd done for years, which, because of size disparity, pro-duced a guaranteed end result favoring Chris and myself. The next stage was the rumble, which we always won, and then of course the final part of the strategy—us getting the best seats. It worked every time. I settled back and relaxed. It was comforting to know not everything was going crazy.

A different game plan

I went through the week wondering what the next move was. Chris was all for me coming down after training to meet Mark—apparently the guy was good enough for the reps side as well as the Sunday comp. But I told him I thought we'd established it wasn't Mark I was after.

I knew I was becoming a pain in the arse, like Chris had said. I had to stop complaining and get on with it. I went to the next rehearsal ready to rip off what I knew was going to be a really scabby Band-Aid. It would hurt. But hopefully it was going to be worth it.

I waited until the end of the day. Andrews and Mark were going over the last scene, which meant Elizabeth was finished and on her own. I stood and watched her laughing with the other girls. She talked to everybody, including the adoring Year 7 chorus girls. I figured that would have to work in my favor: if she talked to everyone, then the odds were she would talk to me.

I began to walk toward her on three occasions and chickened out each time. I was on the fourth attempt and about two meters away when her mobile rang. It was right about then I tried really hard to look casual, like I wasn't trying to talk to her at all. I focused intently on the wall and kept walking. Idiot!

I got to the wall. I knew I needed a reason for being there, and fast. I was dead certain she'd watched me walk all the way to the other side of the hall and was retelling the whole story to whoever she was on the phone to. I was desperate. A discarded *St. Andrew's Angles* was lying on the floor near where I was standing. I haven't in my whole school career found a newsletter so fascinating. Let's face it, it was probably the first time I'd ever read one. I walked back across the hall reading every word of it. As I passed her I was determined not to look. I repeated in my head, *Don't look up, don't look up*. Just as I reached the point of intersection, I looked up. And, even worse, I was mouthing the words *Don't look up* when I did. Elizabeth was looking directly at me. In fact she didn't take her eyes off me as she continued her conversation. She could have got an instant tan I was giving off so much heat.

Then I had one of those déjà vu moments. I was positive I had done this before—stood in front of her like an openmouthed idiot. But there was no going back now. I'd made myself look like a prize dickhead so I might as well sit it out and wait till she was off the phone. My heart began to make dangerously loud drum noises and I was breaking into a sweat.

Yes, Mum. OK, Mum. Yeah, I'll be waiting out the front of the hall.

This was my chance.

The phone call was drawing to a close. I began to walk closer. She half watched my approach. Nearly there. I opened my mouth to speak when . . .

Will?

Wrong! Wrong! Wrong! That was the wrong voice and it was definitely coming from the wrong direction. Sighing, I turned around, still clutching the *St. Andrew's Angles*. There standing in front of me was the Romeo to my Juliet, and Juliet was now walking out of the hall to meet her mother. Bloody typical! I felt the same intensity of heat from three minutes before start to radiate from my body as I wondered if he'd been witness to everything I'd just done. It was then I became aware of the *St. Andrew's Angles* newsletter I was clutching. I dropped it and watched as Mark's eyes followed its path to the floor right in front of his feet. He decently made no comment, although I could have sworn he had a grin on his face.

Yeah . . . Hi. I stared at him for a moment and then realized he was waiting for me to shake his hand.

Mark Newman.

I shook his hand.

Yeah, I know.

Look, I was at training on Thursday and Chris was telling me to come and introduce myself seeing as we seem to be the only seniors in the place.

So this was all Chris's fault!

Yeah, he mentioned something like that to me too. Except I wasn't having any of it.

Jock and Tim have been sharing some stories . . .

I could just imagine.

Don't listen to Jock and Tim, they compete with one another to see how much shit they can talk.

I noticed. You should hear the crap I get about being in the musical. Playing football and being in the musical are mutually exclusive activities according to Jock. He's convinced I'm only doing it for the girls.

For the first time in his life Jock may actually be right.

That's why I introduced myself. They've just texted me to say they're throwing the footy around at the park.

I thought about it for about two seconds. I wasn't in the mood to bond with the competition.

Thanks, mate, but I've got to get home.

My first reaction was to be pissed off. Why would the boys text Newman and not me? Just then the phone beeped. It was Jock. I proceeded to text him where he could shove his football and felt just a little bit better.

I watched as Newman drove away and waved from his cozy, warm car as I put on my beanie and climbed onto my beaten-up old bike. Just once I would like a rehearsal to end with me coming out on top. Just once.

This week's game plan—there is no game plan

When I saw Chris at school on Monday I told him what happened. He cracked up laughing and gave me grief about not coming for a run. It turned out the boys went out for pizza and continued the bonding session. Then I had to put up with Tim and Jock carrying on during bio about how much of a good bloke Mark was.

Not that what Newman did was going to worry me anymore. I'd decided on another game plan for the Elizabeth, Mark and Will triangle . . . I was buying out completely. It was causing me way too much hassle for absolutely no gain. I wanted my life to go back to normal. It was too much energy and uptightness. I was determined to just turn up at rehearsals, do the band thing, yell at the geeks, save the Freak and go home. It wasn't as if I was some social reject who needed to make more friends. I didn't need to get hung up on a girl who didn't even know I was a part of the cosmos, let alone the human race.

I couldn't shake the Freak, but he was becoming bearable in an annoying kelpie cross fox terrier puppy type of way. I hadn't had to save him from any nerd bashing since Wednesday. Brother Pat had insisted I attend the Wednesday band rehearsals instead of detention. He was all fired up about the excellent job I was doing with the geeks, and he carried on about it being unfair not to reward me by canceling detention and allowing me to attend band, and he was going to make sure Waddlehead understood. What could I do, he thought he was doing me a favor.

Anyway, last Wednesday at band practice the geeks raided the Freak's lunch box. His dad had taken to giving him afternoon tea as well as recess on Wednesdays and the geeks found out about it. I conducted my own investigation and applied some gentle encouragement for the goods to be returned at the next rehearsal. This week was like a food drive, there was so much of it. The Freak invited Brother Pat, any of the other teachers who came by to listen, and the geeks who had taken it in the first place, to have afternoon tea with him. I tried to tell him to leave out the guys who had stolen from him, but he said it didn't matter. Maybe this kid was one of those Dalai Lama midgets that the Buddhists hadn't found out about yet. Anyway it turned into a food fest. The Freak was at the center of it and he was stoked. Needless to say his lunch box hadn't been touched since.

If I was really honest, I liked hanging out with the kid. He didn't expect anything from me. He was happy and I was happy. I just wished he'd shut up more often.

On Saturday I rode in thinking that it wouldn't be long before I would have my life back.

Hey, Freak!

Hey, Will!

He wasn't doing his usual hello dance so I could tell something was up. I looked around quickly for any sign of the geek gang.

What's up, mate? You're usually pogoing all around the place at the beginning of rehearsals.

I can't stay. We have family commitments and Dad thinks it's important we both go.

I pointed out to him that this was also a commitment but he wouldn't budge.

I thought of my mum and how family things like that were a big deal.

I know what it's like, Freak, but your dad wouldn't have said it was important if it wasn't, right?

He nodded his head in agreement but still looked pretty tragic.

Cheer up, mate. I'd love to break out of here.

But you're not me.

He had a point.

So how come you're here then?

I told Dad it was important I explain why I can't be here to Brother Patrick and Mr. Andrews.

He paused. I wondered if he'd been given any trouble.

So have you let them know? I'll walk in with you if you like.

No, I've already seen them. I was waiting for you.

Me?

I wanted to let you know we can't have our breaks together. Sorry, Will.

And the kid was genuinely sorry. That's why you couldn't help but like the little guy.

Hey, don't you worry about me. I'm the one who has to watch your backside, not the other way round. But it's going to be a really boring day without you.

The Freak started to pogo again.

Really?

Well, yeah, who else am I going to flog all that great food from?

I looked at him quickly; you've got to be careful with the Freak.

It was a j—

I know, Will. I can tell when you're joking now.

Maybe the kid was going to turn out OK.

It looked like I'd have to deal with the love triangle on my own.

And that was more difficult than I thought. As much as I wished the Freak would be struck dumb when we were stuck all day in the pit, he did provide a constant source of distraction. In his absence I spent a lot of time listening to my MP3 player and mucking around with my guitar. And there's only so many ways you can restring a guitar. By lunchtime I was getting desperate. I was about to bolt to Chris's, even talking to Brother Pat was looking like a good option, but in the end it didn't matter. I watched Mark and Elizabeth and some other people go off in Mark's car. Fine by me. I scoffed Mum's sandwiches and played really sad songs on my newly tuned, newly restrung guitar.

Brother Pat had to go somewhere after lunch, which meant I had to step in. Conducting meant that everything else went out of my head. The geeks were so full-on about their playing I had to take it halfway seriously. It was a quick finish to a bad day. I packed up as Andrews was doing his usual roundup, grabbed my stuff and bolted.

And then the day got even worse. What the . . . ! I found myself sprawled facedown in a pile of St. Andrew's festering rubbish—you know, the type that no one ever picks up when the teacher on playground duty asks.

What's your problem? I began as I removed my guitar case from the two-day-old squashed banana and tried to eyeball the dickhead who had just laid me out. I couldn't quite make him out but I knew that voice. Bloody Romeo again!

Hey, Will, sorry. I got to my feet and glared at him. He took my guitar case and began to clean it off on the grass. **I was keen to get out of there, if you know what I mean.**

I tried to get rid of my pissed-off tone but it didn't work.

Yeah, right. Don't worry about it, Mark. I'm used to ending up in shit. In fact I'm pretty good at it. You seem like you're in a hurry, going anywhere special?

I've got an Economics assessment due tomorrow and I haven't even started yet.

Well, if he was that bloody worried, he should have worked during lunchtime and not gone off somewhere with Elizabeth, shouldn't he! He offered me my guitar case, which now had banana and grass stuck all over it.

Thanks. There was no point even trying to hide the sarcasm.

He just stood there looking uncomfortable. Not so smooth now, Romeo!

Look, I'm driving, can I give you a lift home? Apology and all that?

I weighed up whether I was going to get more pissed off by riding home or by spending time with Mark. It took about an eighth of a second to decide. Call me a hypocrite but he owed me. The bike could have another school sleepover.

That'd be good.

You don't live thirty k's away, do you?

I was tempted to say yes and get him to drop me at a mate's place just to make him suffer, but even I thought that was pretty sad.

About fifteen minutes by car. Down near the BP servo.

I think I know the one.

We arrived at an old Holden. I'm pretty sure it was an FJ or the next one out; whatever it was it was pretty cool. I had to give him that.

Nice car.

Thanks.

I bought it in Melbourne. Well, Dad did.

Yeah, Chris said you were from there.

Shit, did Chris tell me that or did I pick it up from Elizabeth and him in that conversation I wasn't meant to hear? I tried to move on quickly.

How long have you been in Sydney?

We moved up at the end of last year.

Big difference?

Yeah, I suppose it is. I don't know, I haven't really seen a lot of it. It's been school and around here mainly with the footy boys. St. Andrew's is different to the last school I was at. Girls make a real difference.

I bet they do.

Mark grinned at me. **No, I mean everybody just acts more normal, more natural.**

Could you imagine Jock and Tim in a coed school? They couldn't cope.

But that's just it. They wouldn't stand a chance. The girls would pull them into line straightaway. Most of the blokes don't carry on with all that tough-man stuff because if they do there's always someone to tell them to pull their head in.

St. Andrew's could do with a little more of that, just ask the Freak.

So how come you had to leave in your final year—that would be pretty hard, wouldn't it?

Yep . . . but there was no way around it. Dad was retrenched and got this great payout but he . . . couldn't get another job. He's pretty old and I'm the youngest. He started stressing about everything: Mum, retirement, me, uni.

He reached over to the glove box, opened it and rummaged around until he found a cigarette.

Don't tell the boys, they'd give me shit on the field. I just

started again, but not for good. He took a drag. I watched Dad turn from a hotshot businessman to this major stress-head. That went on for six months and then the job in Sydney came up. It was Mum and me who convinced him to take it. I could put up with leaving more than I could see Dad crack up. He didn't say anything but I reckon he bought the car to say thanks.

That would suck. I changed the subject. So you know what you want to do next year?

As soon as I asked I knew that he would. He was just one of those guys.

Law at ANU.

That'd be right.

He stumped out the cigarette after three drags. What about you?

I figure I've got at least another year and a half before I have to decide. Right now, I'm pretty happy just cruising.

Let him know I don't need to overachieve to be a success.

Right. So is the musical going on the CV?

Well, at least I didn't volunteer to be involved! Sarcastic wanker!

I hear your audition was pretty special.

I grinned in spite of myself. Jock and Tim can never keep their mouths closed.

Actually, it wasn't them who told me.

That shut me up.

What do you mean?

He looked over at me and grinned.

Come on, mate, not funny! Just tell me.

Who do you reckon?

I wouldn't have asked if I knew, would I?

He paused for two more seconds. I was over the game.

Elizabeth.

He turned his head slightly to watch my reaction. My whole body snapped frozen vegetable shut.

Elizabeth?

He looked at me as if I was stupid.

Yeah, you know, the one I play opposite, the one I have to kiss.

How did she know?

She said something about being on the bus you mooned.

That would be right. Of course she was.

Yeah. She says you looked straight at her.

My whole body turned an instant microwave red.

In fact, I think she said she was the one who tried to save your arse.

That's where I knew her from! The girl with the ponytail and the killer death stare. Great, so she'd really be interested.

No way, she was majorly pissed off, I remember.

Yeah, she told me she cut you a look but that was because the Year Twelves were giving her a hard time about telling everyone to shut up. It was her who first saw Danielli and Waddlehead. She told one of her friends to let you know but she reckons you just stood there with a big grin on your face. In fact she said you've done that twice now. She thinks it's pretty funny.

The rays of embarrassment were now replacing the clapped-out heating system in the car. Right, well, that's it then. I'd be expelled for pulling out of the musical and be the laughingstock of Lakeside for my entire life.

Mark now had a huge grin on *his* face, the bastard. And there I was feeling sorry for him. What was I thinking, feeling sorry for the bloke? He operated just like the boys, right down to the delivery of the St. Andrew's piss-take.

What? I challenged. **So what if she was the girl who saw me? It doesn't bother me.**

No. No, I can see that.

I looked out the window, trying really hard to look fascinated with the scenery.

OK, I admit it, I said finally. **I think she's pretty hot. Don't you?**

I threw it out there as casually as I could.

Yeah, I suppose she is.

You suppose!

So you *are* interested.

It was a statement, not a question.

Maybe I'm a little interested.

He was nodding and laughing. **I knew it!**

What do you mean you knew it?

It was just obvious, wasn't it? All of a sudden Chris is on at me about meeting you, and he starts to ask questions about the lead girl. Then the other day I watched you stand dead in front of Elizabeth with your mouth wide open . . .

Bastard!

Hey, don't blame me, I saw you pretending to read that stupid newsletter and tried to bail you out of what looked like a really embarrassing situation.

OK, OK! So shut up laughing for a minute and tell me the truth. You can't tell me you're not interested. You're always laughing and hugging and carrying on with her. It's like you're already boyfriend-girlfriend.

Mark took his eyes from the road for a second and looked at me.

Man, you have got it bad. Look, we've become good friends. I'm used to having a lot of girl friends from my old school. We always carried on like that.

Yeah, right. Good comeback, Will! Good comeback!

Look, there's no doubt she's a stunner . . .

So you do—

He cut me off. **And funny, smart and feisty and every now and then, not often, she gets really, really fiery. One time in rehearsals Elizabeth and Andrews nearly lost it with one another and he's a hard man to get started.**

I knew there was a reason why I liked the girl!

But the thing I like about her the most is that she doesn't spend any time thinking about what other people think about her. She is who she is without any crap.

It was around this time I figured I had no hope. **So are you going to ask her out?**

He looked at me, smiled and said nothing.

Come on, mate, I persisted. **Are you going to ask her out?**

Why, are you?

Look, the way I see it, there is no way a girl like Elizabeth is going to give me a second look with someone like you sniffing around.

No, mate, you've got it all wrong.

Give me a break. All I'm asking is that you save me from making a complete idiot of myself in front of her yet again. Just tell me if you're interested. If you're not then I'll eventually, someday, maybe get enough courage to go and talk to her. But if you're keen I'll just back off right now.

He said nothing. It began to dawn on me that maybe there might be the slightest possibility he wasn't interested.

Mark, are you really not interested?

The car went quiet; the only noise was from the dodgy AM

radio station, the only one that worked. It was after a whole chorus of some really bad love song that he finally answered.

No.

She's seeing someone?

No.

Then why wasn't he interested?

You must have someone back in Melbourne then.

Not exactly, no . . .

Got your eye on one of the younger chorus members?

He looked at me like I was perverted.

My brain was still percolating. You could nearly hear the slurps and swishes. He was a good-looking guy who was smart, could sing and dance and play football.

Well, what other reason could there possibly be, unless you've found out something really strange about Elizabeth that you can't tell me.

He was silent again and then let out his breath like an overfilled bike tire.

No, Will, I'm not seeing anyone, I'm not having a secret love affair with an older woman, and Elizabeth is perfectly sane. It's just that I'm . . .

Pause.

It's just that I'm . . . gay.

I was so busy trying to figure out why he wouldn't be interested I completely missed what he'd said.

Will, did you hear me?

No, sorry, I was just thinking . . .

Forget it.

No, what did you say?

I'm not saying it again.

Come on.

Will, when someone outs themselves to a near stranger it's a pretty big thing to do. I'd kind of appreciate it if you were actually listening.

Right, sorry, Mark.

Outs himself, what does he mean *outs himself*?

Will, I'm not interested in Elizabeth because I'm gay.

I sat dead still and didn't look at him.

Gay.

He's gay.

He's GAY!

The bad love song had turned into another really bad love song. It was time to get out.

Right. Look, I'm nearly home. You can just drop me here.

Will, it's all right, I can take you home, just tell me where . . .

No, really, Mark, I'm nearly home and I've taken you out of your way. I'd prefer to walk.

He'd pulled over to the curb and was slowing down, trying to talk to me.

Will . . .

I clutched the door handle and waited until he came to a complete stop.

No, no, I'm fine. Here's good.

Will . . .

I opened the door and got out.

OK, thanks heaps. See you later.

And with that I bolted around the corner.

Gay!

Gay! He's bloody gay! It was midnight and for the past two hours that was all that had been going through my head. That and *You dickhead!* It's not like I was homophobic. I'd sussed that out in Pastoral Care last year. I was cool with it. I didn't care what anyone did. As long as they didn't try to come on to me.

But Mark played footy. Maybe if he didn't and he was just in the musical, it would have made more sense. Because they were meant to sing and dance and stuff, weren't they? I knew there were a couple of famous footy blokes who were gay, but Mark played football with Jock and Tim! Wait till they found out!

It wasn't as if I didn't have a right to be a little freaked out. I mean there I am and I don't even know the guy, he's giving me a lift home and he tells me he's gay. Any normal bloke would feel just a little uncomfortable, wouldn't they?

Just because he gave me a lift doesn't mean anything. We were talking about Elizabeth. And he guessed I was interested, so it wasn't as if he would have thought I was gay. No, no one would think that I was gay . . . would they? I mean, I didn't look gay. Did I? I was in the musical, but I wasn't performing. It was different when you were in the band. You were a muso and musos aren't usually gay, the singers and the dancers are the gay ones. Not the girls, though; they're always the hot ones.

What was I going to say to the bloke the next time I saw him?

Hi, I'm Will Armstrong and I'm not gay? But then maybe that was why he cornered me in the first place. Then he had the perfect excuse to offer me a lift home. And then by bringing up Elizabeth he had the perfect way of figuring out if I was interested in him. Maybe he set up the whole thing to find out my sexual orientation. Maybe I was giving off mixed messages. Maybe, maybe, maybe . . . Shit, maybe he was right. Maybe I was gay!

Monday morning

For God's sake, Will, you're not gay!

Chris had come round to pick me up for school. He'd just got his Provisional license and had managed to scam the car for the day. I'd barely slept all night and looked pretty bad. The recurring theme for the night was my own sexuality. Could you be seventeen and not know you were gay? Could it be possible that I was gay and I had missed it? Maybe I was in, what do they call it on TV, denial? Then I'd get these pictures in my head of me in a pair of tights singing onstage but it wasn't with Elizabeth, it was with Mark! We'd get to the kissing scene and then I'd run screaming from the hall, because of my state of denial.

I knew I couldn't tell a soul. I had to sort this one out for myself.

But then Chris said those magic words.

Will, you look like shit.

Chris, I think I'm gay. I've been thinking about it all night. It makes perfect sense. I play the guitar. I'm good at English. I'm in the musical. And there was that time in Year Seven when I accidentally looked at another guy at the urinal. I didn't mean to, but it's something I've never forgotten and if I wasn't gay I would have forgotten it by now. Sure, he got me by the throat and accused me of being a pervert. But you know, I suppose he had every right, right?

Calm down, mate.

No, really, Chris, I'm wired! I've been thinking it through all night—

Will, you're not gay.

Chris, you don't know. Even you were giving me crap about asking about Mark.

Man, you really have lost it. You're carrying on like some kind of nutter! Wasn't the whole conversation about Elizabeth?

He was looking at me like I *was* a nutter. **A girl, you idiot!**

I told Chris about The Conversation with Mark.

So he's not interested in Elizabeth, then.

That's it? That's all you have to say? Your best friend just outs himself to you and you say, *He's not interested in Elizabeth*!

Then finally it hit me.

He's not interested in Elizabeth.

So he wasn't a threat to me. I could be interested in Elizabeth. Maybe I actually had a chance with Elizabeth!

I'm not gay.

Chris was looking at me very strangely. **OK, you have definitely lost it. Meet me in the music room during homeroom. I'm worried about you.**

I just felt relieved.

The music room

I can't believe this morning was for real, Will. I mean, it was pretty funny but you looked like you were dead serious. You've been all over the place lately. Are you sure there's nothing else going on? You didn't even go on like this when your dad . . .

Chris stopped himself. But we both knew what he had been going to say. It jolted my gut like a mini explosion. We hadn't talked about Dad since the day it happened. That was the way I played it and Chris respected that. In the beginning he asked if I was OK but he stopped eventually. They nearly always do if you say you're fine often enough.

Will? Will, mate, I'm sorry, I shouldn't have even spoken about it.

I could feel myself walking out the door, escaping into the quad and wiping it from my memory. But I knew if I did Chris would feel even worse.

I spoke as normally as I could but my mouth had lost all its spit.

Things are really weird at the moment. I can't explain it. I just want stuff to get back to normal.

Chris was looking at me. We both knew that the kind of normal I was talking about was never going to happen.

The bell rang for the end of homeroom. I walked out before Chris could ask me if I was all right again.

I was seriously thinking about checking out for the rest of the day, but I knew Danielli would be onto me in a millisecond. I was antsy, though, ready for something. It was when I was walking up to the quad from the music room that it came to me. For the past three years Jock and Tim and me had had the plan of Glad wrapping the teachers' toilets. Jock still had the Glad wrap in his locker. But each year we came up with a different reason why we couldn't: Year 8 we didn't have the balls, Year 9 we thought it was too disgusting, Year 10 too juvenile, and by Year 11 we just thought it was really, really funny.

We spent recess scheming. Jock was always good at making sure we'd covered all areas so as not to get busted. It was risky, especially for me, but I'd been Mr. Brownnosed Musical Boy for way too long.

Maths was just before lunch and since we were all in different classes, it worked perfectly. Ten minutes before the end of the lesson, we met outside the canteen. Tim was the lookout. The toilets were outside the main building and were easy access, as long as no one was watching from any of the windows, but the risk only quadrupled the fun. After a minute's debate, we decided just to get the male toilets. There was the potential for way too much explanation if we were busted in the ladies'.

The job was done in minutes, or so we thought, but then the Glad wrap wouldn't stick because the bowl was wet. I didn't have time to think how gross it was as I got a paper towel and wiped the whole toilet seat and bowl down. Once it was completely dry it clung on beautifully. Jock kept flicking it to make sure it wasn't going to come off. I told him he'd have to wipe down the next toilet bowl if he stuffed it up so he stopped. Jock shoved the Glad wrap down his pants and kept it as a souvenir. I went to our own toilets and scrubbed my fingers, hands and arms, wishing I had some of Nana's disinfectant, then went back to maths and waited five minutes for the bell.

There was nothing unusual in us bolting over to the canteen at the beginning of lunch, but this time we weren't thinking about food. The three of us stood in different positions and watched the traffic outside the toilets. Nothing happened, but then two of the PE teachers came bolting out of the toilets—one was cracking up, the other one not so impressed. They went back to the gym and the other teachers came out and went in to have a look. Ten minutes into lunch I reckon at least half the staff were at the toilets. It was only when Waddlehead came over that everyone, including the staff, bolted. No one had a clue who did it. I hadn't laughed so loud and so hard forever. Perfect! Things were getting back to normal—including me.

Retarded homophobe Neanderthal

But normal didn't mean having to face a guy you hardly knew to apologize for acting like an idiot. I was really tempted to forget it ever happened but I couldn't. It must have taken a lot of guts for Mark to tell me he was gay and I'd turned around and treated him like he had some sort of contagious disease. He'd probably told Elizabeth I was a retarded homophobe Neanderthal and she shouldn't have anything to do with me. And I couldn't blame him. I had reacted like a retard.

I had to pretend to Jock and Tim that I was going over to Chris's place instead of catching the bus. They would have been really suss if they knew I was hanging around school on a Friday afternoon and I wasn't about to have that conversation with them. I felt too much like a loser as it was. But after lead rehearsals was the only time I knew I could get Mark on his own.

I could hear Elizabeth's laugh before I saw her. She was in her school uniform and she still looked great. She was pulling on her badge-covered blazer as she spoke.

Are you sure you can't come, Mark? The parents have given me tonight off. And they like you.

Mark shook his head and pointed to his overfull backpack. She dragged her own bag onto her shoulder.

All right, be boring then. Looks like it's a girls' night.

She gave him a quick kiss on the cheek and walked off. I waited until she had turned the corner, took a deep breath and started to walk toward him.

Mark?

He stopped, turned around, saw it was me and kept walking.

I'd offer you a lift but I'd be afraid you'd think I was going to jump you before you had a chance to put your seat belt on.

Fair enough.

Mark, I—

He cut me off.

No, really, Will, you must know that's why I had to leave Melbourne. I went around to every school musical in the area and tried to get unsuspecting, straight guitar players into my car.

Mark . . .

He turned around and looked directly at me.

I . . . acted like a . . . a wanker. I was a wanker . . . I'm sorry.

He took a moment before he spoke, like he was trying to weigh up whether I was worth the effort. When he did, it came out in one breath, like he'd been practicing.

Will, I've put up with this type of shit since I was fourteen. And believe me, I've had a lot worse than your *let me out of the car* routine. I appreciate the apology. I'm not about to get hung up about it. If you have a thing with me being gay, that's your problem. I'm not making any more apologies about it.

I stood there, unsure what to say next. I felt like more of a dickhead now than I did the other night.

It's just that, you know . . . Chris reckons you're a nice guy . . . and a good footballer . . .

The roll of his eyes shut me up again.

What's Chris got to do with it?

It's just that . . .

Anyway, he already knows I'm gay.

Chris knew he was gay, but he didn't say anything! How long had he known? Then that must mean—no, surely he hadn't told Jock and Tim?

I'm not stupid, I've only told Chris. I'm waiting for the right moment to break it to the other footy fellas. Like right about when they're cuddling in close for a scrum.

His eyes had become less dark.

Yeah, or the next time you're at practice and you've got Jock's backside in your face.

There was a two-second pause, which indicated that I may have gone a little too far, but then Mark said, What a tragic image!

And we both cracked up.

Mark started again, except this time it was like he was really talking.

I took a risk telling you I was gay. You know, it's not normally something I do when I first meet someone.

He reached in his pocket for a cigarette, looked around to see if anyone was watching, put it in his mouth and then spent the next minute tapping his pockets trying to find a lighter.

I don't know, I figured since you were a good mate of Chris's and we'd be seeing more of each other at the musical—he took a deep drag and blew out the smoke, waving it away as he did—and I suppose you took a risk in telling me about Elizabeth, I just thought, why not? I get sick of it always having to be this big secret.

He looked at me dead on. Your reaction did spin me out, though.

Typical. I reacted like a jerk and Chris probably hugged him and told him how proud he was of him.

Mark butted the half-smoked cigarette and flicked it into the nearest bin where some sicko Year 8 kid would probably find it and try to light it up.

Look, I came up here determined to make it work, the school, making friends. In my head, me being gay is not a big deal, but you know what a school like this is like. I decided before I left Melbourne I was just going to be honest and get on with it. Other people have to get over it, or not. So if we're going to be mates then that's the score. If you can't deal with it then fine.

It felt like it was up to me now.

So does that mean I can get a lift home?

Are you sure you're not going to freak out again?

No, I reckon I can cope, just keep your hand on the gear stick!

You wish, buddy! You wish!

He grabbed his bag and went through the same routine as the lighter looking for his keys. I thought about the bike in the bike shed. It meant having to get Mum to drive me to rehearsals again but she'd get over it.

We both lightened up on the drive home. I was asking him about Melbourne and he was giving me crap about Elizabeth.

You didn't say anything to her, did you?

I might have said I thought someone was interested in her. But don't worry, she doesn't think it's you.

Thank God.

Yeah, I told her you were gay.

You didn't! You f—

Relax, mate. I'm joking. But I did ask if she thought anyone in the band was cute and she singled you out. But let's face it, there's not a lot of competition, is there.

Thanks.

You've got to have a game plan.

I'm not sure I need to have girl advice from a gay guy . . .

Yeah, well, you're not doing all that well on your own now, are you?

He had a point.

And let's not forget she's already seen the best part of you.

He grinned at me.

Very funny. Back off from my arse, would you?

We were talking about Elizabeth, not me, you loser. This weekend's the perfect opportunity. You've got all day Saturday, and if Andrews is right, we'll be there until late on Sunday too.

No, that's not meant to be happening yet, is it?

That's what Andrews said tonight. He wants to have a complete run-through. Everyone else knows 'cause they had to have permission or something.

No, it must be just you guys. I don't know anything about it.

No way, mate, it's everyone. What's the problem? This is perfect for the planned meeting.

I was not sure even meeting Elizabeth was worth forty-eight hours at school. A picture of her in her school uniform appeared in my head. Then again . . .

I'll introduce you during the break.

No. No, you can't do that.

Why not?

She'll know straight off.

Know what?

That I like her.

By introducing you?

Yeah.

I'm only introducing you, not—

No!

All right, what do you suggest?

I don't know. Can't we just be talking and then she comes up and I smile at her, and . . .

And I introduce you. Yeah, that sounds like a great idea, he said sarcastically.

Let's just leave it.

We'd been talking so much I nearly missed my street.

That's my street on the right.

Is it really your street?

What do you want me to do, go and get my mum?

He laughed.

Thanks for the lift, Mark . . . and for being all right about it all.

Thanks for the apology. See you tomorrow, nine a.m. sharp!

Making the right move

I'd spent the whole night trying to figure out a way to introduce my-self to Elizabeth. I couldn't come up with anything that didn't seem totally obvious. Maybe Mark was right. Maybe he could introduce us. But that's when you risk the horrible three minutes' silence where everyone is trying to figure out what to say. It's in those awk-ward, not very smooth silences that I begin to glow a rosy, very un-cool red. That just can't happen.

I was still thinking about it during the trip to school.

Are you all right, Will?

Yeah, Mum.

So it looks like from here on in I'll be taking care of the veg-gie patch. . . .

But then it would be better because there'd be other people around so I wouldn't have to be the only one talking.

Will?

Yeah?

As long as Mark didn't carry on.

Meaning . . . it's getting down to the final weeks.

I looked over at her, wondering what she was going on about.

Well, that's what the note on the fridge says, full rehearsals for the next three weekends and then the show.

So that's the only time I have left. I have to make my move today, otherwise there's no point.

Will . . . ? It would be nice if you actually listened while your mother tried to communicate with you.

Yeah, no, it's all good, Mum.

Well, I never thought I would ever hear Will Armstrong say that spending three consecutive weekends at school was good. You must be enjoying it.

Maybe Mark was right, maybe all I had to do was . . .

Have you made any new friends?

I willed myself back into the car and back into the conversation. She had given me another lift to school after all. And I knew she was making up for lost veggie-patch bonding time.

A couple.

Pause.

Any girls, Will?

Left field! Left field! Back up! How did she do that? I looked over at her, trying to suss whether she had one of those *I know everything about you* smiles on her face. Mum always asked a lot of questions but she never asked those types of questions. She left that up to Dad.

Come on, Mum. It's a school musical, not somewhere you go to pick up.

I know that, Will, I was just wondering if there was anyone, well, you know, special?

Anyone special! As soon as the opposite sex is mentioned Mum turns into one of Andrews's walking stereotypes. That was the difference—if I told Dad we'd end up having a laugh, I tell Mum and it's serious. I pushed that thought straight back out of my head as soon as it got there.

We pulled up outside the gates again. The unanswered question filled the car.

No, Mum, but if there is I'll fill you in—as long as you don't ask me if she's *special*.

Deal.

I reached over and threw a kiss on her left cheek. I was getting used to that smile, and I liked it.

As soon as I had picked up the guitar and turned toward the hall the Freak had sniffed me out.

Is that your mum?

I turned to find him doing the fox-terrier jump at my side. I hadn't seen him since last week.

Hey, man, where did you spring from? Nice to see you back.

He nearly did backflips in response.

I was waiting for you. So was that your mum?

Who else would it have been, unless I had this whole older-woman thing going on?

She seems nice.

I looked at him. He was one of the strangest earthlings I had ever met.

So were you waiting outside for a reason? Are those geeks giving you a hard time again?

Nope, they're scared of what you'll do to them. I told them that you're my best friend.

Yet another strike to my almost nonexistent image. I attempted to reset the boundaries.

Ahh, well, I wouldn't go that far. I mean, I'm pretty much older than you are.

But that doesn't matter. I'm used to having older people as my friends. Dad thinks it's good for my development. Anyway, Dad's my other best friend and he's much older than you. I told him all about you and he said I was lucky to have someone as nice and caring as you as a friend.

I gave up then.

All right, mate. Let's go inside.

The rest of the geeks were playing the latest geek craze on their laptops and Zach was very obviously not invited. They might have backed right off him but that didn't mean they were going to let him infiltrate their geekdom. I could feel the confidence in him grow as he walked beside me. He had to get some mates. But for the moment it looked like I was it.

Waddlehead

As the Freak and I set up our gear it took me a few seconds to sniff out that Waddlehead had entered the building. Usually before rehearsals Andrews would say, *I know it's only happy noise but could you keep it down to a yell?* Today there was silence. All the kids knew that in Waddlehead's world there was no such thing as *happy noise,* it was all *bad noise* except when there was no noise. But it wasn't just Waddlehead-associated fear that shut us up. His appearance marked something unusual. On reality TV this would be the scene they'd put on the ads all week to suck people in to watching.

Brother Pat, Andrews and Waddlehead were positioned right at the front of the stage. Waddlehead had his head down, with his hands inside the pockets of a gray parka. Obviously part of his casual gear. He must shop where my grandfather did. Andrews was moving his hands around a lot. Brother Pat said something very loudly once and then said nothing else. He stood there in his usual position; hands resting on his stomach, slowly rocking back and forth on his heels, whistling quietly through his teeth.

At one point Andrews sprang over to the pit, grabbed his production folder and then sprang back. He held it with one hand, right up in Waddlehead's face, and flicked the pages with the other. Waddlehead looked at the folder once and continued shaking his head. Andrews stopped. There was nothing for thirty seconds, then

Waddlehead turned and left by the stage door, hands still in his pockets.

Andrews and Brother Pat said nothing for another thirty seconds, then Andrews ran out after Waddlehead. The entire occupancy of the hall started to gravitate toward the doors just to see if there was going to be some action outside. Unfortunately Andrews came back in before we got there, but he was definitely looking more pissed off than when he left.

Then no noise turned to lots of noise, full of gossip and rumor. Everyone swore they knew exactly what was going on. *Andrews had been busted over the weekend by the cops and Waddlehead had told him he had to resign: Waddlehead had heard from one of the parents that there was full-frontal nudity and a love scene and demanded that the musical be stopped immediately: someone had a contagious disease and we were all quarantined until further notice.*

In my experience no dealings with Waddlehead are ever good. And wherever he went he left a long trail of misery behind him. So I knew it wasn't going to be pretty. Andrews spent another five minutes talking with Brother Pat, who remained quietly rocking with his hands folded, except this time he was doing a lot of nodding.

Andrews moved forward.

Right, everyone. As you have no doubt just seen, Mr. Waverton was here.

Why is it that teachers always state the obvious?

He said to wish you the very best success, he applauds all of your dedication and hard work and he is sure that *The Boy Friend* will be the most successful musical yet.

Yeah right! That's exactly what he was saying!

Unfortunately he also delivered some very difficult news— but nothing we cannot overcome.

Pause.

It appears the hall has been double booked on the dates of our performances. Due to bookings every weekend of the holidays and the HSC commencing as soon as we return next term, we are going to have to bring the performances forward by a week. Which means that these two weekends will be the final two weekends before the actual performances.

For a second time in twenty minutes the hall was filled with noise: high-pitched squealing and dramatic yelling.

You've got to be joking, sir!

No way, that's not fair.

A couple of the more theatrical types actually left the hall, only to come back in again really quickly so they wouldn't miss anything. It was probably the best news I'd heard in a while, if I forgot about the Elizabeth thing. But I didn't think it was that big a deal.

Now I have every confidence we will be ready, but it does mean that the time we have left is vital for all of us. We absolutely must, must, must all pull together as a team. That goes for every single band member, every backstage person, every chorus member, every lead, the prompt, Ms. Sefton, Brother Pat and myself.

As he labeled each group he paused and stared at where they were sitting, even the teachers. When he got to himself he pointed, as if we didn't know it was him he was talking about.

From now on, we do not have time to wait for people who forget their cue, to wait for the Year Eight chorus to repeat their dance to "It's so much nicer in Nice," to wait for people to move stage left instead of right. And chorus, absolutely no more faking with the words of songs!

Leads—he turned and looked to the left of the stage—**there is absolutely no excuse for not having lines learned nor blocking**

onstage. I will be expecting you all to work with me three times a week for the next two weeks.

He looked in Brother Pat's direction.

It is up to Brother Pat what he wants to do with the band.

We'll be ready, Mr. Andrews, don't you worry!

Thank God for that!

OK, people, it is up to you now! Five minutes, then we are on.

So Waddlehead didn't just destroy the lives of students. I watched as everyone did their own thing to try and get their heads around the news. Andrews went outside again. Mark went in the opposite direction, no doubt to have a sly cigarette even though he told me he'd given up again. Elizabeth went straight to the dressing room. Yep, Waddlehead had done his job well.

The aftershock

Waddlehead's news meant that the morning was high pressure, punctuated with mini explosions of steam that escaped from bubbling creative tempers. Mr. Andrews, who is normally Mr. Ice Man, lost it at Mark, who is normally Mr. Placid. Mark then lost it at Elizabeth, who is normally Ms. Nice, who lost it with the music teacher, Ms. Sefton, who is normally Ms. Understanding. Ms. Sefton then lost it at us, the band, who are normally kept out of all that hypertension crap. It was at this time Andrews called for a break and instructed all of us to leave the hall and go for a walk, run, whatever, just so long as everyone lightened up.

I was wondering whether now was the time to make the move. As I made my way to the stage, I caught sight of the back of Elizabeth's shirt walking at top speed out of the hall. It was pretty obvious that she didn't need some guy hanging around right at this moment.

I looked down to find the Freak waiting patiently with his lunch box in his hand. He and Brother Pat seemed to be the only two people in the hall who Waddlehead had not gotten to.

Come on, Will! Little lunch.

We'd been going through the same routine every rehearsal.

Listen, Freak, by the time you get to high school you have got to start calling little lunch *recess* or, at the very least, *play lunch*. Actually, that's just as bad. Just call it recess.

Why? What's the difference, it still means the same thing.

In some way he had a point and maybe if he didn't care then other people wouldn't. But unfortunately that's not how school play-grounds operated. There were so many codes you had to learn to survive your first year in high school. These codes then dictated the pecking order for the next six years or until there was a major growth spurt with a heavy shot of hormones. That was how vital it was to get it right. And persisting in calling recess *little lunch* showed a major lack of understanding of the code.

I peered into the plastic Ninja Turtles lunch box. As usual it was jam-packed with everything good: a pink icing doughnut, a small packet of chips, cheese and crackers, fruit strips. You had to give his dad credit. He sure knew how to pack a lunch box.

Man, you've got enough in here for the whole band.

Zach nodded his head in agreement and with a mouthful of chips offered, **Yeah, lots of people sit with me at little lunch.**

I bet. Do they come back at lunch?

No, I normally have lunch by myself and go straight to the library. The other guys just want to play footy and I don't want to. Here, you can have the doughnut.

He put it in my hand, the pink icing clinging to the outer edges of my palm.

No, I can't have that. It must be your favorite.

It is, but I don't care if you have it. You're my friend.

The thing was, this guy was so honest. He just said what was in his head without worrying what anyone else thought. It was a hard way to live but it seemed a bit more real than the usual teenager crap. Maybe a little too real at times.

We were sitting eating the Cohen feast when I saw Mark. He was talking and having a laugh with the other members of the cast.

It seemed as though everyone liked him, the bastard. Elizabeth was nowhere to be seen.

Hey, Will!

Mark beckoned me over to join the group. I waved back and pointed to the Freak.

Come over and meet these guys, Mark called back. **Bring your mate.**

The Freak nearly wet himself with excitement.

Come on, Will! Let's go. Oh boy! Wait until the other guys see that I know all of the leads. Come on. They're waiting for us. Zach . . .

Too late. The Freak was already doing his doggy leaps over there. I could see Mark extending his hand and Zach shaking it hard. The others did the same. Zach had not shut up the whole time.

Yeah, Will, well, he's like my best friend in the musical. He's the best. He says—

Settle down, Freak.

Everybody looked at me as if I'd said something really bad. I suppose if you call a guy who thinks that the sun shines out of your arse *Freak*, they might have a point. But the little guy loved it; well, at least it looked like he did, and I know he would have no problem telling me if he didn't.

No, that's his nickname. You like it, don't you, Zach?

He nodded and continued talking to the girl who played the second lead. That kid could talk to anybody.

Mark looked at me. **Your new best mate, Will?**

The little guy needs someone to keep an eye on him. I looked over at the Freak, who was still talking. **He's all right. He's really innocent. He doesn't seem to care that he hasn't got any friends.**

Yeah, that type of thing's hard.

I thought that maybe it had been like that for Mark. He shook his head.

I wasn't some type of reject, if that's what you were thinking.

I went to apologize but he was on a roll.

In Years Seven and Eight I rated myself as a pretty cool footy player. The shit hit the fan in Year Nine. That's when everything went crazy. . . . I spent half the year dodging fruit, bags, fists. Even dorks rated higher on the scale than faggots.

I flinched when he said *faggot*; at St. Andrew's it was one of the lowest put-downs. I was about to ask him about it when I felt someone pulling on my arm, an annoying action that could only belong to the Freak.

Hey, listen, Freak, back off, would you . . .

I turned around to tell him to shove off and instead found myself face to face with Elizabeth Zefferelli.

Nooooooooooooooooo!!!!

I couldn't move.

Nothing. I had nothing.

The most I could do was stretch my mouth into a really stupid *I have the IQ of a baboon* expression. I searched frantically for anything to cover up this dithering drongo act, but there was nothing there. She obviously wasn't having the same problem. Her huge smile was teasing me.

The last time I saw you I wasn't looking at your face.

I could hear the alarm bells sounding. The red of the fire billowed around my face; smoke escaped from all facial orifices.

So you were an eyewitness . . .

Uh-huh.

She continued looking straight at me, her smile toying with me playfully. She wasn't making this easy. In fact she looked like she was loving every second of watching me be uncomfortable. The others were just standing back watching the show.

So, she challenged as she moved closer, **do you have a name or should I just keep calling you** *the backside boy?*

At this point Mark laughed out loud. I tried to tell him to shut up but I couldn't speak. After what seemed like a million minutes, I managed my name.

Will . . . Will Armstrong.

I was dying; I reached deep down, trying frantically to find some type of witty response.

My backside is not my strongest point.

Loser!

Oh, I don't know, I thought it was kind of cute.

And with that she turned on her heel and walked away. Now, call me stupid, but I could swear that there had been some major flirtatious action happening there.

Mark gave me the thumbs-up.

I told you she knew your better points. Saucy, huh?

Andrews's voice summoned me back to the present.

Righto, you lot. Let's make a start.

I was left alone with the Freak. Everyone wandered back inside. I was still trying to return to normal blood flow. I felt light, like I could take off. It didn't matter that I had just acted like a complete loser; all that mattered was that I'd met Elizabeth and she thought I had a cute backside. I'd never been so keen to get back into the rehearsal room.

The run

The rest of the day was a blur of scenes, overtures, reprises, dropped lines, some spectacular and some unspectacular solos. The break was the best thing Andrews had done for me in the past two months and I bet if he knew, it would have killed him.

I looked around the hall and all of a sudden I was there, smack bang a part of it, in a way I hadn't been before.

Yeah, the geeks still got to me sometimes in their annoying mosquito in your ear at midnight type of way, but they could play their instruments; the chorus girls still giggled and carried on, but they were doing the right stuff onstage and looked good. I knew how hard the leads had been working and you could see they were trying even harder after Andrews's freak-out. The hall was full of people wanting to make this thing work.

It was like we had all been through a really painful, exhausting, superlong training session and now we were getting ready for the semis. I suppose you could say I was happy to be a part of it. Even if I hadn't done as many laps around the oval as the others, today I was finally off the bench.

It made me think of the number of people who were creative and never got to do anything with it. Because of lots of reasons: you copped crap for doing it at school, it wasn't considered a proper job, everyone thought you were some sort of dropout or wanker and you'd never make it anyway, and if you did then they thought you were up yourself. I'd dreamt of playing for Man U for half my life and I might still have had the occasional dream where I was dressed in the red and white kit. But somehow that dream was perfectly acceptable—you were probably considered weird if you didn't have it. That was normal, but if you wanted to get out there and be onstage, then all of a sudden to some people you were a loser.

My attention was dragged back to the hall by the booming voice of Brother Pat.

Right, everybody! Friday week from twelve-thirty p.m. we will have a complete dress rehearsal in front of the juniors of St. Andrew's and Lakeside. The girls will be bused over in the afternoon.

The geeks giggled among themselves. I looked over at them, shaking my head. As if any of them had a chance. But after the way I had carried on outside, who was I to talk?

We will also invite the neighboring homes for the aged to watch the afternoon's entertainment, and of course all your parents, if for any reason they cannot make the evening performances, are most welcome too.

I won't be telling Mum about that one, she's already coming to both performances.

Because we were coming back tomorrow, most of the stuff could be left out overnight. I put my guitar away in its case, glad that the dress rehearsal was only in front of the juniors. If it was the whole school it would be a different story. I could just imagine Tim and Jock revved up by the rest of the boys. I would keep hearing about it until I was a hundred.

Will, can I see you for a moment?

I started guiltily, wondering if Brother Pat had somehow been reading my thoughts.

Yes, Brother.

Now, Will, I was just saying to Mr. Andrews that I have been very impressed by your commitment and talent.

Thanks, Brother. I eyed Andrews nervously.

He tells me you have befriended young Cohen. Lovely boy but a bit of a loner. He seems light-years ahead of the other boys.

Oh, I don't know about that, Brother, he's a—

Now, now, none of your modesty. But that's not why I called you over. I have a special request.

Great!

You do realize St. Andrew's Day is also on Friday week, which is part of the reason why we are allowing the juniors to have a little bit of time out of class to watch our performance. The rest of the school will complain, I know, but what with the curriculum the way it is, it's just not possible.

Thank you, God!

However, before the performance, we will be having our regular St. Andrew's Day celebration for the whole school. And this year I would like you to lead the school band. It's clear you have much to offer musically and you may as well let everybody share in your gift.

I stared at him. Hard.

Right, good. I'm pleased that's settled. This will be very good for you, William. It will enable the school body to recognize your talents and see you in a totally different light. We have singing practice in the hall on Friday for the whole school. I'll need you up the front on the stage.

I continued staring, mute.

No need to thank me, I can see you appreciate what I am offering you. Must be getting back. Good evening, Phil. I'll see you tomorrow, William.

The man was serious!

Goodnight, Brother, Mr. Andrews called.

I looked over accusingly at Andrews.

Don't look at me, Will. Brother Pat came up with that all on his own.

I gave Andrews one of my best fake smiles, grabbed my stuff and got out of there.

This was a prime example of what I was trying to get through the Freak's head. It was all about not messing with the code. And singing practice and being in the band . . . well, it didn't just mess with the code, it destroyed it and whoever was involved. I'd already stepped dangerously close by being in the musical, but at least it was punishment, and you weren't on display in the pit. Singing practice meant the whole school, the teachers, the mums on tuckshop duty, the secretaries, everyone could see you.

Yep, it was just one big public humiliation.

Pizza?

I came out of the hall to find Mark, the Freak and Elizabeth all waiting for me. My filthy mood lifted instantly.

We thought you might appreciate a lift home. Zach told us your mum dropped you off this morning, so I figured you might be looking for one.

Zach had it more sussed than I realized.

Yeah, sure. Thanks.

I watched Elizabeth mucking around with Zach just ahead of us. He was talking to her like he'd known her his whole life.

Mark broke the silence.

So what did Brother want?

Elizabeth had stopped and waited for Mark and me to catch up.

Have you been dropping your pants again?

This girl had no shame.

You wish!

It was out of my mouth before I could take it back. There was a second's pause and then she let out a full belly laugh and hit me on the shoulder.

That's a bit *cheeky*, isn't it?

The bad pun wasn't wasted on any of us, except maybe the Freak, who was looking a little bit confused but he laughed along anyway. I forgot being embarrassed and started to feel more relaxed.

Actually, Brother Pat was taking the time to tell me what a wonderful asset I have been to him.

You're full of it!

Wait, there's more. He thinks I'm such a fine role model that he's asked me to play at the school liturgy and the school singing practices!

At this point Elizabeth and Mark cracked up laughing. You see, they understood the code. The difference was they didn't care about it. Only the Freak was looking like I'd just been named Best New Performer at the Arias.

That's really cool, Will! This means we get to hang out at school too!

Mark threw in his twenty cents' worth. Yeah, Will, that will be really cool!

I could easily have thumped the bloke.

Shut up, you sarcastic bastard!

Mark bolted to his car and the Freak followed.

Elizabeth fell back to walk beside me. Any thought of anything else but her evaporated. My body was on sensory overload. I could smell her shampoo, hear her breathing and I burned all over every time we bumped shoulders. How was it she could manage to string sentences together and I couldn't?

She patted me on the shoulder and spoke in a really sincere voice.

It won't really be that bad, Will. I think you'd look cool even playing the guitar in a school singing practice.

I was still trying to recover from the impact of her touch. The fact that she thought I looked cool playing my guitar was way too much to handle. I finally worked up enough courage to look directly at her.

Really?

She laughed.

No, not really, but it made you feel better, right?

You . . . She took off across the playground and I followed. **You girl!**

Good comeback, Will. I'm really offended you called me a girl!

I cornered her out by the old chapel. It was an ancient sandstone slab that seemed permanently in the shade. The juniors carried on about it being haunted but it was more likely rats had set up home there than lost spirits.

I moved closer toward her. And she stayed exactly where she was. . . .

You act all tough but I can see you're worried.

Her laughter bubbled out of her.

Yeah, Will, really worried . . .

I stopped one footstep away from her. Our eyes locked. The world slowed down.

If I'd reached out my arms I could have touched her, but I didn't. We just looked . . . looked at each other for what felt like the first time . . . for what felt like a really long time. No grins, no playful smile, no awkward embarrassment or red faces, just us.

I took one more small step. Elizabeth matched it with her own.

Mark says that if you don't get *your sorry arses into the car,* he's going to leave you here and send Brother Patrick to find you.

What?

Will?

I felt a familiar tugging on my sleeve. The Freak, right on cue!

Come on, Will, I think Mark's getting cranky.

All right, mate, calm down.

As I was pulling myself together I watched the Freak grab Elizabeth's hand. He made it look so easy.

Come on!

Elizabeth smiled, waved and followed. I was the last one to get to the car and tried hard to appear normal.

I thought you said she was a nice girl? I said to Mark as I jumped in the back with the Freak, who I was deliberately ignoring.

Well, she is to me.

Yeah, but that's because you deserve it. I watched her reach over and pat Mark on the knee.

Nice and sweet, that's our Elizabeth.

He returned the pat and I felt a small twinge in my gut. The gay guy and the Freak were doing better than me.

I could feel the Freak's eyes cutting into my back like lasers. I turned to face him.

What?

He sat there grinning at me.

What are you smiling at?

He was about to burst, he could barely contain himself.

Oh, nothing!

He kept grinning.

Cut it out!

Then he started to flick his head in Elizabeth's direction, roll his eyes and burst into giggles.

I grabbed him in a headlock and silenced him. But he was laughing so hard I had to release him so he could get his breath and then I resumed the headlock.

Just as I was about to tell him that he was going to meet a very premature ending it dawned on me that he shouldn't be there.

I stopped mid-pummel. **Hey, Freak, does your dad know you're here? Don't you need to ring him?**

No, he rang and said he couldn't pick me up for another hour. I told him that I would be fine because I'd hang out with you guys.

Yeah, but I didn't even know I was getting a lift home, so how did you?

Because I heard Mark and Elizabeth talking about going to get a pizza and I asked if we could come.

You asked if *we* could come?

Yeah. Well, I thought you'd want to too.

The headlock changed into a kind of bear hug. I loved this kid! There was no denying he was a Freak, but he was a great Freak! Not one trace of embarrassment.

Hey, Will, if you'd prefer to go home I can drop you off?

Mark was looking at me really innocently. He truly was a master of the subtle piss-take.

No way, buddy, I'm not missing out on pizza, even if it means I have to be seen out with you rejects.

The car erupted with all three of them telling me to get stuffed. Elizabeth was whacking me with her script, the Freak was attempting to king-hit me from my left and Mark tossed an empty water bottle at my head.

All right, all right. I'm sorry. I didn't mean it. Now let's get out of this dump!

The love-in

The local pizza place is where all the kids stuck in the *can't legally go to the pub or a club but are sick of Macca's or the car park of the local servo* hang out. It was also a pretty usual spot to find St. Andrew's boys and Lakeside girls. I nodded to a table near the door where a mixture of Year 11s and 12s sat with their girlfriends. Normally these guys would see me with Chris and the boys or the soccer boys. The last person they would expect to see with the new guy, the Year 7 dork and the assistant head of Lakeside's Green House was Will Armstrong. As we walked past them they leaned in and started talking in a way that could only mean hot gossip.

Mark took control.

What does everyone want?

Let's get one with everything on it and super big!

The Freak obviously liked pizza.

Right then, Zach, how about you and I go and place the order?

The Freak consented happily and bounced his way to the counter with Mark. It was clear that the kid was as happy as the proverbial pig in shit. It also meant that Elizabeth and I were left alone at the table. I looked up to find her smiling at me.

Is it true you're only involved in the musical because you were forced to be?

I thought about saying I would have joined up anyway but she didn't look like she'd fall for it.

Yeah.

Was it because of the mooning?

Yeah.

That's a pretty weird punishment, don't you think?

Yeah.

OK, that was three *yeahs* in a row. I was beginning to sound like an idiot.

It was Andrews's idea.

Elizabeth looked at me, wanting more of the story.

I don't know, the last six months he's been on my case the whole time. He reckons getting me onto the musical was going easy on me. But the amount of time I've had to give up would be equivalent to five years' worth of detentions. The musical, well . . . it wasn't exactly my thing . . .

I wanted to say that now, right at this moment, it didn't feel anything like detention, but . . . I didn't. **What about you?**

I wanted to do the musical. It *is* my thing.

I didn't mean . . .

Great! I might as well have called her a loser to her face.

No, it's all right, Will. I don't care. It's different at Lakeside anyway. It's a big deal. It's like what Mr. Andrews was saying today, it depends on all of us to make something like this work and it doesn't matter if you play in the band or have a solo or are in the chorus, everyone has to do their job or it doesn't work. I like being involved in something like that. And I really enjoy singing.

You're good at it.

She looked down at her drink. **Thanks.**

Mark and Zach came back after what must have been the fastest order in history. The Freak did not stop talking until the pizza arrived.

Hey, Freak, try and give it a rest for a little while.

Mark more diplomatically suggested he actually take the time to eat some of the pizza he so desperately wanted.

Yeah, it's funny, my dad says that to me all the time. He says that if he didn't remind me to eat, I would just keep talking until everything on the table was eaten and then I'd wonder why I was left out.

At this point I shoved a slice of pizza in his mouth. He got the idea after that, and plowed through another three pieces, leaving the table oddly quiet.

What are you two going to do with all the free time you have after this is over?

I couldn't think of anything better to say. Anyway, I was genuinely interested. In Elizabeth anyway. Mark volunteered first, however.

Well, that's easy for me, the HSC and rugby.

Is that all?

You wait till you get to Year Twelve and see how much time you've got!

Elizabeth shook her head and grinned at Mark.

Stop being such an old man! You've got to make time to have some fun!

She changed direction from Mark to me. **What about you, Will?**

Pretty much the same old stuff . . . you know, hanging out with the boys, playing my guitar . . .

You play soccer, don't you? The boys reckon you're pretty good.

Not this season. Mostly I just kick the footy around with the boys down the park.

We should all try and meet up after the musical's over, like on a regular basis.

The Freak had evidently finished his pizza and wanted to exercise his vocal cords.

Yeah, that'd be good. Elizabeth was looking at me again. I could feel the telltale blush begin its ascent.

Sure, a new kid in town who's gay needs all the friends he can get, Mark threw in.

I caught the Freak out of the corner of my eye. He was looking at Mark with renewed interest. He was going to let loose with one of his father's philosophies, I knew it.

Are you really gay? he asked.

Zach, I cautioned.

It's all right, Will, let him ask. Yes, mate, I am indeed one hundred percent gay.

Wow, you're the first real gay person I've ever met. So have you really kissed a boy? What's it like?

Zach! This time I kicked him under the table.

Zach looked at me, wounded.

What? He said it was all right to ask him questions. I'd ask you what it was like to kiss Elizabeth, when you finally get around to it.

At this point I put my head in my hands and seriously thought about dragging the little jerk off his seat and giving him a good bashing. I felt Elizabeth watching me across the table. She was laughing hard. Needless to say Mark was carrying on like it was the joke of the millennium.

Eventually everyone died down a bit and Zach burst out, **Wait until I tell Dad about you, Mark! He won't mind, you know. He** believes everyone should live their life the way they want to, as long as it doesn't hurt anyone else.

He sounds like a smart guy, Zach. You're lucky to have a dad like that. Mine's only just coming around to the idea.

The Freak nearly caused an electricity surge he was so stoked that Mark had complimented his dad. I was more interested in Mark's father.

Is your dad still strange with it?

Mark picked up his glass of water and turned it in his hand.

Yeah, it's taken him a while to get his head around it. He's older, you know, so when he hears the word *gay*, he only thinks of men who put on women's clothes, wear bad makeup and mime to really bad songs. And hey, if that's what makes them happy . . . Mark put down the glass and picked up the coaster. **He didn't say much when he first found out. I think he figured I was going through a stage because no one who was really gay could possibly be such a good footballer. I still reckon he secretly hopes I'll grow out of it.**

I wondered about what Dad would have done if I'd gone home and told him I was gay. With all he went on about blokes giving each other such a hard time on the site, you'd reckon he'd be all right with it, but you never know. And I'd never get to ask him now.

So what do you reckon your dad would do, Will?

An innocent question—they always are—but it hit me in the belly like a concrete pylon.

Ahh . . . I felt the ancient eyes of the Freak pierce through my skin. **I don't know . . . hard to say really . . .**

I could sense the Freak was gearing up to ask me one of his killer questions. Self-preservation dictated I get in before him.

Hey, Freak, it might be better if you kept that bit of news around this table. Don't you think, Mark?

Well, I'm OK with it, but he might cop it a bit, and if things are already tough, saying you're mates with a gay guy isn't going to do you any favors.

I don't care what they say to me. They say plenty now and I can handle it. But if you think it's going to be better for you this way, Mark, then I won't say anything.

Thanks, mate. I think you're smart enough to figure that one out.

The kid grew five centimeters in five seconds.

We got off the gay topic, and spoke about Elizabeth's dream of being an actor.

They're waiting for me to grow out of wanting to act and sing too—she inclined her head in Mark's direction—and I keep telling them that it's not going to happen. Mum wants me to go to Sydney Uni, like she did, and do Economics-Law. Which is why she adores Mark, because that is exactly what he wants to do.

ANU, not Sydney.

Whatever, she still loves you.

He held his hands in the air. What can I do, mothers love me!

She threw a piece of pepperoni at him.

How come your parents are making such a big deal of it? I asked.

I don't know. Mum goes on and on about how Nonna and Nonno worked so hard to make sure she had a good education. They sent her to a private girls' school. Mum wanted me to go to one too but all of my friends were going to Lakeside so I said no. It was the first major fight we'd ever had. Up until then I was Miss Goody-Goody.

Right, Miss Assistant Head of Green.

Shut up, Mark!

Anyway, thank God Lakeside was getting written up in the paper as one of the best state schools so she let me win that one. My brother wasn't as lucky, though.

I put on my most sympathetic face. **That's harsh.**

What?

Sending your brother to a private girls' school.

She nearly choked on the drink she was sipping, she laughed so loud. Mark and Zach joined in.

Sorry, go on. I wasn't at all sorry.

She shook her head. **It's not over yet, anyway. I want to learn how to do something that I already love and Mum wants me to do something I know I already hate. Subject selections next term should be fun.**

Yeah, if your mother is as fiery as you, I want tickets.

She ignored Mark.

What about your parents, Will?

Silence. I made myself answer.

They're different. They only ever said that I should do the things I'm interested in. They were cool with the subject selections. I mean, I think Mum would have loved it if I'd chosen physics and chemistry and extension two maths like Chris and this nerd—Mark gave me the finger—**but they knew that was never going to happen, so they accepted that. I guess I'm pretty lucky.**

Pause.

It's not as if I'm dumb or anything, though. I couldn't quite believe that had come out of my mouth. Andrews and Danielli must have been rubbing off on me.

Elizabeth thankfully ignored this last comment.

You're so lucky.

I guess I was lucky. I grew up in a house where both my parents had their heads in books, where music was always on—bad music but music nevertheless—and where Dad stuck his guitar in my hands when I was three.

So do you want to play music when you leave school?

I'd never thought about it.

I don't know. Yeah, maybe.

I didn't know whether Mum would be *that* cool.

Once again the little guy came to my rescue.

I intend to be a trombone-playing physicist.

None of us laughed. It wasn't a joke.

Do you like school, Zach? Elizabeth asked.

He nodded his head.

I do like school, it's just that sometimes I don't like what happens to me there.

What happens?

Her voice had softened and she looked at him encouragingly.

Some of the kids always have to give me a hard time. It started right at the beginning of school when some of the boys from my primary school told everybody I get really angry. They say I click it. I don't lose it so much anymore, but if someone is trying their hardest to get you to click it, it's hard not to. So I clicked it a couple of times and ended up in Mr. Waverton's office.

You've been in Waddlehead's office!

Zach nodded at me admonishingly. **And I don't know why you don't like him because he was very nice.**

I had a comeback ready but I figured it was the little guy's moment, not mine.

He told me he wanted to help me and find the boys who did it. So I told him. But it didn't help much. Well, most of them stopped but two of them didn't.

He took a quick breath and carried on. **Dad got really angry and came up to the office and yelled at Mr. Waverton and said he was going to take me out of the school. But I didn't want to go. I like it here. Things are OK now. Mostly they leave me alone. Dad told me that the best way to deal with it is to ignore them so I do. And some of the other guys tell them to stop. Anyway, like I said, it's different now.**

He reached for another slice of pizza and held it in his hand right close to his mouth. It waved in front of his face as he talked.

Since Will and I became friends everyone has shut up. And because of you too, Mark. You know how you say hello to me at the tuckshop, well, they know you play football and you're friends with Chris Holden and even though you can see they want to say something they won't because they're scared.

Eventually the cheese started to drip down his hand.

There's a couple of kids in the band who are all right, but I like hanging out with you guys. He shoved the slice in his mouth.

Well, you can hang out with us anytime you want, Zach.

I hoped Elizabeth meant it, because I knew from experience that he would.

Zach beamed back at her, chewing. Elizabeth looked at me and smiled a huge smile.

Mark grinned over at me. I put my head down and groaned.

Just as the evening was about to end as a huge love-in Elizabeth's phone rang. It was the first time I'd ever heard her panicked. She looked over at Mark, who jingled his keys and nodded.

Yeah, all right, Dad. Mark's giving me a lift and I'll be home soon.

She put her phone away. **It's so typical! They said I could go out after rehearsals but they're already stressing about tomorrow and schoolwork.**

Yeah, but if you go home now you'll have more chance to go out tomorrow night, right?

Mark gave her a push as she collected her bag and she eventually smiled.

I thought about the drive to school this morning with Mum. Who would have thought the day was going to end up like this? This was exactly the type of girl information she would love.

Except that conversation was never going to happen.

In need of
Bubble Wrap

The next morning I actually looked forward to rehearsals! Even the thought of singing practice on Friday wasn't freaking me out so much. So the boys would give me heaps, but that would be nothing in comparison to what I planned for my revenge. I'd pull off one of Will Armstrong's finest schemes and order and balance would be restored. Yep, things were definitely looking up.

I rode to school and was nearly as early as the Freak. He was waiting out front as usual. This time it was me who felt like pogoing all over the place.

Hey, Freak! I circled him on my bike. It had become a little bit of a game and it wound him right up. He didn't know whether to laugh or to tell me to get lost. But he loved every second of it and it amused the crap out of me.

Watch out for my trombone, Will.

He was trying to be serious but every time I kept trapping him he'd giggle even louder.

Trust me, Freak, have I hurt it yet? You know, you need to get another love in your life other than that bloody trombone.

What, like you and Elizabeth?

And he giggled so hard he nearly fell over.

Right, that's it! And I circled round, got up speed and went straight for him.

He ran the fastest he ever had in his life. I called a truce.

I'm not coming back until you get off your bike!

All right, all right, I'll get off.

As he approached me, I went to get on it again. I did it every time and every time it completely threw him. It was just another one of those codes he hadn't cracked yet.

You promised! he screamed as he hid behind the Dumpster I first rescued him from.

All right, mate, relax, it was just a joke.

The little man did have a tendency to lose it. But he was slowly lightening up. He edged up beside me and we made our way to the hall.

Hey, Will? Can I ask you a question?

Yeah, sure, mate. As long as it's not about Elizabeth.

No, it's not about her, I promise.

OK then, go right ahead.

Your dad's dead, isn't he?

Where the hell did that come from?

It's just that we were talking about Mark's dad last night and then Elizabeth asked you about yours and you didn't say anything. I remember one of the older boys telling someone else that your dad had died in some sort of accident.

The sound of my dropped bike echoed around the playground. The Freak looked at me, waiting for a reply. I willed myself to answer him.

Yeah, he is.

I had my back to him, bending down to pick up the bike. It was so like Zach to fire out this kind of question. He wasn't doing anything but trying to understand. It was just that I didn't want to understand.

Look, Freak, I don't really talk about it.

I was just wondering how long ago it was. Whether it was ages ago or . . .

I dropped the bike again and put my head in my hands, nearly pulling out every bit of hair that was attached to my head to prevent myself from ripping out his.

It happened during the Christmas holidays last year.

My mind went back to that time. I could feel the pull of the tunnel dragging me down.

Me at Chris's house. His mum saying my mum had called wanting me to go home. Mrs. Holden driving and Chris *coming along for the ride*. It was after New Year's and Mum was having one of her famous clear-outs. Whenever Dad and I sniffed one was in the air we made a really quick exit. She'd listen to bad hippie music and sing really loudly and constantly be bossing us around, moving stuff everywhere. I thought that was why she had summoned me home and I wasn't happy.

I saw Uncle John's car in front of the house. He had been Dad's work partner and best mate for as long as I could remember. I wondered why Mum hadn't conned him into helping instead. I came into the house about to say exactly that when I saw her. I knew there was something wrong. She was sitting dead still at the kitchen table, surrounded by old scarves, coats, hats and dresses. Fleetwood Mac was blaring in the background. Uncle John didn't even look at me. He excused himself to turn down the music.

She looked at me, a look I had never seen before. And I knew. You always know, you just pretend you don't.

Darling, there's been an accident. . . .

And at that point I went straight to my room and didn't come out.

I could just make out Zach. He was looking at me intently and his eyes were sad, really sad. If I kept looking in those eyes I knew I would never make it out of the tunnel again.

Will! Hey, Will?

Freak was patting me on the shoulder and trying to pick up my bike.

I'm sorry, Will. Don't be sad. I'm really, really sorry.

I felt like I was going to throw up. I took the bike from him and made my way to the hall, hoping the movement would shift the shadow of the tunnel.

I don't want to go there, Freak. You've got to understand that not everyone talks about everything the way you do. You've got to back off people, give them some space.

Don't be mad, Will.

By this time the Freak had run in front of the bike and blocked my path. I couldn't look at the kid. I knew he was sorry and he needed to know that things were OK. I tousled his hair.

It's all right, Freak. Just leave it.

We walked into the hall together. It was the first time he'd shut up since I'd known him. An oxygenated bubble wrapped around me; I'd been using it for most of the year. It allowed me to see the world and be in the world but nothing from the world could get to me. It was a familiar and comforting sensation and I gave in to it completely. The rehearsal was going like always but I watched from a long way away. Disconnected. I saw Elizabeth and Mark onstage and at one point, when I remembered last night, I felt some sort of pull.

I tried my hardest to avoid everyone at lunch but the Freak must have said something to Mark because I could tell he was concerned.

Hey, Will, why don't you come over?

I nodded and smiled but said no.

Come on, mate. You and Elizabeth were sparking last night. She's going to think you're not interested.

I could feel the smallest of rips in the bubble.

I was thinking we could all head up to the pizza place again. Look, we've got to work with Andrews now, but I'll see you afterwards.

After Mark had left, the Freak came over and offered me my choice from his lunch box. The kid had looked like he was going to cry all morning. Straight after that Brother Pat, who had been giving me strange looks all rehearsal, rolled over to me on his conductor's stool, asking if I was all right. I told him I wasn't feeling well but I'd be fine after I'd been outside for a while.

I walked out of the hall and thought about last night, and then the past five weeks started to roll out in front of me. I figured with everyone asking me how I was it was just as hard to stay in the bubble as it was to rip it off.

It was Zach's face that really did it. The bugger looked so miserable. By the end of lunch I came up behind him and took off with his lunch box. It was another familiar game along familiar lines. He bolted off his seat after me the quickest I'd ever seen him move.

That's not very nice, Will. Give it back. And with that he attempted to kick me, his giggling preventing him getting anywhere close.

That's not very nice, Zach, I repeated in exactly the same tone.

Well, it's mine so give it back.

I hung it over his head just out of his reach.

Not until you say sorry.

His eyes clouded over and he stopped jumping instantly. **I am really sorry, Will.**

I know, mate. I know.

I relinquished the lunch box but only after I'd taken the last doughnut—he was keeping it for me anyway—and chased him back to his seat. He was cracking up laughing as usual and I was nearly back to normal.

By the end of the afternoon I knew I was back because I started yelling at one of the geeks to get his bloody timing right, and during the break I shoved a whole lot of toilet paper in his clarinet. Juvenile, I know, but he thought it was hilarious and took it as some sign of his increased state of coolness because I was paying him out.

I nearly bailed on the pizza night but I could tell the others were looking forward to it and they'd be disappointed if I wasn't there. Elizabeth must have done some major work on her parents because she was allowed out again, and I figured that if I was serious about her I'd better lift my game. It was then I thought about getting Chris to come along. He was always studying, playing football or looking after Jessie. And if I was being shoved out of my comfort zone, he may as well be too. It turned out that Elizabeth was already inviting some of her friends, which was even better. I didn't say that to Chris when I spoke to him on the phone. There's only so much shoving a person can take in one day. I knew that better than anybody.

Pizza again

It was a different night to last night. Last night was fantastic but it was pretty full-on with everyone spilling their stuff. Tonight the vibe was more up and everyone was just having a laugh. I made sure I was sitting next to Elizabeth and I didn't care who noticed, especially her. If she'd got up and moved I would have felt like a complete loser but she didn't. She just smiled and slid over on the booth. I sat back and listened to her friends going on about school and boys and stuff, throwing in my own stupid comments, trying to get them to laugh, trying to get Elizabeth to laugh.

Chris seemed to be doing all right over on the other table. He'd been talking to the same girl for the last half hour and she didn't look like she was going anywhere. Zach and Mark were sitting on either side of him, like his security blanket, but from where I was sitting he didn't need them. One of Elizabeth's friends kept going on about how cute he was. It nearly killed me not to give him heaps about it in front of everybody, but even I couldn't be that cruel.

But there was no way I was watching out for Chris all night. No, my attention was firmly on Elizabeth. She was something else. If you tied her hands behind her back she wouldn't be able to speak. And her eyes danced along with what she was saying. Her friends were really nice too. You could tell they were trying to scope me out, but they weren't too obvious about it. For a while, anyway—and then they started.

So you were the bloke who showed us his bits at the bus stop?

It was right about then I started to rethink my *nice* opinion. I could feel the familiar sound of the fire engine alarms starting up. What do you say to that? And what did she mean my *bits*? It was just my backside. Wasn't it?!

I looked at Elizabeth for support but she was loving every minute of it.

I shoved another slice of pizza in my mouth and nodded.

Yeah, we thought that the guy who did it must have been such a try-hard.

I stopped chewing for a split second. That's a bit harsh, isn't it?

But it seems like you're all right.

Yeah right, thanks heaps! Queen of the backhanded compliment. Then the one called Milly started up.

Yeah, Elizabeth says you're really funny.

I looked over at Elizabeth and raised my eyebrows.

So you've been talking about me to your friends?

I only said you were funny in a really annoying way.

I resorted to familiar territory and got revenge without words. I grabbed her bag and proceeded to fill it with all the stuff from the table: salt and pepper shakers, serviettes, coasters, the works. By the reaction I got it was working. She tried for a good three minutes to grab the bag from me, but I had the advantage of height and strength and we both knew it. Eventually she gave up and collapsed back into the booth laughing. She tried to grab it again when she thought I wasn't watching, at which point I threw the bag to Milly and asked her to finish the job. This allowed me to catch Elizabeth's hands and pin them behind her back.

Eventually Milly relinquished the bag but only after Elizabeth had threatened to get *her* bag and spread out all of its contents on the table. I wondered for a moment whether I might have gone a little too far when the salt shaker spilled all over Elizabeth's bag, but she just laughed even harder and when I wasn't looking grabbed a handful of salt and threw it over my head.

And I thought you were meant to be Miss Maturity!

At that point Milly said she had to leave, and since her mum was giving a lift to the other girls, they all stood up to go.

Wanna lift, Elizabeth?

Ahhh . . .

She sounded unsure, which was a good sign. She was definitely stalling, I could tell. I just wasn't so sure if she was waiting for me to say something. Chris could give her—

I can give you a lift, easy. As long as your dad doesn't come out and give me grief for getting his precious daughter home late.

Mark and the boys had grabbed their stuff and were moving tables. He must have overheard the question. Smooth. Thanks, mate!

No. He likes you. Besides, I told them we had to stay late for rehearsals and that I needed time to unwind afterwards.

Mark was barely listening to Elizabeth's reply because he was too interested in grinning pointedly in my direction. The Freak was giving me the thumbs-up really obviously.

It was good ending the night with just us again. Even though Chris was a ring-in, he fit right in as usual. For the final hour Elizabeth and I relaxed and didn't jump every time we accidentally touched. By the end of the night we were resting on one another and it felt great. So great that when Chris said that he had to get the car home so as to prevent parental stress, I nearly told him to go without me. But Mark grabbed his keys and jangled them.

Yeah, me too. Are you ready, Miss Elizabeth?

She didn't seem very keen to be going anywhere either. But eventually we all stood up and moved outside, saying our goodbyes. I felt my palms go sweaty and jittery when I knew it was my time to say goodnight to Elizabeth. But she came straight up to me, gave me a kiss on the cheek and said she'd see me next weekend at rehearsals . . . and to give her a call during the week if I wanted. Thank God Chris started to drag me away, otherwise I would have stood there like a speechless idiot. I yelled out goodbye to the Freak and Mark and followed him.

I knew Chris was going to start as soon as we got in the car and he didn't let me down.

Willo! You are completely gone, mate!

Give it a rest, Chris.

Yeah, well, her friends were saying she's into you too. He put on a fake girl voice. **The talk of the musical.**

Shut up, you wanker!

The cutest guy in the production. He kept going with the girl's voice. **And you're really funny and it's great how you look out for Zach and help Brother Pat. You're just a big softy underneath the tough-man act, aren't you, Will?**

If he hadn't been driving he would have copped one right in the gut. Instead I started on him.

So what about that Maree chick, then? She was hanging off everything you said and, mate, I know you, you're just not that interesting. Elizabeth's friends kept going on about how cute you were. They were even more impressed when I told them you were going to be school captain.

Got him. This time it was Chris who went red.

You what?

He hated it when I raised the school captain thing, really hated it. I moved on quickly. **Look out, mate, your life is just about to get a whole lot more interesting.**

Chris freaked out all the way home, but he was loving it.

And I was loving it. In fact, something strange was happening, because for the past two days almost everything was good.

The phone call

The week went pretty quickly except that every five minutes I thought about Elizabeth and the fact I hadn't rung her yet. Andrews had organized three rehearsals after school for the actors, and after band practice on Wednesday I figured I'd give her a ring and see if they were up for pizza again. It was a great plan, if I actually did anything about it. Brother Pat was also full of plans, but he, on the other hand, had no problem getting on with them.

Now don't forget, Will, I will need you to be out of classes on Friday morning before singing practice. Make sure you give me a list of the teachers I need to notify so they don't think you are up to any mischief.

For the first time in my whole school career I wasn't looking forward to missing time out of class.

You know what, Will, I can help you if you want.

I looked down to see the Freak, waiting to walk out after practice with me like always.

Sure, Freak, that would be great.

At least it would give him a chance to tell the other losers to pull their heads in.

That all right with you, Brother?

Absolutely!

We left Brother Pat on the sax, practicing for his regular Wednesday-night gig with his mates.

We both stood on the veranda of the music room and looked out into the junior quad, not saying anything. The Freak must have been figuring which one of the geeks he was going to tell off first on Friday, and I was practicing what I was going to say to Elizabeth.

I got out my phone to check the time.

Are you going to ring Elizabeth?

No! Why would you say that?

'Cause you keep looking up to the hall and then going to get your phone out. I can't go out tonight because Dad said not during weeknights.

Right.

But you should ring her because you said you were going to.

Right.

Thanks, Freak.

Silence.

What time is your dad coming?

Now.

I took a deep breath.

Do you want me to come out and wait with you?

Pause.

Nah, it's all right. You can meet him at the show.

Exhale of breath.

All right, well, if I don't see you around tomorrow, I'll catch you on Friday morning in the hall. You can help me set up.

He made contact, his ancient eyes reflecting a very busy head.

I've already been thinking about that, Will, don't worry.

He stopped mid-pogo. **You really should call Elizabeth.**

Thanks for that. He left me nodding to his back.

He was right, I should call. She told me to ring her. She'd given me her number, made me put it into my phone. So considering she said to, there's no reason why I shouldn't. It's not as if I'm stalking her.

I went over to get my bike. I knew I could just as easily have gone over to the hall, but I didn't, it would look too desperate. And Andrews would seize the opportunity to ask me in front of the whole cast exactly why it was I was spending even more time at school than I had to.

I put down my bike and reached in my pocket for my phone. I scrolled down to Elizabeth's number. Don't think about it, Will, just do it. I pressed the key.

Elizabeth?

Hey, Will? Have you just finished band?

Breathe, you idiot. She sounds completely normal.

Yeah. Are you guys in the hall?

Yep, but Mr. Andrews says he thinks we won't be finished before nine. So it's going to be a very long evening.

Right, no pizza then.

Pause.

It was definitely my turn to speak. **Has Andrews lost it again?**

OK, so it wasn't great but it kept the conversation going.

No, he's fine. Just giving us his usual motivational speech. Telling us how good we are, you know what he's like.

I wanted to say he had a completely different delivery for me but I didn't.

Will . . . I had a great time the other night. The girls haven't stopped talking about you all week.

Ahhh . . .

I'd love to do it again but, but . . . maybe just us next time?

Ahhh . . .

I could hear Mark in the background telling her to get onstage.

199

Will, I've got to go.

Speak, you idiot!

Yep . . . OK . . . Elizabeth, I had a great time too. . . .

So definitely next week then? Just us two?

Yep, that would be—

I've really got to go. Thanks for calling.

I got on the bike and floated home. Finally a victory! Brother
Pat was right, I was the man!

The dark side

There was a completely different story going round my head when I sat in homeroom on Friday morning.

Right, just a warning, boys, there's a memo that says period three will be taken for singing practice.

The news was received in one of two ways: half the boys cheered and instantly swarmed their diaries to see what period they were going to miss; the other half groaned. It was hard to hear which side had the majority. It was around about then I began to have another meltdown.

Settle down, mate, it's not that bad. At least you get to miss out on maths.

No, Chris, you don't get it. Brother Patrick's conned me into being a part of the school band. You know, being up onstage in front of the whole school, looking like a prize idiot.

Chris stared at me as if he'd been waiting for this moment all his life. Which is exactly why I hadn't told him. He was now about to get his revenge.

Me and the boys had given him constant crap about being the school brownnose ever since he had been made the class representative in kindergarten. Not that it had ever stopped him: he just gave us the finger and kept accepting the badges. But now, after twelve long years, he had the perfect revenge and he didn't have to raise any fingers to make it happen.

You mean you have to get up there in front of the whole school and actually play when Brother Pat's doing his wailing banshee stuff on the mike?

Yep.

He didn't even wait one second.

Hey, Jock!

Shut up, Chris! Come on . . .

But Chris was going to bleed this for everything he could get.

Did you hear that Willo's going to be up onstage this morning?

No way, man! It can't be true! The man who dacked himself at the girls' bus, one of the finest moments in St. Andrew's history? You're part of the Brother Patrick Show by personal invite? Will, you've crossed to the dark side.

Others, overhearing Jock's accusing roar, came flooding over to throw in their gold coins' worth. After five minutes of being slammed, I'd had enough.

Yeah, yeah, you're all a bunch of bloody comedians!

Just at that moment, I mean at that exact moment, Brother Pat's voice boomed over the PA, entering every room in the school.

Could William Armstrong of Year Eleven please meet Brother Patrick in the hall immediately.

Naturally, this was too much. The whole class fell over one another, some in pain they were laughing so hard.

Whatever fragments of my armor were left clanked to the ground with each step. By the time I reached the hall I was unarmed and defenseless. Last night's bravado had evaporated along with any semblance of credibility.

Singing practice

Brother Pat loomed from the stage. **Good to see you heard the message, William. We have a lot to do! You are to be in charge of the band, as I will be up the front leading the school.**

What do you mean, in charge of the band, Brother? I asked, edging nervously toward the front of the hall.

He stopped unwinding the mike cord and stared down at me, incredulous.

What do you mean, what do I mean? I mean you will be conducting, of course.

My pace slowed significantly. He'd only asked me to look after the band—he hadn't said anything about *conducting* it.

But Brother, I'd really rather play. I'm not that confident conducting.

Rubbish, with your ear, you're a natural!

What about Ms. Sefton? Isn't that her job?

Oh no, she's far too busy. She's playing the piano and accompanying me with the flute. It will have to be you, Will. He placed his hand on my shoulder. **Now, there is no time for self-doubts. I know you will do a wonderful job.**

I stopped.

I've set you up on the stage so that everyone can see the band. It's time to give them a much higher profile in the school,

especially considering how hard they are working in preparation for the musical.

This was it. This was the point of no return. Goodbye, Will the funny man, Will the I don't give a . . . Will the soccer hero. Hello, Will the geek, Will the brownnose, Will the loser, Will the nerd.

I watched as the midget geeks came piling through the doors of the hall full of excitement, oblivious to any code of cool conduct. The Freak came bounding up the front ready to carry out any instruction I threw at him. I knew I could still pull out one of my finer escape moments, of which there have been many, but for some reason I didn't. I kept on my slow path to the stage. And as I edged closer I knew I'd crossed over to the unknown and relinquished myself. I had made contact with my inner geek.

Come along, boys, called Brother Pat. **Take your positions.**

Hey, Will!

I looked down to see two big eyes staring up at me, radiating excitement.

Hey, Freak.

Isn't this exciting?

Yeah.

I still had to hide the sarcasm. I may have made contact with the inner geek, but it was only a flicker of recognition.

I climbed up onstage and turned to face the band. Their expectant faces looked up at me with complete trust. I tried not to think too much about the responsibility angle. This was enough of a head trip for one day.

I was as articulate and as gracious as ever. **Hi.**

Hi, Will!

Let's start with Brother Pat's favorite, "Amazing Grace," before the animals arrive.

At this moment the hall began to reverberate and the foundations shook. All doors were invaded and the hall began to swell with its inhabitants. A very strange phenomenon, the singing practice. A thousand adolescent boys crowded into a confined space, led by an elderly man, singing religious songs written two centuries ago. Weird.

Packs of students took their seats and waited. Expectant. Alert to any opportunity to take the piss.

I could make out the Year 11s as they nudged one another and pointed at me. Guys were shaking their heads in disbelief; others were laughing and being told to shut up by Danielli. Chris, Jock and Tim stood up and waved.

Brother Pat yelled into the mike.

Right, thank you, gentlemen. As you all know, next Friday is a day of great celebration for St. Andrew's College. It falls to every single one of you in this hall, students and teachers alike, to make sure we honor the day in the best way we know how. This means singing up loud and strong. So let's hear you sing up, St. Andrew's! OK?

A few boys mumbled, **Yes, Brother.**

I can't hear you, St. Andrew's!

Yes, Brother! they chanted.

That's better!

This was just the beginning of the rev-up.

I would like to introduce to you a young man of special talent who has taken pride of place in our wonderful school band. He has been working tirelessly with these youngsters to whip them into shape for the musical. He has proven to be a wonderful role model for them. A big round of applause for William Armstrong.

The school body broke into applause, some obligatory, some a piss-take, not much of it genuine. Some teachers were left with their mouths open. Andrews threw his head back laughing and turned to some of the other teachers. I didn't even look in Waddlehead's direction. Year 11, on the other hand, went wild, led of course by the Tim and Jock cheerleaders. I heard a chorus of *Go, Will!* and the beginning of the wave. I attempted to throw the ringleaders a death stare but it only provoked them more, with them throwing me fake kisses in return.

Right, over to you, Will.

I turned my back and tried to develop the select hearing my mum reckons I have.

OK, geeks, let's get this right.

They started.

And I forgot that I was onstage in front of a thousand potential savages. That was until at one point while we were waiting for Brother Pat to finish one of his rev-ups, I looked up and saw Tim and Jock maneuvering themselves around to the right, waving what looked like little sticks in the air like fake batons. When I looked over again they were gone. I hoped they'd been busted, but more than likely they'd just got bored and were now poking the sticks in people's ears.

Slowly I started to chill out. The geeks were doing a good job. Everybody else was too busy taking the piss out of the singing to be worried about what we were doing. Brother Patrick wound the kids up and the teachers calmed them down. The boys sang loudly and badly off-key. Brother Patrick yelled how good they were and to *Sing up*; the teachers looked angry and told the kids to *Shut up*.

It all went horribly wrong, however, as soon as Brother Patrick screamed his next announcement.

206

Gentlemen, it's time to take a rest from singing and use our listening skills.

He waited for silence. **I would like to introduce to you our latest singing star to emerge from St. Andrew's.**

Oh no!

Now, he was very reluctant to sing as he wants to rest up for next week. But I'm sure if we encourage him loudly enough, he will pay us this honor. Put your hands together for a new boy to St. Andrew's—so we can't take all the credit—the very talented Mark Newman.

No one ever sang on their own in practices. Brother Pat had no idea how dangerous this was. The atmosphere became hostile instantly. To single someone out from the pack, especially someone who was unknown to most, was potentially fatal. I searched my head for the last bloke who'd sung in front of the school body. The only image I could dredge up was footy boys in dresses at the Year 12 farewell two years ago. Brother Patrick was offering the pack fresh meat. And the boys were licking their lips in anticipation.

I watched Mark leave the anonymous safety of the Year 12s to minimal applause. He was definitely dealing with the situation far better than some of the A-grade footballers, who obviously didn't know that their new star player was also able to belt out a tune. He looked at me as he approached the stage, trying to catch my eye, smiling. It was at this point I was overwhelmed by a very familiar need for escape. It was going to be hard enough for me already; the last thing I needed was to align myself with a bloke who was setting himself up for hassle every day until he left school and even after that. Knowing I was a hypocrite and not caring, I turned my back to him.

It was up to me to count the band in. For those four counts, the hall pulsated with heavy silence. And then Mark opened his mouth and sang, loudly and well. When he'd finished, the hall's inhabitants breathed a sigh of disappointment. They were angry that they hadn't had their flesh. However, they made sure he knew he hadn't got away with it completely. The wolf whistles and catcalls confirmed just how much he was going to cop in the quad.

Thank you, Mark. That's a taste of what you will hear when you come along to the musical to support your school. But for the moment let us all stand for the school song.

The atmosphere lifted again and everyone competed to make the funniest, crudest, rudest version of the school song they possibly could. It was something I'd been getting a laugh out of for the past four years, but this time it wasn't funny. My gut had concreted over. I knew there was a reason why I should feel like crap but I couldn't, wouldn't think about it.

From where I was onstage, I watched three of the more well-known St. Andrew's hard boys looking over in Mark's direction, shaking their heads and trying to throw him death stares. Mark wasn't paying attention, he was dealing with Jock and Tim and the other footy boys who were now giving him crap to his face. Something was about to go down. I knew it.

My need for escape had intensified. I had to get out, to get as far away from the hall as possible.

I dismissed Brother Pat's thanks at the end of the song, threw down the baton and left the Freak in charge of clearing up. I had to get to the safety of the music room before the pack began to feed.

The fallout

Too late.

I made my way out to the senior quad, feeling more exposed than when I'd dropped my daks.

As I walked past a group of Year 12 guys, they stopped their conversation, watched me walk past and then laughed. There was nothing unusual about that. Hassle was to be expected.

As I moved just out of range one of them yelled, **Nice baton twirling!**

I told him where he could shove the baton. He replied that, unlike myself, he didn't like taking things up the arse. If I'd hung around I would've hit the guy in the face.

I increased my pace, trying to regain control. I made my way over to the tuckshop and stopped when I saw a crowd was gathering. For once the top priority was not who was served first. This was a very different fight for position, a fight between Mark and the three try-hards from the hall.

They were known throughout the school, something they took great pride in, and belonged to some gang that ended in *boyzzz*. Jock always took them off behind their backs. Australian white-bread boys acting like some American TV version of kids from the hood. As expected they had tracked and stalked their prey, except Mark wasn't looking very threatened.

I couldn't hear Mark's comeback but it must have been good

because the three shut up and the whole tuckshop line cracked up. These blokes weren't used to their victims having any sort of comeback, let alone one that made them the butt of the joke. They didn't fight with words. Mark was getting himself farther and farther into dangerous territory. As if to confirm the increase in aggression, the action moved out of the sight of the tuckshop ladies. The three circled Mark now, shoulders back and chins jutting forward as if to knife his face.

I moved closer.

So, mate, you're a songbird, are you?

Mark attempted to move out of their way. The main guy, flanked by the other two, deliberately stood in his path.

Come on, mate, why don't you give us your own little concert right here?

You sing really sweet, mate. Are you sure your balls have dropped yet?

By this time the crowd had swollen, loving the fact that they were being treated to a second show for the day.

Hey, one of those geeks in the band reckons he heard you saying you were a faggot! Is that right, mate? Are you some sort of faggot?

Instantly the mood changed. The crowd visibly recoiled; echoes of *faggot, poofter* filled the four walls of the area. I watched as Chris, Jock and Tim moved closer, their faces impassive, their bodies tense.

Mark walked slowly up to his stalker and stared him in the eye. They stood silent, a space of no more than one centimeter between them. The crowd was hushed now. For more than a minute no one moved, until Mark smiled.

Why, mate, what's it to you? Are you interested?

Victory! And the crowd knew it. The tension vaporized instantly. Mark walked away, leaving the try-hard to his moment of humiliation. He didn't have to do much more: the fickle pack did the rest for him, until word of a teacher's imminent arrival wiped the crime scene clean. For now.

I remained fixed to the spot. I should have gone over but I wasn't going to incriminate myself further.

Will! Hey, Will!

That was my cue.

Mark's voice was behind me. I pretended not to hear him and kept walking. This time he was more persistent. I felt a hand on my shoulder.

Will! Didn't you hear me? I called out three times. He looked at me quizzically.

Right, sorry. Must have been thinking about something else.

Nice scene, huh? Mark pointed toward the tuckshop.

Yeah! Are you all right?

I've had worse. Dickheads like that just need to be confronted.

I looked over my shoulder. We were standing in full view of the senior quad. I had had enough of being on show. I just wanted to hide, become anonymous.

Mark, look, I've got to go . . . I mumbled, not making eye contact.

Will, are you OK?

Yeah, I'm fine. I've just got to . . .

Go. He finished my statement, his voice slightly challenging. **Yeah, you already said that. You're acting really weird, Will. If I**

didn't know better, and I do, I'd say you don't want to be seen talking to me. Is that why you blanked me in front of the whole school when I got onstage?

Another pile of concrete landed in my gut. I couldn't say anything to him. All I wanted to do was disappear. I walked away.

As I was reaching safe ground Jock came toward me.

Hey, nice work with that little stick, Will!

Get stuffed, Jock!

I kept walking, leaving Jock openmouthed and shrugging his shoulders.

Music theory

I locked myself in the music room, reefed up the amp and didn't stop to hear or think. It was only when Ms. Sefton knocked on the window and pointed to the adjoining classroom that I figured we had theory. It was too obvious to ignore her and I was in no mood to explain anything to anyone. I grabbed my stuff and made my entrance. A couple of comments flew my way but they crashed midair as I turned on them. Chris had moved his stuff so I could sit in my usual seat. I sat on my own.

Ms. Sefton had set up some sort of listening exercise. Fine by me. She turned on the music. Old. Classical. The type of stuff your grandparents listen to. Cellos. They always sound so bloody depressing. Miss sat at the front with her eyes closed, looking like she'd been teleported to another universe. I felt progressively more like shit.

It was then the images started. Woven in and out of each melancholic chord were snapshots of the assembly, the playground, the tuckshop and the conversation. Me watching from a distance, Mark in among it, in their faces. I shook my head to stop it but the scenes kept looping: Mark; the three wannabes; Chris, Tim and Jock stepping up; me watching, me walking away.

The cellos continued. My thoughts responded to the music, weaving, releasing, spilling. I fought hard to get the bubble on for guaranteed protection. But somehow I knew this time it wasn't going to work. There was too much erupting its way to the surface, other images that had been censored, prohibited for the well-being of Will Armstrong.

The pain of recognition ripped through me. I had forgotten what he looked like. He became movie-theater big, looking down at me, shaking his head, disappointed. He was speaking, but all I could hear was distorted sound.

I tried to push the delete button, but I had uncovered a private stash of do-not-remembers and, once unleashed, there was no stopping them. I looked to the door ready to make an escape, but I couldn't move.

The presentation was set to automatic slide show.

Photos of Dad and me flashed one by one on the screen.

Click: Dad and me just born.

Click: Dad and me, first birthday.

Click: Dad and me and my first bike.

Click: Dad and me and my first guitar.

Click: Dad and me and my first soccer boots.

Click: Dad and me and my first soccer jersey.

Click: Dad and me and his soccer jersey, his beer and his ball.

Click: no more Dad.

Hundreds of images and with each flash an electric bolt. The music intensified the enormity of my pain. Ripping at the bandages that had been caked on for so long.

Will?

Ms. Sefton was beside me, her voice calling a halt to the images.

Will, are you OK?

What, miss?

She was crouched beside me, whispering, eyes concerned. I frowned, disorientated.

Aren't you feeling well?

It was only then I became conscious of my head in my hands. I didn't answer. I couldn't.

Will, are you all right? You look upset.

I looked around to see if anyone else was watching. Chris. I looked down.

Will?

I spat out each word.

Yeah, all right, miss. I'm all right. Just leave it.

Flight.

I reached around and grabbed my stuff. I was out the door before she could say anything else.

Will!

That was all I needed. He must have still been helping Brother Pat move the gear back after the rehearsal. I kept on toward the gates. Exit was the only thing on my mind.

Will! Wait for me!

I heard his footsteps behind me break into a run.

Will, where are you going? You're not allowed to leave school before Admin.

For fuck's sake, Zach! Do you ever shut up!

Exposed. Ready to attack, destroy.

But that's the problem with you, isn't it? You can't shut up, you have to tell the world everything.

No, Will, that's not true. My dad says—

Shut up about your fucking father. I'm so sick of hearing about him. Do you think you're the only person in the world to have a fucking father?

No, Will . . . I'm just—

Jesus, he sounds like a king freak anyway. No wonder you are

such a geek when you've got the father of all geeks showing you the way.

That's not very nice, Will.

Nice? I'll tell you what's not *nice*! What's not *nice* is opening your mouth about stuff that is none of your fucking business.

By this time Zach's normally ancient, innocent eyes had filled with tears. It should have been enough to shut me up. But I couldn't stop. All I wanted to do was to hurt and I didn't care who or what I hurt as long as I didn't have to feel the pain myself.

Don't give me that look, pretending to be Mr. Fucking Innocent.

What?

You couldn't help yourself, could you? You had to go around pretending that you had friends. That's it, isn't it. You couldn't keep your trap shut. You had to show off that you knew Mark was gay. Well, now the school knows about it. Good on you, Zach, you're a real fucking hero.

But Will . . . I really—

Don't bother, you reject! And you know what else? Don't hang around me anymore. I don't want anything to do with you.

By this time I had found my way to the gates.

Do you hear me?

I looked up to see him standing in the middle of the playground, bag by his side, face crumpled. For one second I felt the urge to make him better again.

Do you hear me?

He called out a very husky **OK.**

I disappeared around the gates.

He was left in the middle of the playground. Alone.

Bed

That night I shut myself in my room and didn't go anywhere all weekend. Mum kept asking if everything was all right. I told her I was feeling crook. Chris rang. Elizabeth rang. Mark didn't ring. Zach didn't ring. I wanted to be left alone in complete blackness, in a void where I didn't have to think, where I didn't have to remember, where there were no more images. I lay in bed in fear of the slide show starting again. But it didn't. Eventually, under the doona, in the blackness, things became blank again.

I convinced Mum I was too sick to go to rehearsals. I could tell she was concerned but she didn't say much. I knew Brother Pat would be expecting me, but I couldn't front this time. Mum rang him and said I was in bed.

I wrapped the doona firmly around me and tried to sleep. I was vaguely aware of different voices outside my door, but each time I would roll over and eventually fall back to sleep.

Sunday night I got up, had a shower and made it to the lounge just to try to decrease the Patricia Armstrong stress. She'd been trying to get me to eat all weekend. Sunday's attempt was some sort of soup for *beating the winter blues*. It was healthy and full of vegetables and I couldn't touch it. But I didn't tell her that. So I sat and watched the telly and pretended to eat.

One good thing was I didn't have to worry about school. Mum already had that covered.

Well, if you've been sleeping all weekend and can't eat, you can't go to school tomorrow. Musical or no musical! I'll ring Helen and let her know that you'll definitely be off tomorrow. If you're not any better by the end of the day, we'll make a doctor's appointment for Tuesday.

I left the doctor's surgery with a certificate that declared I had a virus and was off for the rest of the week. It was one small victory because it meant, to Mum and the rest of the world, that I was legitimately sick.

I didn't know what I was. All I knew was that the world felt a hell of a lot better when I was asleep.

On Thursday afternoon I heard something being slid under my door. I pulled on the doona even tighter and turned to the wall. I made up scenarios in my head about what the note contained: Elizabeth telling me how much she missed me. Zach saying he didn't hate my guts. Mark telling me he understood why I'd acted like a dickhead again. And for a flicker of a second it was Dad, saying I hadn't disappointed him, that he was back and everything would return to normal. It was only because I couldn't deal with any more scenarios that I pushed myself out of bed and picked up the envelope. I found myself staring at my name written in swirly, old-fashioned writing.

Dear Will,

I am very sorry to hear you are ill. Your mother tells me you have a heavy flu.

I wished to write and tell you how much support you have offered me over the past weeks throughout the musical. Even though I may not have openly acknowledged the reasons why you were initially involved in the musical, I of course knew. However, I always believe in giving people a clean slate, and I must say over the past weeks you have filled yours admirably.

Your work with the younger boys has been marvelous. You have demonstrated kindness, good humor and great patience in your dealings with them. You have guided them masterfully and diligently, making sure they offer the best of themselves as young musicians.

Your own skill as a musician is also worthy of note, not only on the guitar but also in conducting the band. You are in fact more talented musically than you realize. This is something I urge you to continue with.

I doubt you are aware of just how much you have achieved in such a short amount of time. Your leadership capabilities are very strong and obvious, Will. People respond very warmly to you because you are open and friendly. Your dealings with young Zachariah Cohen in particular have shown compassion and brotherly care.

I am aware that the musical was not the place where Will Armstrong ever thought he would find himself, but you have certainly lived up to the expectations of those people who spoke so highly of you. Congratulations, Will. I'm not the only person to have noticed this but I did think I should take the time to let you know and perhaps assist your recovery.

We will all be very disappointed if we don't see

*you tomorrow; however, if your illness prevents
this from happening, please know you have all of
our blessings.
Yours sincerely,
Brother Patrick Murphy*

I sat there for a good ten minutes on the side of my bed looking at the letter. At times it blurred. I was an emotional cripple, that much was pretty obvious. Who would have thought? I'd always assumed I had Brother Pat fooled into thinking I was in the musical for the love of it. I knew what this meant. As much as I would have loved to have pulled the doona over my head I knew I couldn't ignore it. The slides started again but this time it was a different show: Brother Pat, the geeks, Elizabeth, Andrews, the chorus girls, the Freak and Mark. The last two slides kept repeating.

The old bugger had worked his mysterious ways again and I bet he bloody knew it too.

The incredible shrinking hypocrite

The next morning I pried the doona off and pushed myself out of bed. I could picture Chris telling me how much I looked like shit. The way Mum was carrying on in the kitchen she would've obviously agreed with him. I managed to delude her into thinking I was on some heroic mission to save the musical and Brother Patrick couldn't survive without me. The more she zapped me with her beams of pride the more I shrank into a very tiny hypocrite. Man, did I have her fooled. I only just succeeded in getting her to let me ride my bike to school. I told her I needed to clear my head. At least that part was true.

I arrived just after homeroom and hid in the hall. I figured if I stayed out of people's way, did my job and went home then I couldn't hurt anyone else. Part of my gut kept nagging me about the unresolved stuff with the Freak and Mark. But there was only so much facing-up a guy could do in one day. Today was about keeping Brother Pat happy and me from having some sort of breakdown.

Good to see you here, Will.

I nearly fell off the stage. Brother Pat had appeared and was standing behind me.

You don't look too good, Will, maybe—

I cut him off.

No, I'm fine, Brother, really. You just gave me a bit of a shock.

I stopped. **And thanks for the note.**

Nothing but the truth, Will. Sometimes we all need a bit of encouragement to keep going.

He began to arrange the music stands as we talked, and I automatically fell into helping.

I said as much to your mother when I rang to find out how you were. I told her the young ones wouldn't know what to do without you. Especially young Zach.

He looked directly at me when he said it.

He's looked quite lost over the past couple of days.

I busied myself with the stands, shrinking with each word.

No doubt he will pick up when he sees you.

I reduced even farther in size. The incredible shrinking hypocrite.

Brother stood facing the hall doors and sighed appreciatively.

Here they come, right on cue. Come on, boys, set yourselves up. Look who's back!

I looked in the direction of the Freak. I was sure he'd seen me because he was making it so obvious he hadn't that he must have. He was either going through his bag or cleaning out his mouthpiece or looking the other way. His awkwardness was killing me. I had just decided to go over and tell him what an arsehole I was when Brother started with the school song for the St. Andrew's Day service. Considering I was the guy who was leading them I figured I'd better not stuff up that job as well. I faced the band, made sure I didn't look at the Freak and started. It was good to have an excuse to stop thinking and have something to do, even if I did have to wave a little stick at some geeks in front of the entire school. All my energy was going into getting the job done. I was too tired to worry about anyone and the potential for anything. Let them go for it.

We didn't have time for a break after the service. The band stayed onstage practicing for the run of the musical. I liked my state of unthinking and unfeeling and was determined for it to stay that way. I led the geeks through all the numbers and we sounded good. If I hadn't been feeling so wiped out I might actually have felt proud.

I sensed the change in atmosphere before I saw the girls arrive. Excitement and hormones buffeted the air. It wasn't often girls found their way onto St. Andrew's turf. I was aware that maybe I should be a little concerned about how the boys would react to Elizabeth, but I figured that she and the other girls were more than capable of looking after themselves. After all, they were only performing to Years 7 and 8 and they would have been snuck in the back way to avoid testosterone-driven groupies.

I had plenty to do to keep me out of the way. Brother Patrick had given me a whole list of jobs, including making sure that everything was present and accounted for and in the right spot—meaning instruments, music stands, leads and amps—overseeing sound checks and the tuning of the instruments, and ensuring the sheet music was in the right order and ready to go. I wondered fleetingly how someone like me who did everything to make sure I had a low profile had become so high profile. But for the moment it didn't matter because it kept me busy, and out of the way of the leading man and lady. Elizabeth did call out and ask me with her hands why I hadn't returned her calls. Mark didn't even acknowledge my existence.

I was the only person in the hall who wasn't pumped. Having the juniors there made it work. They were excited enough about missing out on school. The oldies from the homes were already in love with the show before it even started. It was exactly the type of audience you wanted for a practice run.

The geeks were noisier than usual but, unlike most other times, I didn't tell them to shut up. I sat back and happily let Brother Pat run the show. The Freak hid behind his trombone and didn't move. I could hear Andrews delivering his third last motivational speech to everyone backstage.

The lights went out and we started with the overture. Elizabeth opened with her first line and it was on. . . .

Only ten hours to go before it was over.

One down, two to go

Brother Pat seemed to think it was a good run-through. I wasn't really watching, although I did notice that one of the Year 7 girls came on wearing the wrong costume, but I think that was about it. Most people were hanging around school or meeting up early before opening night. Me? I left school the way I'd arrived, slinking out, grabbing my bike and riding fast all the way home.

After I'd had a shower Mum said I looked better than she had seen me all week. Which was a good thing considering I had some serious spade work to do with Elizabeth about not returning her phone calls. I couldn't even think about the Freak and Mark.

I tried to tell Mum I was happy to ride to school but this time she wasn't having it. When we pulled up outside the hall I got myself and my guitar case out of the car. Foolishly, I thought I was safe. She leaned over across the seat and spoke to me out the window.

Will?

Yes, Mum?

I am so very proud of all that you have achieved.

I shrank to the smallest I had shrunk all day. Her eyes were glassy and she had one of those *I'm going to cry* smiles.

I couldn't deal with any more scenes or any more praise. If only these people knew what a hypocrite I was. I was only just keeping it together. I knew I had to make a speedy exit before she mentioned the D word.

Thanks, Mum, I mumbled, then I grabbed my stuff and ran.

Mum's words stayed in my head. What did she mean, achieved? Yeah, I had achieved in hurting people and acting like a cowardly dickhead. And proud? Proud of what? It wasn't as if I had transformed into bloody Chris! I mean, had she forgotten how I'd gotten into all of this in the first place?

I changed into my muso black and made my way out to the band. The unfeeling, uncaring state that had got me through the day evaporated. My guts started to churn like they do before you have to sit a big exam or play in a soccer final. I walked toward the pit, telling myself to chill out. I looked over at the Freak and watched Mark do his final warm-up and my guts began to churn even more. I sat down, pulled out the guitar and knew that at least for the next three hours I was going to be safe.

I wasn't the only one on edge. Andrews was too, but considering this was all his doing I didn't have any sympathy for the bloke. He was onstage throwing instructions with the accuracy and speed of one of those dart players from England.

Everyone should be in their positions!

Offstage and behind those curtains!

Where's the stage manager? Make sure that the props are where they should be.

You, yes you, get out of the wings, you can be seen!

Right, band, two minutes until we start the overture. For God's sake, someone give the kid with the clarinet a hand!

OK, the lights are dimming and one-two-three, play . . .

Brother Pat, on the other hand, looked as laid-back as any jazz player who'd been around the scene for fifty years.

Right, Will, are you ready to go?

Yes, Brother. . . .

I became anonymous in the darkness of the pit. I listened to the geeks start the first bars of the overture and for the first time that night I relaxed. It was nearly always like that with music for me. I knew for the next three hours I was safe, but more importantly I knew it was three hours where I wouldn't stuff up. It was only when the whole audience stood and clapped and the house lights came on that I came back to reality and realized that the first night was over. There was no way anyone could not be lifted and carried around by the buzz in the room. It was like the kids were Hollywood stars from the amount of applause and whoops and hurrahs they were getting.

The Year 7 geeks were all over themselves with excitement. Brother Patrick was pumping the hands of old boys who were offering their congratulations.

The best one yet! The best one yet! he exclaimed.

I could feel myself being carried away with everyone else. I figured after the last few days I was going to get on and ride for as long as I could. I watched Mark and Elizabeth kiss and hug each other, with Andrews, Brother Pat and Ms. Sefton right in among it. I was overwhelmed by a need to make things right. I watched Mark leave the stage and I followed.

Round one

Great show, Mark.

I caught him just before he went into the change rooms. His face shut down as soon as he saw it was me.

Thanks.

I continued. **Look, I've been away, I've been—**

He interrupted. **Sick, yeah, Chris said you were crook. So how are you feeling now?**

His voice was distant.

Yeah, no, better.

I was no longer floating anywhere. It was pretty obvious that Mark wasn't OK, and knew I wanted to apologize for being piss weak in front of everybody and not backing him up. I knew what I wanted to say but I couldn't say it. Looking at Mark, I began to wonder whether saying anything was going to make any difference anyway.

I tried to get things back to normal.

So I suppose I'll see you at the pizza place once you've said hello to everyone?

No, I don't think I'll be going tonight.

He continued to stare at me, his face unreadable.

Right.

We both looked at one another, neither one of us saying anything. Quiet. He wasn't going to speak first, it had to come from me. I took a deep breath.

Mark, I'm sorry.

His eyes flashed, the first sign of a reaction.

Sorry for what I didn't do the other day. At the tuckshop, you know when those—

He cut me off. Yeah, yeah, I know what you're talking about, Will. What have you got to be sorry about? You didn't have to do anything, you weren't involved.

That's the point, Mark, I wasn't involved and I made bloody sure I wasn't. Then when you tried to talk to me afterwards I dogged you completely.

He fired up now.

Look, Will, as far as the tuckshop incident was concerned, I dealt with it. Those wankers won't say anything to me again because they're cowards.

He turned to walk away, then thought better of it.

But you know what I thought you might have apologized for? For treating me like I was some sort of freak in the quad. You said it, Will, you did completely dog me. It was pretty obvious you didn't want anyone to know we had anything to do with each other. So why is it so different now? Because no one can see us? That's not being a mate, Will! I don't even treat people I can't stand like that.

Silenced. Burning.

Mark, I . . .

Yeah, you're sorry. But you know that's a bullshit easy word to say, especially when you've already said it once. It doesn't mean anything unless you back it up with what you do.

With that he turned away and walked toward the crowds of people who wanted to congratulate him. I stood there not knowing what to do or say.

Round two

I felt myself engulfed in a bear hug of the kind I'd had all my life.

I told you I had every reason to be proud of your accomplishments.

Round two and I was still reeling from the KO Mark had just served. I wasn't sure I was going to be able to stay upright.

Thanks. I tried to deflect Mum's praise. I couldn't stand any more. **But it's those guys who should get the biggest rap.**

Just as I said this Elizabeth looked in my direction and waved. All week I had waited for the next time I saw her but not now! Please not now! She made her way over.

I began to feel the familiar reddening of my cheeks.

Goodness, dear, you look a little flushed all of a sudden, maybe you haven't fully recovered.

Hey, Will.

She hadn't changed out of her costume. She was shining, like she had one of those spotlights on her as she walked through the crowd. She looked at Mum and introduced herself.

Hi. Mrs. Armstrong? I'm Elizabeth.

Mum looked at me inquiringly and smiled. I willed her to say nothing.

Elizabeth, I thought you were wonderful. Such a beautiful voice.

I needed out. Mum and Elizabeth were so bloody happy and

laughing and proud and I continued to head farther and farther into a deep, dark space. I looked over at Brother Pat and found my escape.

Sorry, you guys. Got to go and pack up.

Mum beamed but Elizabeth looked confused and a little angry. Someone else to add to the list.

Round three

For the second time that week I felt like I was going to throw up, really throw up: dry mouth, foul taste in the back of my throat. I changed direction. I figured one hour of Mum drilling me on why I had left and a telephone apology to Elizabeth were better than a full-on public meltdown.

I made my way round the hall, trying to stick to the walls, as far away from the backslapping and congratulations as possible. I had just about made it to the doors when I heard my name.

Will? William Armstrong?

I turned around very slowly. This was all I needed.

Yes, sir?

I came face to face with the man the Freak would become in twenty years' time, except he didn't have that dorkiness about him. He looked pretty much like any guy his age who was dressed in jeans and a jumper.

Pleased to meet you. I'm Frank Cohen, Zach's father.

No!!!!!

Nice to meet you.

Bad. Bad. Very, very bad!

I really wanted to introduce myself.

OK, so all I could do was apologize for traumatizing his son for life. I might be told where I could shove my apology for the second time tonight, but what else could I do?

Look, Mr. Cohen, I can—

He interrupted. I braced myself to be ripped apart.

No, Will, let me speak.

I shut up and he stared at me with those familiar ancient eyes.

I wanted to thank you.

Right. So this guy was clearly mad, which would explain a lot about the Freak really.

Thank me? No, Mr. Cohen, you really don't need to . . .

I started to feel sick in the stomach again and that filthy taste right at the back of my throat made me want to gag.

I needed you to know just how much you have done for Zach over the past couple of months. He hero-worships you. He doesn't stop talking about you at home.

This was one trillion times worse than the bloke giving me a proper serve. I tried to interrupt him again, to tell him he'd got it all wrong, but he wouldn't let me.

No, Will, let me finish. I think what I am about to tell you is important for you to know. You know Zach's had a really difficult time fitting into high school. It looks like he's one of those kids that the boys target. But he's such a nice kid and he's had far too much to deal with already.

There were no words for how bad I was feeling.

He never talks about it, but his mum left when he was nine.

This time I gagged.

Are you all right, Will?

Idiot! Idiot! I was such a huge idiot! He always went on about his dad, never his mum. I should have known something had gone down there.

That was when he started to withdraw. He just didn't want to get involved in stuff that the other boys did.

That explains the library at lunchtime.

I suppose I didn't help much because I'd tell him he should stand up and be an individual, but that's hard for any twelve-year-old.

I thought about Zach at the pizza place telling Mark he had nothing to worry about, he wouldn't tell, and me in the quad walking away from Mark. There was only one coward in that scenario.

That's why I wanted to thank you.

Thank me! The guy should be shooting me!

You obviously have the right connections, because as soon as the word got around that you and he were mates everyone backed off. He's a different kid.

I was so, so sorry. And so screwed up I couldn't do anything about it.

I'm very thankful, Will, really.

It was just like the Freak to keep his mouth shut. I knew that he would never have said anything about Mark. Mr. Cohen was still looking at me. I could barely raise my head.

Your parents are very lucky to have a son like you. Are they here?

I tried to find my voice but only managed to gag again. I collected the spit in my mouth.

Mum is. I paused and Mr. Cohen stared.

Ahhh . . . say it! Say it! Just say it! **Dad . . . couldn't make it.**

Well, that's such a shame—he missed a wonderful performance. I'm sure he's very proud of you anyway.

He extended his hand again and I shook it. We were the last two left in the hall.

234

Are you coming over?

No, I've still got stuff to do here. I pointed to the safety of the empty orchestra pit.

Well, make sure you see Zach, I'm sure he'll be waiting for you.

Meltdown

I watched speechless as Mr. Cohen left to join everybody else in the library for Brother Patrick's after-performance drinks.

I leaned over the pit, wanting to throw up, needing to throw up. I felt a heaviness in my legs, a sensation I remembered from once before. I'd run out of places to hide. There was no bubble, there was no doona, there was no blank nothingness.

I threw my guitar case across the hall and heard it thud against the wall. What the hell was going on with me?

The hall began to rotate. I attempted to sit down but landed on the music cases, scattering them all over the floor. I tried to get a grip and took hard, deep breaths, trying to stop the concrete that was slowly filling my lungs. Somewhere in my head I knew I had to get rid of all of the crap that had lodged inside me but I continued to fight.

Eventually the spinning stopped. My sweat made a dripping tap noise as it pinged onto the cases. I couldn't go anywhere without making a scene. I had to stay here and do something normal. I focused on the music stands and arranged them one by one. My head went blank as I fell into a rhythm.

Will, what are you doing in here? Everyone's waiting for you in the library. Including Elizabeth.

I didn't answer Chris, I just nodded and kept stacking.

'll! Hey, Will, didn't you hear me?

At that point Chris stopped and said what I knew he'd say.

Will, you look like shit.

I shrugged.

Just stop for a minute. Leave the bloody music stands and sit down.

He grabbed me by the arm and tried to pull me away. Instinctively I turned on him, ready to fight.

He caught me by both shoulders and wrestled me into a chair.

Mate! What's wrong with you?

My heart was thumping. I felt like I was being beaten with a piece of metal rod. I tried to take in a breath. To slow everything down. Once again I sat with my head in my hands.

Will, you're freaking me out. Do you want me to get someone? Your mum?

No! Three music stands flew across the pit.

Then just tell me what's going on!

I knew I was arriving at breaking point, but I didn't have the strength to fight it anymore. I was exhausted. I could barely find the words.

I screwed up, Chris. I really screwed up.

What do you mean? Everyone's raving about how impressed they are with you.

But they've got no idea. They've got no idea just how much I've stuffed up.

I lifted my head out of my hands and looked up at Chris, speaking very, very quietly.

Did Zach tell you what I said to him? Did he tell you I deliberately stood in front of him and told him he was a piece of nothing? How I completely ignored Mark, blanked the guy because I was worried about how the boys would treat me?

Will—

And then—I spat out the words—**Brother Patrick sends me a note to say how grateful he is for my help, Mum's going on about how proud she is and Zach's dad comes up and tells me how grateful he is to me for helping his son.**

The silence in the hall engulfed both Chris and me. I knew what was coming next, but I wasn't stopping, I couldn't stop.

And all the time, all the time I know he's watching all of this and not saying anything, not doing anything . . .

Will, you should have heard your mum going on about how—
I'm not talking about Mum, Chris!
Silence.

I stood up from the chair and walked across the hall.

And you know what else? When I see him all I want to do is scream and yell at him and tell him it's all his fucking fault. That none of this would have happened if he hadn't died. None of this shit would be happening right here and now if he hadn't gone to that stupid fucking work site and he'd taken us to the beach instead.

Every part me of became wet. Sweat dripped off my body, collecting in dirty pools on the floorboards.

But that doesn't make sense. I know that none of this is his fault. I did it. I did it all by myself. And I don't know how to undo it. That's what I wish most of all, in the whole world—that I could undo all of it. Undo every single part and he was back and Mum and me and him and everything was back to the way it should be.

I couldn't sit. I had to move, to get away from what I was saying. I walked to every corner of the pit. I kicked cases, stands, scripts, anything that was in my way. And still I couldn't find a way out. There was no way out. What I'd been afraid of most was dredging its way from the pit of my gut.

No one gets it. One day everything's normal and then in one second everything's blown apart. And people expect you to talk about it. But how do you talk about something that has just blown your head away? How can you talk about something that you can't even think about?

The snot and sweat came flying off my face as I wiped my eyes to try to focus, to have some clarity.

I thought about it once. About one month after he died. I thought about him and the accident. Him lying there dead. Alone. Completely alone.

And then I swear to God, Chris—I swung around and glared at him—**I felt like I was falling down this long dark tunnel. Its . . . its guts were covered in bits of glass . . . jagged bits of glass . . . to stop you from ever getting out. . . . But you still grab on like some crazy man because you know that if you fall to the bottom you'll be destroyed . . . exploded into minuscule fragments that will never fit back together again. So . . . so you jam yourself onto the glass and rip your flesh and guts trying to get out, clawing your way to the top.**

I balled up the snot and tears that leaked like toxins down the back of my throat and spat.

And it doesn't matter how cut up, how much blood there is or how much skin hangs off your bones, because you made it out. And that's when you take whatever you can find and wrap it around you like bandages. They never come off. Because if they do, you won't ever be able to put yourself back together again.

And then you spend the rest of the time walking around hiding the bandages, looking and acting like everything is normal, but you know that nothing will ever be normal again.

Every part of me was shaking. I was saturated. My face was caked with layers of salt, snot, dirt, pain. The enormity of it nearly threw me to the floor.

I moved slowly, cautiously onto one of the music cases and for the first time since Dad died I cried.

I cried and Chris sat.

Holden bear hug

Slowly, I became aware of where I was. It was the most exhausted I had ever felt, even on the day of the funeral. I could feel my breathing come back to normal. It was only then I felt Chris's presence on my right. I didn't remember him walking over or sitting on the case next to me. My eyes felt like sandpaper and I could tell my face needed a wash.

I looked over at Chris and made a halfhearted attempt to appear normal.

Looks like I'm cracking up, huh?

His eyes were far more serious than his voice.

Yeah, pretty freaky.

We didn't say anything else again for a while.

So do you reckon everyone knows I'm a basket case?

Yeah, pretty much, but they thought that before your dad died.

The word *died* hung in the air.

Will, I can't believe I just said that. . . .

My gut shrank like a chip packet in front of a heater, but I actually managed a little bit of a laugh, mainly at how tragic Chris looked.

It's all right, Chris. Really. Dad would want to see the Holden versus Armstrong piss-taking tradition continued. He always gave you heaps.

I looked over at him. He was smiling and nodding and wiping his face.

You know what, Will . . . I miss him too.

That blew me away! And I didn't think that there was any part of me that had been left intact.

He was always so ready to be up for something. He'd always have time and I didn't have to line up behind four others. He was like a cross between a mate and an uncle.

I'd never figured Chris might miss him too.

But you never talked about it.

Well, I wasn't going to, was I? It was pretty clear that you were never going to and I had to go with that. I might miss him, Will, but he was your dad.

Yeah. I could feel the tears start again but it didn't matter. It felt better just to let them fall.

We sat in silence for a while longer. I wiped my face with my sleeve and tried to move the conversation away from Dad.

So what do you think I should do about Mark and Zach?

Talk to them.

I tried to do that with Mark and he basically told me to get stuffed.

Well, let's face it, the guy's got good reason.

I nodded in agreement.

So let him calm down. As for the little fella, God, you're his hero, Will.

Yeah, and that's what makes all of this so bad.

So tell him that. Tell him you were a complete dickhead and you're sorry. And give Mark another twenty-four hours and try again.

Something came into my head that I'd wanted to ask Chris for ages.

How come you never told me he was gay?

He shrugged. **'Cause he asked me not to.**

You see, that's why you are going to be school captain and I'm king of the geeks. I tried to stand up and rocked on my feet. **I feel like I've just done twenty laps of the oval and headbutted Jock fifty times.**

You've looked better.

Cheers, mate.

I looked over at him and grinned. I was exhausted but lighter. And there was Chris doing the same thing he'd been doing for the past seventeen years—just being Chris. You've got to love the bloke for that. I walked over and offered my hand.

No really, Chris, thanks. I couldn't have done that with any-one else. You're family.

I extended my hand. He pushed it aside.

Well, in that case, he said, grinning, **Dad would expect us to give each other a Holden bear hug.**

I bolted as soon as he got close.

Yeah, I know what one of your bloody bear hugs are like! I could barely feel my nipples for a week after the last time.

He ran straight after me, jumping over the various music stands and cases that were lying all over the pit.

Come on, mate, that's what families do.

And with that he grabbed me in a headlock and wrestled me to the ground. Then he proceeded to move through the repertoire of nipple cripples, the typewriter and other Holden favorites.

Get off, you—

Chris had my shoulders pinned back and was just about to inflict more pain when . . .

Here I was thinking that something had happened to you and you're male bonding!

It was Elizabeth. Chris and I froze like we'd been busted by our mums. She might have looked hot but she sounded angry.

You left me with your mum so you could wrestle with Chris?

Chris winked, unpinned me and said very loudly that he was going over to the library.

I called from where I was still trying to get up, **Chris, could you tell Mum to go home without me? I can't do the library meet and greet tonight.**

Sure, mate, I'll tell her you're very busy being responsible Will and that I'll make sure you get home safely.

Chris said goodbye to Elizabeth and mouthed *Good luck* to me.

I suppose Elizabeth did have a right to be pissed off. I just wasn't sure how I could tell her about what happened. But I knew if I didn't come up with something soon I could add her to the list of people who thought I was a drop-kick.

Look, Elizabeth, I'm really sorry, but I have to clean up this mess, otherwise Brother Pat will . . .

This time she looked more disappointed than pissed off. I tried another tack.

But how about once I've done that we go to the pizza place and I'll tell you why everything's been such a stuff-up tonight? I mean, why *I've* been such a stuff-up tonight.

She took a deliberately long time to answer.

Well, Mum and Dad have already gone home after finally saying I could hang out with you guys, but then Mark went and piked it, so I suppose you'll have to do.

Her tone shifted slightly. It was less angry and more teasing.

And if it were anyone else I'd offer some assistance but since it's you, consider it payback.

A cup of Italian coffee

About fifteen minutes later, Chris and Elizabeth walked in together, Chris jangling his keys and Elizabeth pointing to her watch. I was just locking the cupboard with the instruments in it.

All right, I'm ready, let's get out of here, I said as I started switching off the main lights.

Chris, being a true gentleman, has offered to give us a lift to the pizza place, but I said I'd only accept if he came too.

I liked hòw she went out of her way to include Chris. I'm not sure he was feeling entirely comfortable with it, though. He went a faint tinge of pink and shook his head.

Nah, I've got stuff to do when I get home.

What, on a Friday night? There's no game tomorrow, I challenged. **I'll shout you a cup of Italian coffee to say thanks for everything.**

But Chris remained unmovable.

Nah, maybe next time. He grinned at both of us. **Besides, don't you want some time on your own?**

The comment had the desired affect. Elizabeth and I looked at each other. The telltale redness began to glow. Why did I keep doing that? It was so uncool.

Elizabeth wasn't playing as smoothly as she had been earlier either, I noticed.

That shut you both up. Chris grinned. **Come on, it's bloody freezing in here.**

Oh yeah, Chris continued, **I told your mum you were heading out with Elizabeth and you'd be home late.**

What was all that about brotherly love? The bastard knew giving that piece of information to Patricia Armstrong meant certain all-day harassment and interrogation for me tomorrow. But I couldn't say any of that and he knew it.

She said to remind you that you haven't been well and not to be home too late because you have another big night tomorrow.

He said it the way he would talk to Jess and cracked himself up. Elizabeth followed. I pegged the program at Chris's head.

Thanks for that, you wanker.

Alone

Chris dropped us off at the pizzeria and for about two minutes Elizabeth and I were strange around each other. It felt like a date, but the thing was I hadn't had time to prepare for a date. I had barely had time to recover from my freak-out. And then I just shut up that really annoying voice in my head. *Just grab her hand and get over it!*

And I did. **Come on, let's go in, it's freezing out here.**

After we'd placed our order, I knew for about the tenth time tonight that it was up to me to speak first and apologize.

Elizabeth, I'm really sorry for not ringing and for walking off tonight. It's just that—

It's all right, Will. Chris let me know you've had a pretty big night.

She put her hands over one of mine.

Are you all right?

Yeah, I think I am. I don't know what Chris said . . .

No, he didn't say much, Will, he just said not to be too hard on you. She smiled at me. **He's a really nice guy.**

Yeah, he is.

Your mum seems really nice too.

Thanks.

She was talking about your dad and how proud he would have been of you. She must have missed him tonight.

I looked at her in surprise. I hadn't even thought about how Mum would feel.

Yeah, I reckon she would have.

Did you miss him?

Yeah.

I looked up, not saying anything. I knew I had to take a risk. I knew I could trust her, I just wasn't sure I could go through it all again tonight. But then I figured it had to get a little bit easier every time.

Will, we can talk about something else. I'm sorry, I didn't mean to—

No, it's just that I had kind of a meltdown about Dad tonight. The first one I've had since he died.

I found myself telling her all about the practice in front of the school, dogging Mark, the music room, seeing Dad and tearing up the Freak. I must have talked for over an hour and she just listened and held my hand and it honestly all felt OK.

I think it was Zach's dad that sent me over the edge. He told me how proud Dad would be of me and I just lost it.

And you haven't ever cried before now?

Nah. That's what I was saying to Chris, it was too hard to even think about. So I just blocked it out. But the last months I started to crack. I didn't have a choice about being involved with the musical. Andrews made sure of that, and then Zach attached himself to my leg, and you walked out onstage and I started to think you and Mark were together and that, well, that drove me nuts, then I met Mark and you . . .

I looked up to find her smiling at me. Man, I didn't have a chance of keeping it together if she smiled at me like that.

So what was he like? She asked this really softly, really carefully, like she was worried the question would wound me.

I don't know really. He was a good guy. The type of guy that people admired, looked up to. He was always on about things being fair and justice being done. He was really big on treating people with respect and making sure everyone was treated equally. But at the same time he could take a joke and lighten up.

I grinned. **He was a really good soccer player, or he thought he was. I don't know . . .** I finally said the one thing I didn't want to say, the thing that made me realize how much I wasn't like him. **What I liked about him most was that, well, he was who he was and it didn't matter who he was speaking to.**

He loved Chris coming around. I reckon Dad respected him because he was always who he was without any bullshit. Like you and Mark and the Freak. He would have respected Mark and probably given him heaps about being gay, once he knew him. And you. Well, he would have loved you. He always went on about how Mum was smart and feisty and beautiful. . . .

The tablecloth blurred for a second or two. I felt a strange combination of embarrassment and sadness.

She squeezed my hand really tightly. **You obviously take after him then.**

Me? Nah. I think I missed out on all of the Armstrong genes.

Oh, come on, Will. That's exactly what you're like. Look at how you stopped those little guys picking on Zach, and how you looked after him. And Mark.

I started to say that she had it completely wrong but she got in before I could.

Yeah, OK, so you stuffed up, but he'll get over it. Look, you

made him feel accepted and liked because you liked him. Some guys would have kept well away. That was important to him. He acts all together but he's not.

She stopped talking and played with the pizza that had been sitting untouched on the table all evening.

I looked up to find her staring at me. The kind of stare that said she wasn't afraid, that she was ready for anything. I stared back, not as fierce but I tried. To be honest, I found her stare a little bit scary. I thought I was the one who was meant to be in control. We kept staring, silent. My heart thudded. I was certain its pulsating could be seen through my jacket. My face became red hot as usual but this time it was not due to embarrassment. I knew I had to do something! But maybe she didn't want to. Maybe she was sitting there wondering what was wrong with me. My head was moving closer and closer to hers.

Our lips touched. They were gentle, soft kisses, as if we were shyly introducing ourselves for the first time. Slowly our bodies gravitated toward each other. She reached her hand to my face, I reached my hand around her back. The more relaxed we were, the greater the intensity of our kisses. I was blown away by her presence, by her smell, by her taste . . . by her. We stopped. We smiled at one another and said nothing.

Thanks. I mean, thanks for everything you just said and for what just happened. . . .

What a pinhead!

You're welcome, Will. I meant it. All of it.

I felt myself becoming all uptight again and then I made myself relax. What had just happened was the best thing that had happened to me in the past decade and I wasn't going to stuff it up. She'd taken the risk and I knew that it was my turn now.

I reached over and grabbed her hand.

You know, I was gone on you the first time I saw you. You came out onstage and I became a blubbering idiot.

She looked up at me playfully.

Yeah, well, I can do better than that. From the very first moment I saw your backside, I knew that you were worth investigating.

More bloody talking!

Even though I had been asleep for most of last week, last night was the first night I'd really slept.

I didn't wake up until my phone rang.

Chris's number flashed.

Chris, not everyone has a Jessie alarm clock, I grumbled.

What's your problem, lover boy, it's midday.

It is not!

It bloody is.

What! I'd planned to make an effort to go over to the Freak's. But it looked like I'd run out of time. I'd have to give him a ring and ask him to meet me at the show early.

The boys are going down to kick the footy around, are you in?

Nah, I can't, I've got to get ready and head up to school.

Excuse me, is this Will Armstrong?

Shut up, you tosser. I said to Brother Pat I'd make sure everything was set up again and I've got to clear stuff with the Freak.

And Elizabeth? Chris teased.

Yeah, well, since she's one of the stars of the show, I suppose she'll be there too.

You weren't so bloody sure of yourself last night when I drove you to the pizza place. So what happened?

Nothing. We went out for pizza.

And?

And we . . . I don't know, we spoke about everything. And it was easy, and she's fantastic.

Chris laughed.

So you're gone! Have you spoken to your mum?

No. But thanks to you I'll cop twenty questions as soon as I walk out the bedroom door.

You're welcome!

I paused.

Chris, thanks again for dealing with the meltdown and smoothing things over with Elizabeth.

Sweet. Just make sure you pass on to some of her friends what a nice guy I am. I'd better go, I told the boys I'd see them down there five minutes ago.

Hey, Chris? Don't say anything to any of the boys about Elizabeth.

Chris's laughter filled my right eardrum.

I don't have to, mate. Tim's already rung me this morning. Costa saw you at the pizza shop and said there was a bit of passion going on!

Shit!

Oh yeah, I nearly forgot, I mentioned to the boys I saw the show last night and they're all keen to come tonight. To show some school spirit and obviously to offer you and Mark some support. The sentence dripped with Chris Holden sarcasm. **It's got nothing to do with checking out the girls or your new girlfriend.**

He hung up before I could tell him to get stuffed. Great, so the boys were turning up and they already knew about Elizabeth. I could just imagine the amount of hassle I was going to get.

The kitchen

I ventured out to the kitchen, where Mum was reading the book section of the paper. She had her reading glasses on and she looked up and squinted.

Well, I was wondering when you'd surface. Have a good night?

She smiled at me, the type of smile that said she knew something and she wanted to find out more.

Yeah. I opened the fridge for something to do.

Elizabeth seems very nice.

She looked at me sideways and there was a semi-knowing smile hovering on her lips.

So I suppose I'll be seeing her a little bit more often from now on?

Yeah, I suppose you might. I grinned at her.

She returned the grin. **Good.**

Then she put her glasses back on and started to read her paper again. That was it? That was all she was going to say? Not possible! Ripped off. I wanted an excuse to talk about Elizabeth, considering she'd been in my head all night. And now my mother chose to shut up?

Something that Elizabeth said last night came into my mind— maybe that was how Mum felt about Dad. Maybe that was why she wanted to talk about him all the time, because it made her feel like he was around. It was like Chris said—he wouldn't speak about Dad because he knew I'd spin out. Pretty bloody selfish of me.

I put the orange juice back in the fridge and talked to Mum from the bench. I figured if I could expose my insides to Chris and then again with Elizabeth, I could manage to ask Mum something about Dad. I felt the familiar clenching in my stomach, but this time I knew it wasn't going to kill me.

Mum?

Yes, love? She had her head down, reading.

Mum, did you miss Dad last night?

Mum flicked her head up and forgot to hide her look of absolute shock. It would have been pretty funny if I hadn't been so nervous.

Yes, Will, I did. I missed him very much.

That wasn't so hard. I forced myself to keep going.

It's just that Elizabeth said you were talking about him.

She took off her glasses and carefully put them into their case.

Actually, I was telling her how much you reminded me of him.

She waited for a response. Normally by now I would have run screaming out of the room; well, I wouldn't have bothered with the screaming part, I would have just turned around and walked straight out.

That's what Elizabeth said, but . . . I stopped to get the words out. **I'm not like him, am I?**

This time there was no hesitation.

Will, you are more like him than you realize.

She paused, allowing me to digest what she'd said. She was moving cautiously, like someone who was helping a hurt animal. My gut clamped down hard like I'd been winded in a tackle. I wasn't walking out this time, though, and I wanted to know. I think I needed to know.

How?

Because you're funny, you get on well with all sorts of different people. You go out of your way to help people, and you have a very quiet, sensitive side that you don't like to admit to and only show to a handful of people.

She said it like it was no big deal I was asking and I liked that. But what I couldn't tell her was that I didn't believe it. I mean, I'm not that much of a victim that I think I'm a complete write-off— well, not today anyway. But it didn't take away how I'd treated Mark or Zach or Mum even. I couldn't get rid of this feeling that I'd let Dad down somehow and he was disappointed in me. But I didn't know how to tell Mum that. If I ended up telling Mum then she'd be disappointed too.

Yeah, but Dad stood up for what he believed in, didn't he? On the work sites he always made sure that everyone was treated fairly and he never acted better than anybody else. He wasn't afraid of what people thought of him.

No, you're right, but he wasn't perfect, Will. He'd hate it if you remembered him as being perfect. God, that's the last thing he'd want. He prided himself on how much he could act like an idiot. Something else you also inherited from him.

She threw this comment over arched eyebrows. She paused again and then slowly straightened the paper in front of her.

Look, Will, he was a man, a human being who was decent, loving, compassionate, just, but who could also be a pain in the backside, broody, quiet, an idiot and angry, just like all of us.

We're all human, Will. We all muck things up and hurt and fall in love and make idiots of ourselves and do the wrong things. I can't tell you the amount of times I was furious with your father about something he did or said or didn't say, but the thing was I

knew he never meant to hurt me. And as soon as he figured out what was going on he'd apologize. In fact he was far better than me when it came to giving and receiving apologies. I always tended to hang on to being cranky for a while . . .

She trailed off, smiling. It felt as though she had gone somewhere else for a minute. I turned away from her, trying to brush aside some of the tears that had landed on the bench. She stood up from the chair and hugged me for a moment, then stood beside me. Both of us stared out at the veggie patch.

Darling, you have gone through one of the toughest things you will ever have to face in your life, and at such a horribly young age. It breaks my heart to watch you struggle to make sense out of something that has destroyed your world. I worried for a time that you were going to disappear. But you haven't, Will, because you're stronger than that. Because, like your father, you refuse to give up or to accept that everything is serious all the time. Because you have surrounded yourself with people like Chris, Mr. Andrews and Brother Patrick, who all care about you. Because you are who you are. Your dad was a good man, Will, but he was made a better man because you were his son. And no matter what you do, he will always, always love you.

She was crying by this stage—not big heavy tears, just gentle ones. I was too. I'd never cried with Mum about Dad. And maybe I wouldn't again, but I needed to let her know that it was all right and I was all right. I tried one of the Holden bear hugs. It felt a little uncomfortable but it worked.

She eased herself out of the hug, glassy-eyed but not crying anymore.

And I am so proud of everything you have achieved in the musical, Will, and I don't care how much you pretend you haven't

done anything. I know for a fact because so many people told me last night. Mr. Cohen came and introduced himself and told me about young Zach. Brother Patrick went on about all of your support with the band. Mr. Andrews says you've improved out of sight in English.

That stumped me. Maybe there was a chance of getting an extension for the English assignment.

And Elizabeth, she's lovely, Will. I am very happy for you.

The mention of Elizabeth's name was a sign to get everything back to normal again. There was only so much heavy emotional stuff a guy could handle and I reckon I'd had enough in the past twenty-four hours for at least another decade.

Mum was about to put her glasses back on when she stopped and looked at me.

Will, one more thing. She paused. **Talk to him.**

I thought she must be referring to the Freak. **Yeah, no I am, that's why I need you to drop me to school early.**

She continued looking at me.

No, Will, your father, talk to your father.

I didn't know what to say to that. I just stared at her.

She smiled at me. **You haven't looked at me like that since you found out there was no Santa Claus. I mean it, Will, talk to him. They never leave you if you keep them alive in your heart.**

She put her glasses on and went back to her paper, leaving me standing like that seven-year-old kid. Just like the Santa Claus thing, I wasn't ready to hear it.

Zachariah Cohen

Mum dropped me at the gates. It felt like a lifetime ago since I'd winked at the brothers' main man that Friday afternoon. Lucky the musical was nearly over, otherwise they'd be carting me off for intensive therapy.

I could see the Freak waiting out the front. He'd taken out his trombone and was making sure it was tuned. Anyone else would have cracked up about the fart noises, but the Freak just kept on with the job. I called out to him.

Hey, Zach.

Hey, Will.

It was then I realized that the fart noises were not just coming from his direction. There were three others, just like the Freak, all tuning their instruments, listening to him like he was some sort of guru. They stopped playing instantly as I approached and stared.

Zach, do you reckon I could talk to you for a minute?

Zach didn't seem that angry. In fact he didn't seem that much of anything.

Sure.

He stood up and walked over to where I was standing. He was waiting for me to speak. I looked at him curiously. Surely he knew why I'd asked him to meet me early?

I met your dad the other night.

Yeah, I know.

He's a nice bloke.

He looked at me as if I was really strange.

Yeah, I know.

You look just like him.

Yeah, I know.

Zach, I'm sorry, I'm sorry about the other day.

He looked at me dead on. Yeah, I know.

I was freaking out. I didn't mean anything I said. I was angry and you were the one who copped it.

Yeah, I know.

How do you know?

'Cause Chris came running out after you and asked me what you'd said. He told me you were upset about something else, not me.

He was quiet, really quiet. Then he looked straight up at me.

Other people have said that type of stuff to me, and even though it hurt it doesn't matter because they're not my friends. But you are, Will. You're my friend and I trusted you. He paused. You shouldn't have said those things to me.

I felt like I did when his dad spoke to me last night. I wished he'd screamed and carried on. But he didn't, he just told it to me straight and that's what cut me up the most.

I know, Zach. I'm really, really sorry.

He looked at me again with his ancient eyes for a long time.

Yeah, I know. And you know what else, Will? It wasn't me who said anything about Mark.

It was my turn.

Yeah, I know.

I wouldn't do that to Mark.

Yeah, I know . . . Listen, Freak, the dad stuff's no excuse,

I know. But things have been really weird lately. I never set out to hurt you, mate, never. I know that sounds like such a bad excuse, but it just happened. And you wore all of the fallout.

It's all right, Will. I know what it's like.

His eyes had darkened and become sad.

There was this one time when I went psycho in Year Four. It was straight after Mum left. I remember throwing chairs around and yelling and screaming. It was so bad they had to ring Dad to get me to stop. When he arrived, he came and talked to me. He said I was angry at the world for taking my mum away. I figured you were angry at the world for taking your dad away.

I was speechless. No one this little was meant to be that smart.

You threw chairs around the classroom?

Yeah, pretty cool, huh? The kids've thought I was mad ever since.

He gave me his first smile of the day and patted me on the arm.

It's all right, Will. I know you're sorry.

I grabbed his hand and spun it behind his back and then grabbed him from the back and lifted him up.

Thanks, Freak. Nice to have you back.

I tousled his hair like my dad used to do to me when I was Zach's age. Then I looked back over to where the geeks were trying really hard to look like they hadn't been listening to our entire conversation.

So who are your mates?

Just some of the geeks from the band. They're all right. No big deal. He walked over toward the geeks and his trombone. But they did tell me you and Elizabeth kissed last night.

Great! It had even made it to the Year 7 geek section of the St. Andrew's news network.

The final performance

I walked into the hall and started getting everything set up. The Freak told me he'd give me a hand after he'd finished having a jam with his mates. I had to shut my mouth before I made a smart-arse comment. As I walked toward the pit I caught myself feeling proud of the little guy.

By the time I'd finished the setup, the hall had begun to fill with the whole crew for the last time.

Good evening, handsome!

Elizabeth was walking through the stage hall doors. Her hair was out and reached halfway down her back. She was dressed in jeans and a T-shirt like she always was, but this time when I looked at her it was different. I don't know if I was different, she was different or we were both different, but it didn't matter because it was good different.

She had her costumes thrown over her shoulder and was carrying at least three other bags. I walked over to meet her, grinning and not caring that the entire hall had stopped to watch the show. I grabbed the gear like some bloody knight in not-so-shining armor. She leaned across and brushed my lips with hers. The whole hall erupted. Back to reality. I didn't know whether to laugh or to tell everyone to find their own love life to feed off. As for Elizabeth, she just laughed up at me, not bothered by any of it.

Yeah, all right, settle down! I managed as we continued on our path to the change rooms.

She stood in the doorway and I handed her the gear. She looked straight into my eyes like she had last night.

Thanks for last night, Will, I had a great time.

I was thankful the others had not overheard. Their perverse little minds would have become too excited.

No, yeah, it was good.

How could I have spent all last night talking to the girl and still not manage a decent sentence today?

So are you coming to Mark's after-show party?

I continued to struggle.

The thing is, I'm not sure if I'll be wanted at Mark's party.

She took the rest of her stuff, turned me around and gave me a shove on the bum with the only thing that was free, her foot.

Go and talk to him, Will.

I knew I had to. I didn't want to stuff up the after-show vibe for him like I had last night. Anyway, this time I figured if he didn't accept my apology there wasn't much more I could do.

I knocked outside the blokes' dressing room and watched the younger chorus guys run out. I walked straight in and found Mark in the corner, putting on what looked like a really bad, really bright 1920s jacket.

Hi, Mark.

He looked up and nodded.

Well, at least he didn't tell me to get out.

Nice jacket.

He continued to look at me without comment. OK, so a joke was not a good way to start.

Mark, I know you're pissed off with me and you should be. And I know everything you said last night was true. Just give me a chance to say some stuff to you, OK?

He sat down in front of the mirror and swiveled the chair toward me.

You were right yesterday. You were right. I was worried about what other people would think. And it was a stuffed thing to do to you. I don't think you're a freak. I'm the one who's been acting like a basket case.

I looked up over him.

And I know if I say it won't happen again, you'll think that's what I said last time. So I guess I'm just going to have to prove it to you.

Mark continued to sit and say nothing.

But I want you to know that I really am genuinely sorry.

The room filled with the sound of him swiveling on his seat. It was a good three minutes before he spoke.

I was still really pissed off yesterday, Will, but you deserved it. And I appreciate you backing up today. But I still mean what I said: I've learned the hard way that it's all got to be about trust, otherwise it doesn't count.

We both waited in silence. Mark stood up from the chair and I thought for a moment he was going to leave, but instead he extended his hand.

Thanks for apologizing, Will.

I reached out and shook his hand a little uncertainly.

So you like the jacket then? I'm wearing it to the party.

He was dead serious. I looked at the jacket again; he had to be winding me up, but I wasn't taking the risk.

Yeah, I said cautiously, **it's great.**

Joke, Will. It was a joke!

He was grinning at me. **You are coming then?**

Yeah, yeah, of course.

You and Elizabeth can get a lift with me after the show if you like. That is, if you two don't want to go alone.

You've heard then?

Who hasn't? The chorus girls have been carrying on all afternoon.

He looked over and grinned again.

About bloody time if you ask me. It's taken you practically the whole term to pull your finger out.

This time I returned the grin.

You're just jealous, mate.

I felt like Chris must have when he made the Dad joke the other night. I didn't know if I was about to crash and burn. But he grabbed his boater hat and sliced it through the air at me.

You wish, buddy, you wish!

I caught it and threw it back to him. Things were instantly easier.

Look, I'd better get going, the geeks are getting restless. Are you nervous? Last night and all that?

Yeah, I am a bit. I've got some mates up from Melbourne.

It was nearly out of my mouth to ask if it was anyone he wanted to impress, but I thought that might have been pushing it. I said goodbye and headed over for my last time with Brother Pat and the geeks in the pit.

Good evening, Brother. Are you ready for yet another fine performance this evening?

You sound remarkably chipper, Will. It wouldn't have anything to do with a certain Elizabeth Zefferelli, would it?

I looked at him incredulously.

Not too old to notice, young man. Very good. Very good indeed. Nice girl. Now let's get this show under way.

After the show

Willo! Loved the show, man!

I looked up from among the band gear. It was the boys, led by a widely grinning Chris.

Yeah, that's because you couldn't take your eyes off the can-can dancers.

Nah, that's not true. I spent a lot of time looking at Polly. But some loser cut my grass. I'll never forgive you, Willo.

I gave Jock the finger and said hello to Chris and Tim.

Nice gangsta outfit! Show us your moves, homeboy!

Jock came over to my left side.

No, seriously, man, she's cute. So do you reckon you can introduce the one who played her friend? You owe me!

I pushed him aside and continued moving music stands for the last time. Something I was definitely not going to miss.

Did you have to bring them? I said to Chris.

I pointed over to where Tim and Jock had taken some of the geeks' instruments and were trying to play them, which wasn't working, in an attempt to wind up the geeks, which was working.

I couldn't stop them. They wanted to make sure you knew who to set them up with.

Chris looked over to where the Freak was giving them a very thorough talking-to.

If you're not careful, the little man over there is going to become a William Armstrong clone.

Jock and Tim were giving up the instruments and telling the Freak to settle down. He was doing an all right job of it too. I thought I'd give him some backup.

Hey, be careful with those, you idiots! I shouted.

But it looked like Zach didn't need any assistance, he just looked over and waved.

So you two are mates again?

Yeah. It was like he understood what was going on before I did. I mean, look at me last night about Dad, and I'm seventeen—imagine what you'd feel like if your mum walked out on you when you were nine. Nah, he's a really cool kid, in a geeky kind of way.

The Freak made his way over and shook Chris's hand.

Are you coming tonight, Chris?

Sure am.

I'll see you there then. I can't talk. I've got to organize these guys to get the gear down to the band room, otherwise Brother Patrick and Ms. Sefton will freak.

Sure, Zach, I'll catch you then.

Quite the confident socializer, your Zach. You have taught him well, Yoda.

I hit him with a drumstick.

All right, all right. So are you going to Mark's tonight or are things still strange?

I spoke to him before the show. I think he's OK. You could tell he was keeping himself distant, but we had a bit of a laugh. He said he had mates coming from Melbourne. You'd want to make sure that the boys are told to pull their heads in.

Chris was smiling at me.

What?

I'm sorry, am I hearing William Armstrong speaking to me about being responsible? Man, this is great!

You know what I mean, after the tuckshop incident and all.

Yeah, Will, I'm the one who gets it. The boys'll be fine. They're just up for a good party where they can check out the ladies.

I looked around and saw we had at least an hour's packing-up to get through.

Chris, do you reckon you and those two idiots could give us a hand?

Chris was shaking his head as he started with the instruments. Jock had obviously overheard and he came up and slapped me on the shoulder.

It'll cost you, Willo.

I wouldn't expect anything different, Jock. All right, I'll introduce you. But you've got to act halfway human.

Come on, it's me you're talking to!

At which point Tim called over to him and pretended to play the trombone by farting at the same time. Jock couldn't speak for five minutes he thought it was so funny.

Forget it!

The Newmans and the Zefferellis

There were after-show drinks again—and rumors of a small party hosted by Brother Pat. I reckon that's one of the main reasons he gets involved, for the drinks afterward. I headed over to the library, feeling pretty happy with myself. Things had sorted themselves out and I was about to see Elizabeth again. I found Mum talking to Danielli and Brother Patrick. I hoped it was another one of those sessions she'd told me about this afternoon. Mr. Cohen was there with an older couple in suits. They'd have to be Mark's parents.

Here he is! The man of the moment! Did you get all of the instruments away?

Brother Patrick boomed this at me even though I was right in front of him. Obviously the sherry had been flowing already.

Everything's good, Brother. All the little guys did their bit.

That's all down to your good guidance, Will.

Mum beamed.

Well now, no room for false modesty here. We all know you were a right troublemaker before, so we may as well give praise where it is due.

Danielli moved himself beside me.

Brother Patrick has been telling us about what an excellent job you have done. Well done, Will, well done!

I saw Andrews looking over in our direction. He excused himself from a bunch of very happy parents and headed over. I watched him, wondering what he was up to.

Truce?

Here we go.

What, sir?

Come on, Will, I haven't exactly been your favorite person lately.

What was I meant to say to that?

No, sir, I mean, yes, sir.

It's all right, Will. He was smiling at me like he always did.

He extended his hand.

Congratulations on an excellent job, Will. Really. It's been a pleasure working with you.

This was more like it.

He was called away by someone over on the other side of the room. As he turned to leave he threw over his shoulder, **Don't forget about the assignment due on Monday.**

Bastard! He'd done that deliberately.

Mum came over and led me to the older couple who had been standing with her.

Will, these are Mark's parents, Mr. and Mrs. Newman.

Hello, Will. Well done. It was all excellent.

I remembered what Mark had said about his dad. He sure fit the hotshot businessman description, all decked out in his pinstriped suit. He needed to relax, though. He was jiggling up and down on his feet as if he was nervous about something. Maybe if he loosened his tie a bit he'd chill out. But at least he'd made an effort to be here. Mark's mum was completely different. She and Mum were nattering on like they'd known each other since kindy.

Well, it's Mark and Elizabeth who are the real stars.

Oh, I don't know about that, you can't have a musical without a band. No, I think we can say that you were all brilliant!

No wonder Mrs. Newman and Mum got on. They both spoke the same over-the-top language.

Will you be coming to the party, Will?

Oops! Hadn't quite got around to asking Mum about that.

Ahhh . . .

Mark had just reached the group and answered for me.

Yeah, sure he'll be there, he's one of the guests of honor.

I smiled over at Mum sheepishly. I knew we'd be talking about this later.

Hello, darling, we thought you were wonderful. Mrs. Newman kissed Mark on the cheek. **I don't know where it comes from—it's not from my side, that's for sure. Mind you, your father has a very good voice, don't you, Stephen?**

Mr. Newman looked uncomfortable. **Oh, I don't know about that.** He extended his hand rather formally to Mark. **Well done, son. I admire your bravery.**

Thanks, Dad. It wasn't much but you could tell that Mark rated the compliment.

There was a moment's silence while everyone looked at one another and smiled. Then Mark glanced at his watch and said, **Right, well, we'd better go home to make sure everything's ready for tonight.**

Oh no, you can't go yet, Brother Pat boomed. **No, there are far too many people who want to meet you. Some of the old boys and their wives think you're the best thing since . . .**

I grinned wickedly at Mark, who gave me the finger and then turned to give a hasty smile to Brother Patrick.

Hey, Will, Mark called out to me as Brother Patrick marched him off. I nearly forgot. **Elizabeth's waiting for you in the dressing room.**

What?

It was pointless. He'd run off. What was she waiting in the dressing room for?

I excused myself while Mum and Mrs. Newman were at it again. Nervously, very nervously, I found my way to the girls' dressing room and knocked.

I heard a **Just a minute.**

Elizabeth?

God, what kept you? I was beginning to think you weren't coming.

She opened the door and started to look around, then she stared at me.

What's wrong with you?

I was speechless. She looked stunning. I mean stunning. She had on a deep red dress that tied at her neck and hugged her body. I didn't know backs could be so sexy. I was blown away.

Will, what is it? You're worrying me now.

God, y-y-you look great! I stammered eventually.

This time it was Elizabeth who blushed.

You don't think it's too much, do you?

No way, it's fantastic!

She moved closer to where I was standing.

Thanks, Will.

We stood looking at each other for a while. I began to wish I'd made a little more effort with my own gear.

Here. She offered me a glass of champagne. **Mark's mum and dad gave it to us at the beginning of the performance.**

We clinked our glasses Hollywood style and, in keeping with the theme, I reached over and kissed her.

So, what's with the *meet me in the dressing room*? I said eventually, once my heart had stopped hammering. **Mark nearly forgot to tell me.**

She seemed a little nervous.

I wanted to see you before you met my parents.

Why?

I just wanted to explain. Look, they're really conservative . . . in an up-to-date way. I just wanted to warn you.

I know, you've told me all this.

All of a sudden I had this vision of the Godfather holding a horse's head with my name on it.

Dad's nice and everything, but he would have freaked if he knew we were on our own last night. It's not that they won't let me have a boyfriend, it's just that they like to meet him first and meet his parents. They're protective, that's all. She paused. **Maybe it's better you don't tell them how you got to be involved in the musical.**

It's not exactly something I advertise, Elizabeth.

Please don't be offended, Will. She paused and lowered her head. **It's just that I don't want anything to muck us up and I know what they're like.**

I pulled her toward me and let her lean against me. I was full up with the need to make everything all right for her.

Don't worry, it'll be fine. How could they not like me? I grabbed her hand, threw the champagne down my throat and opened the door. **Come on, I was enough of a basket case for both of us last night. No more stressing, let's go and have some fun like they keep telling us we spend all our time doing. Now *skol*!**

Will, you're very, very sad. She threw back the champagne. **But I really like that about you.**

We walked up to the group and were watched with every step. I was still holding Elizabeth's hand tight, but her grip was tighter. It looked like Mum had done the hard work for us, though. She'd obviously been talking to Elizabeth's parents already. She was always good at that sort of thing.

Here they are! You look beautiful, Elizabeth, Mum said as she kissed her hello. **And this is my son, William.**

I shook hands with Mr. and Mrs. Zefferelli. Mr. Zefferelli nearly managed to end my nonexistent career as a lead guitarist before it even started, his handshake was so full-on. I hid my pain and tried a bit of Patricia Armstrong small talk on him. After the third grunt in answer to my third question, I figured the man either hated my guts or just didn't do small talk. I moved over to Mum for some support. She was doing well with Mrs. Zefferelli and since I'd already scored some points with the only other female in the Zefferelli family, maybe I'd stand more of a chance there. Just as I was about to launch into a *you can't help but love me* hello, Elizabeth, who had been chatting with Brother Pat, came over and Mum took that as her cue to excuse herself. There was no way I was going in there on my own so I also made my escape. As I did I overheard the Zefferellis saying *wonderful, spectacular.* Apart from the lack of small talk they seemed like pretty normal parents to me.

Thanks, Mum. You're good at the meet and greet thing.

Thank you, Will.

So Brother Pat invited you to his party?

She grinned at me knowingly. **Yes, Will, he did. When were you going to ask me about yours?**

Yeah, sorry about that. I meant to tell you about it, but what with everything going on—

It's all right, Will, just promise me you'll behave yourself.

I'm not a five-year-old. Besides, how much trouble can there be at a wussy after-musical party?

I caught Mark's eye across the hall. He pointed to his watch. I gave Mum a kiss, told her to go off, have a good time and stop stressing, then went searching for the Freak. There was no way this kid was not coming to the party. Mr. Cohen smiled at me and shook my hand.

I know he's in safe hands. Thanks, Will. But, Zach, midnight and that's final!

Elizabeth had disentangled herself from her parents, who were happily moving off with Mark's parents and Mum to join Brother Pat.

Be good! they chorused.

We all waved and smiled.

Don't worry, we will!

The party

When we arrived the music was blaring and there were plenty of people around already. Mark's Melbourne mates had left right after the show and got things organized. We were cheered as we entered. Well, I wasn't, but Mark and Elizabeth were.

Mark made a beeline for his friends: three guys, two girls. I wondered again if he was keen on any of them, the blokes I mean. I watched from a distance as he kissed two of them hello. He seemed to act pretty normal but he was paying a lot of attention to one guy in particular and he took a cigarette off him, waited for him to light it, then had three drags and put it out again. I was standing there watching when I had this horrible feeling I was turning into my mum so I started to turn away.

Just as I did, Mark motioned for me to come over.

Yes, this is the man who had the freak attack in the car.

I suppose I deserved that. I wonder when payback time is over.

Thanks for that, Mark.

He introduced me.

But now he's a mate.

I nodded in his direction and shook hands with all of them.

And I also set him up with my gorgeous costar.

Shit, I'd been so wrapped up in Mark's love life I'd forgotten about my own. I looked over to see Elizabeth talking to the boys. I excused myself and went straight over. I knew most of them would behave themselves, but I wasn't so sure about Jock and Tim.

As I approached, I could hear Elizabeth laughing as usual and Jock telling a story, obviously a really funny story. It was when they shut up as I reached them that I figured it was a really funny story about me.

All right, Jock, shut up.

He looked at me innocently.

What, Willo? I was just giving Elizabeth here all the background info she needs on Will Armstrong.

She looked over at me and grinned.

I tried to defend myself. **You know no one listens to Jock, Elizabeth. He's full of it!**

Oh, I don't know, I was enjoying the story until you wrecked it.

The boys went into their usual chorus response of **Oooooooooooohhhhhhhhhhhhhhhh!**

Chris offered to get drinks. **Why don't you give him a hand and Jock can finish his story?** said Elizabeth.

I bowed my consent and left to even louder applause. Dad would be proud I'd ended up with a feisty one. I knew she'd be fine, and it was pretty obvious the boys were falling over themselves to impress her. I found Chris by the coolers. He pointed his bottle in the direction of the boys and smiled.

She's a really nice girl, Will.

Yeah, I know.

I've got to say, mate, I'm dead jealous.

I looked at him strangely.

No, don't get me wrong. You're my best mate and it's great you're happy. I just want you to know that she seems like a really

sound girl and it's obvious she's totally into you. It's great and I'm jealous.

Chris was jealous of me?

Thanks, mate. Not that you're jealous, just thanks for saying it.

We were both quiet. Silence wasn't a big deal between us, but I got the feeling Chris was a bit embarrassed. Talking about girl stuff was new coming from him. He was normally the one dishing out the advice.

Right, well, that's it then. Come on.

I grabbed hold of Chris's arm and pulled him over toward Elizabeth's friends.

What are you doing?

Well, you were doing all right the other night with Elizabeth's friends. What was that girl's name . . . Maree? It's time for you to meet them again. Before you start hitting on Elizabeth!

The night was getting louder and more revved up. There were only a couple of people out of control; mostly everyone was still hyped from the show. Considering it had taken nearly a whole term of hard work, it was a pretty major event. And it had been a success. I know it wasn't a Broadway show or anything, but they were good, we were good. People were buzzing about the funniest moments, who stuffed up their lines and how real the Elizabeth and Mark kiss looked. I kept out of that discussion.

Zach was right at the front doing the now infamous terrier routine. Elizabeth was standing with Mark, who had his arm around her. I looked over at the boys a little fearful they'd be taking the piss, but they were too busy showing off. Some had even resorted to talking to some well-known nerds so they could get introduced. Chris was in deep conversation with the Melbourne girls. A very long, involved conversation. Of course he'd have to find someone who lived a ten-hour car ride away.

One of the footy boys who had come with Jock and Tim called over to me. **Hey, mate, you want to keep an eye on your woman.**

He nodded over to where Elizabeth and Mark were standing arm in arm at the front door, talking to the geeks who were being picked up by tired parents. Midnight was obviously the latest any of them had been allowed out by themselves in their lives. Zach was there, reluctantly waiting for his dad. I figured I should move over and say goodbye.

I turned around and looked the footy bloke square in the face and smiled. Let him think what he liked.

I waved at the Freak as he got into his dad's car and continued toward Elizabeth.

Hey! I slid my arms around her. It felt really good.

I've been waiting for you to come over.

I looked at her and wondered how I'd gotten so lucky. The whole night had been a success. I was riding the crest of what felt like the world's biggest wave. I'd been dumped, chewed up, nearly drowned and spat out, but now, right now, I felt like I was riding it.

This was not the time for fear or fumbling. I drew her toward me, running my fingers over her face. I nearly pulled them away, worried that they could scratch something so incredibly soft. She looked at me without flinching. Outside the old chapel, at the pizza place, at school today; each time she had looked at me in exactly the same way. Open and honest, and really, really hot!

I felt her hands navigating my back, her touch sending shivers of excitement up my spine. Our breathing quickened and our bodies pressed together. It had been a whole two hours since we had last kissed and it was time for plenty more. . . .

I, uh, hate to break up this moment of young love, but we have visitors!

What? I managed to mumble. It was Mark and he was looking a little concerned and rather a lot pissed off.

I said we have visitors and they're not the kind that were invited.

Elizabeth was looking at the two of us. Her face seemed to be a mixture of dismay, anger and puzzlement.

Don't tell me that one of the most beautiful moments of my teenage life has been interrupted because you two have come over all territorial and full of testosterone.

Mark and I looked at one another. Neither of us knew how to respond.

So someone's gate-crashing the party, ring the police! You don't have to prove anything to anyone.

Little did she know I had plenty to prove, but I wasn't about to get into a deep and meaningful talk about it.

And besides, she continued, **I thought if you were gay**—she looked at Mark—**and the musical, sensitive type**—she looked at me—**the Neanderthal gene was recessive.**

Mark turned to her.

Now, now, you're more intelligent than to rely on stereotypes, Elizabeth.

She rolled her eyes and told Mark to go away. I went to give her a kiss.

Don't bother doing your hero's farewell kiss on me. This isn't a damsel in distress, thank you. I will do the most sensible thing

and ring the police. **Now if you will both excuse me, I intend to save you from getting your rather handsome faces pulverized into a bowl of mush.**

Mark and I raised our eyebrows and went to the front door. The rest of the boys were already there. Chris was standing in the doorway trying, in his very Atticus Finch way, to speak reason.

Listen, there's no need for any trouble. The party's over and the parents are asleep. Why don't you all go home?

Mark's parents weren't home yet and Chris knew it. But it wasn't a bad tactic. There were five of them. I didn't know their names but I knew who they were. They were mates of the tuckshop boyzzz who were smart enough to keep away because of what would happen at school, and even smarter to send their mates around to finish the work they couldn't the other day.

Their tag was in every bus stop in the area. Jock reckoned that was about as hard as they got, but they weren't looking exactly friendly standing on Mark's front step. They looked like they'd already been to about ten parties and were ready for a bit of action.

The biggest bloke spoke really slowly, like he was speaking to an idiot.

We don't want to go home, mate. That's why we came here. So we could party.

He began to shoulder his way past Chris and attempted to make it through the doorway. I felt Jock and Tim move forward. I moved with them. Mark cut through all of us. His voice was deliberately light but with an undercurrent of strength.

Well, you're going to have to go home, mate, because this is my house and you're not invited here.

The bloke looked at Mark and shifted his head as if he recognized him.

Hey, aren't you that new bloke my mates told me about? Aren't you the faggot who sang in front of the school and then acted like some tough guy afterward?

This time he spoke to the other four, who were still standing behind him.

Boys, it looks like we've stumbled on a party full of fucking faggots. So is that it? Are you all a bunch of filthy shirt-lifters?

By this stage the boys, joined by two of the guys from Melbourne, were ready to knock Mark out of the way and start on all of them.

Jock was red in the face and already swinging his arms. **I'm not having a dickhead like you call me a faggot! Who the fuck do you think you are?**

The bloke stepped back a bit. Jock was not a forward for nothing. But Mark continued to be the one in front, like a barrier. He was doing it deliberately. I knew he was trying to stop a full-on fight, but I didn't reckon he was going to have much luck. The thug just kept going, itching for someone to make a move.

So is that it, are all of you pretty rich-boy faggots?

I could see Mark's broad shoulders shaking with rage and the amount of control he was using so as he didn't reach over and push the guy's tiny brain out of his ugly head.

No, that would be me you're talking about. And I don't want scum like you insulting me in my own house.

The bloke looked a little disconcerted for about three seconds. You could see that Mark did not fit the image he had in his head of a typical poofter. The boys were moving forward; the room was filled with testosterone-charged aggression.

Then the other losers started to fly as many names as they could through the doorway.

You filthy freak!

You arse-licking pedophile!

Pretty-boy faggot, bringing dirt into our area . . .

I don't know whether it was because I felt I had to prove something to Mark, whether I didn't want to be accused of being a poofter, or whether I just wanted the ignorant wanker to shut his mouth, but I pushed past Mark and swung hard into the bloke's gut. He stumbled but regrouped and came back swinging. I knew I was in it bad but I didn't care. I felt removed from all of it, focused and controlled, fueled by anger. Behind me I could hear the sound of fists meeting flesh.

It didn't stop until two cars pulled up. The big guy who had the mouth yelled at his mates to bolt, but it was too late. The cops had already made their way onto the front yard, followed by what looked like the majority of the street all dressed in their pajamas, some looking scared, others looking really pissed off.

I looked around for Elizabeth and found her standing next to the other car that had pulled up. The one with Mark's parents in it. It turned out she had to ring the school 'cause she didn't know the address. They were all talking to one of the cops, who was writing down what they were saying. They were keen to take us all to the station, but Mark's parents did some serious talking. Mark's dad looked totally wound up and from what I could see he wasn't going to let these cops take his son anywhere. I could hear his raised voice saying stuff like *thugs, lawsuits, illegal entry, harassment* and *vilification*. So the iceman could lose it when he wanted to. Now I could see where Mark got it from.

Eventually we moved into the lounge room. It took about an hour to give our statements. We looked like we'd all had the hardest game of rugby in our lives. One of the Melbourne guys was going to

283

have a black eye, and I reckoned, considering I could only see out of one of mine, so was I.

Mum wasn't going to be happy. It was then I figured she'd be really worried. I asked if I could use the phone. Walking out to the kitchen I found Elizabeth helping clean up the rest of the party. I hobbled over to her, hoping for just a little bit of sympathy. She looked at me and I could see she was upset. It must have been pretty scary to watch. She went to touch my eye and I flinched.

You bloody hero, she whispered as she gently put her arms around me.

Aren't your parents going to freak?

Yeah, I don't want to think about it. Mrs. Newman's already rung. Dad will be here in a minute. I heard her ring your mum too.

At least I didn't have to face that.

I was having a great night up until you and Mark had to come over all macho.

I looked at her out of my good eye. **That's a bit strong, isn't it?**

I don't understand why you didn't just shut the door in their faces.

I could tell she was serious and I half knew it wasn't only the fighting she was worried about, but I was too tired, too sore to go into it. It was at that point when her dad and my mum arrived. I figured it was best I kept right away from Mr. Zefferelli. I didn't want to risk another black eye. I limped over to Mum, worried that she was going to start on the same theme as Elizabeth.

Hello, darling.

Well, at least that was a good start. Better response than anticipated.

Come on, let's get you home and we'll talk tomorrow.

She ushered me into the car and made sure that everyone else was all right and had a lift home. Chris, who was driving, was going to take three of the boys. We picked up another two. Just before I left, Mark came over to me.

Thanks, mate.

For what? I think I came off worse than anyone.

You know what I mean.

No big deal.

See you Monday, I said as I shook his hand.

Seat belts, boys, Mum chorused, and there was something wonderfully familiar about the instruction, the tone and the resulting groans.

The phone call

It was 3:00 p.m. on Sunday and I was sitting at my desk trying to get my head around the fact that I had to get the English assignment in to Andrews tomorrow. The fallout from Mark's party had taken up most of the morning. Mum had the obligatory *violence leads to worse trouble* talk. But this time it was edged with a touch, just a touch, of *I'm pleased that you felt you could stand up for Mark and challenge the other boys.*

Yeah, right. As if any of those brainless losers were going to listen to reason.

It was 3:02 p.m. and there was still nothing happening on the assignment front. At 3:04 Elizabeth rang. I knew there was something majorly wrong as soon as I heard her voice. I couldn't cope with any more drama so I carried on as if everything was normal.

I was going to ring you, but Mum's been doing the whole parent thing all day. She's been really cool about it, though. Heaps better than I thought. I mean, she was upset and gave me the usual *fists don't prove anything* talk. But it's not as if I'm grounded or anything. So all in all I reckon it's turned out all right.

Silence.

I was getting a little freaked out. Normally it was me who didn't know what to say. I tried again.

Don't you think?

Silence.

Elizabeth?

I heard something very faint coming from her end.

Elizabeth, don't cry—

She cut me off before I had a chance to get going on the sensitive and aware routine.

I'm not crying, you idiot ... I'm furious! I haven't said anything because if I told you what I really thought of you, you wouldn't speak to me again for the rest of my life. You've wrecked everything!

What the hell was she going on about?

What do you mean, I wrecked everything?

A really big sigh came rolling down the telephone line straight into my ear.

Will, you knew my parents were strict, I told you enough times, but you still had to go off and prove yourself in front of the boys. And now they won't let me see you at all. They think you're a nice boy, but Dad reckons he can't trust me to go out with someone who's going to get involved in fights all the time.

Say what?

Now hang on a minute, that's so not fair! Did you tell them that I was stepping up for a mate? And that I wasn't one of the losers who turned up on the doorstep looking for a bit of biffo, calling one of our friends, your mum's precious Mark, a faggot?

I was getting charged up by now.

Did you tell them that, Elizabeth?

Of course I told them. Do you think that I don't want to see you? But come on, Will, you've got to admit part of the reason why you got into the fight was because you felt like you had to prove something.

What did Dad say about strong, opinionated girls?

It had only been forty-eight hours and we were already having our first fight.

Look, that doesn't matter now. What are we going to do about Mum and Dad?

Well, I don't know, Elizabeth, but it sounds like you pretty much agree with your parents, so maybe we had better do what they say and not see one another.

Silence. Yeah, let her know she needed to apologize.

Fine.

What? She wasn't meant to say that. Her voice met my anger and raised it by a hundred.

Fine, Will. That's fine by me. Nice to see you can be so mature about it. I was going to suggest that you come over and talk to them about it. But obviously you've got far more important things to do, like hang out with your mates. So I'll leave you to it then.

Great, that would be great.

Another **Fine** and the phone exploded in my ear.

What was that all about? One minute we were talking normally and the next we'd broken up. So now I was left with a black eye, no girlfriend and a stupid assignment to write in six hours.

Welcome back, Will. Welcome back.

That bloody assignment!

It was now 3:17 p.m. and in the space of thirteen minutes I had managed to destroy all the things that had been good in my life. OK, so maybe I was exaggerating, but this was no time for restraint. I tried to imagine Andrews's face when I explained how my life had fallen apart in one phone call and that was why I couldn't complete the assignment I'd had roughly six weeks to do. But I knew the heartless bastard wouldn't have a bar of it. In fact he'd love it. It was exactly the ammunition he was waiting for, so I'd just have to put up with the black eye and wrecked love life 'cause I wasn't going to give him the satisfaction.

I stared at the computer screen. I typed in STEREOTYPES and spent half an hour changing the font and size. It was killing me.

I tried to go back over it step by step. I remembered Andrews going on about how I had to use the musical as a text. What the hell was that about? How could the musical be a bloody text? The guy was obviously having a laugh.

I played about ten games of solitaire in disgust and arrived back at the same blank screen. OK, so stereotypes in the musical . . . But the people in the musical were people, not bloody stereotypes.

I guess I could talk about the geeks. Fair enough, in the beginning I might have written them off as stereotypes, but when I got to know them they became individual kids. They were still a bit geeky, but when you got down to it they were only kids who happened to like playing their instrument and staying indoors more than team sports.

Then there was Zach, who didn't give a rat's whether he was a walking stereotype or not. And then when you got to know him he became a kid who understood stuff because he was smart and he'd had someone in his life walk out on him and he'd spent the last few years trying to understand that. So he kind of understood other people's stuff as well. He was different, but there was no way he was a stereotype. He was too bloody unique to be a stereotype.

Then there was Mark, who looked like the walking stereotype of the footy player but was gay, and smart. Chris was a mixture of types—the all-around nice guy, responsible jock who reckoned he'd never make it with the girls, but that's not all he was. Elizabeth was the same, I suppose. Miss I Will Succeed and Miss I've Got It All Together, but she had paranoid stress-heads for parents who wouldn't let her have a boyfriend unless he was a bloody saint.

Come to think of it, if you pulled apart anyone you knew, they could never be just a type because if you bothered to get beyond the bullshit you'd get to see them as individuals. It was as simple as that.

And me? Well, I was the walking stereotype in comparison to all those other people. But I don't reckon I knew it. I was walking around trying to be exactly what everyone expects an adolescent male to be.

I worked hard at being the guy who was always in trouble with the school but still kept his head above water. The kid who was well known for not doing outstandingly at school but who could pull it out when it counted. The kid who was popular with the popular crowd but still accepted by all. And you know, it was all crap.

I started to get some of my ideas down on the screen. It still didn't make total sense, but I think I was starting to get it. And even if I wasn't, Andrews was getting it anyway.

It was 9:35 p.m. My eyes were aching and my head hurt. But I went and got another glass of OJ and settled in for what was going to be a long night.

Special delivery

I walked in the school gates and patted my mate the statue on the head. It had been 1:04 a.m. when I'd shut down the computer and printed out the assignment. I was tired and sore but I was bloody happy to be rid of it. I walked over to the senior quad feeling that things were finally settling down. The boys had moved from hand-ball to playing touch footy with one of those little balls. It was a fairly disjointed game, though, because they'd stop whenever Danielli came out of his office.

I copped it as soon as they saw me.

Willo, mate. That's one to be proud of!

Jock was reaching his grubby mitts out toward my eye.

Does it hurt?

I pushed him and his hands away.

Back off, Jock, go put your fingers in your own eye.

Then Tim started. **So how's Elizabeth? She's hot, man!**

There was no way they were going to hear that sad story.

Yeah, she's great.

I just had to figure out a way of letting her know I still thought that.

Jock was looking at me really strangely. I looked at him as if to say **What?** and then it finally came to me. He wanted me to ask him about the girls.

So how about you, Jock? Any luck?

Funny you should ask, Willo, but there was a certain chorus girl who caught my eye. Mark said he'd get her number for me.

That's great, Jock. I turned to scan the quad. **So have you seen Mark?**

Nah, I don't think he's in yet.

I knew St. Andrew's well enough to know that things could get a bit messy for Mark, especially if the tuckshop boys started again. And not just that, what happened on Saturday night would be around the school by morning admin. But I reckoned he'd handle it. We'd handle it. Even Tim and Jock. I had to remember to ask Mark to invite me when he let them in on the fact that he was dead serious when he told the thugs that he was indeed a poofter.

Andrews's assignment was weighing as heavy as twenty bricks in my bag. The boys reminded me we didn't have English until tomorrow but I didn't care. Andrews had gone on and on about Monday and I was going to make a special delivery just so I could see his face. I went and knocked on the staff room door and asked for him.

Andrews came to the door carrying his trademark mug of coffee.

Nice eye.

I nodded. I wondered if the news had made it to the staff room.

I heard there was some trouble. Did things turn out OK?

And they reckon us kids are bad for gossip.

Yeah, sir, I think so. I haven't seen Mark yet, but yeah.

I didn't want to go on about it. After all, it was really Mark's business and he knew Andrews well enough to tell him himself if he wanted to.

I reached into my bag.

Sir, I wanted to give you this.

I handed him the assignment. I wish I could have taken a picture of his face, he was so shocked.

But, Will, we don't have English today.

I know that now, sir. But did you know that, sir?

Whatever it takes, Will. Whatever it takes. We called a truce, remember?

Yeah, I remembered, but would he? I thought for a moment about telling him that I could see now how me, the musical and the special assignment were all part of his tough-love policy, but I wanted to suss out how that truce went first.

The best I could do was nod in acknowledgment.

I'll see you in English, sir.

And I walked away feeling that for the first time in ages I'd nailed *him*.

Something else

I came home that afternoon and for the first time in two months had nothing to do or nothing I should be doing but didn't want to do. It should have felt great but it didn't. I still *felt* like there was something I had to do. Something big.

I was so wound up I even went out and worked in the veggie patch voluntarily. As I pulled up all the crap that had grown since Mum had her last clean-out, I started to think about Elizabeth. I had to sort things out with her. I knew she was too special to lose, I just wasn't sure how to go about it. Sure, every time I thought of her father's handshake after the musical I broke into a cold sweat, but considering I could still barely see out of my left eye, I'd had worse.

As I picked some produce for the latest Patricia Armstrong extravaganza, I surveyed the veggie patch and for a couple of minutes I stopped stressing. It looked good. It was Mum's and my first combined project and to tell you the truth I was proud of it. I was proud of me and Mum and it. And I know Dad would have been too.

I came in to find Mum setting the table for dinner like we used to. Since the success of the Middle Eastern feast she'd fallen back into it. I washed the veggies and looked around for something else to do. There wasn't anything, so I started a lap of the house trying to figure the best strategy to use with the Zefferellis. After twenty laps Mum freaked. She told me to either sit down and watch telly or go and walk around my own room and stop annoying her until dinner was ready.

I stopped lapping the house and started lapping the lounge room. As I lapped, the phone beamed out like a two-dollar shop's bad flashing neon sign. The phone was the answer. The only thing for it was to ring the Zefferellis and leave a message. But I knew it couldn't be on Elizabeth's phone because the parents had to hear it. It had to be on the landline.

I made eight attempts and hung up each time. Finally on the ninth try I did it. I sounded like a complete loser, but I carried on about how I was really sorry about the other night and that it was an exceptional case and how I didn't go around bashing everyone I met. Well, something like that anyway. I'd tackle Elizabeth tomorrow. She'd have to rate the fact that I left myself right open with the landline message, wouldn't she?

Mum called me to have dinner. I put the posh serviette on my lap before Mum had a go at me and knew I'd played the Elizabeth and parents thing just right. But I still felt wound up. I figured food might fix it and dug into the veggie-patch feast. I looked across the table and watched Mum as she lit the candles.

We spent dinner talking about Andrews, the assignment, the veggie patch and stuff. I asked if she'd mind if I invited Zach over for dinner and she suggested I ask both the Cohens. I nearly choked on the mixed lettuce salad.

Midnight

Three hours of bad television didn't help. Around 10:30 I said goodnight to Mum and went to my room. I played my guitar, downloaded some music and was still completely wired. What was wrong with me? Mum's Mr. Cohen invite wasn't worth stressing over, there was no English assignment hanging over me and Andrews was off my back—for the moment anyway. I'd rung the Zefferellis.

But my gut was still churning.

I lay back on the pillow and tried to clear my brain. I thought about Mum and dinner tonight. She seemed so much happier, more like she used to be . . . freer. I know she was still in the *I have the best son in the world* mood because of the musical, but it wasn't just that. Talking in the kitchen, talking about Dad had helped us talk more about everything.

Thinking about that conversation pushed my gut into overdrive. The feeling was familiar, but this time I knew I didn't have to block it out.

I curled myself up in a ball. The screen and slide show projector started again and images came thick and fast—but this time I made myself watch them, made myself remember each moment, each time. It finished on a photo of Dad looking straight into the camera, straight out to me. I was surprised by how wet the pillowcase was as I moved my head to get a better look. I sat up cautiously, nervously, but this time I didn't want him to go. . . .

I tried to speak but nothing came out.

I tried again and found the words.

Hey, Dad. Hey, Dad, it's me, Will. . . .

A Note on Australian Football Codes

Firstly, I find it incredibly ironic and just plain funny that I'm providing a guide to Australian football codes, because if you ask anyone in my life—my family, my friends, the boys I teach—they can all attest to the fact that I know nothing about any of the technical aspects of the games. Football, to me, whatever the code, means men chasing one another around a field in pursuit of a particular-shaped ball so it can be either kicked through goalposts or pounded down over a line as many times as possible in order to score as many points as possible.

So the technical aspects of the games mean not a lot to me but, from observing the different men and boys in my world, I am fascinated by how the supporting and/or playing of particular codes of football in Australia often defines what type of male you are: your class, your level of testosterone, your ethnicity, your level of education, your intelligence, your sexuality, what part of the country you live in and even what suburb.

In Will's mind, Mark can't be gay because he plays rugby union. Mark also comes from Victoria, which means he should be playing Australian rules football, but because he went to private school, he plays union. In his friend's mind, Will shouldn't be playing soccer because he isn't Australian European or a "wog," and soccer is thought to be "soft" in comparison to the other codes. And Jock should be playing league because, well, quite frankly, he is not very bright.

So what on earth is the difference between AFL, rugby union, rugby league and soccer? If I was to ask a league supporter to define "league," or a union player to define "union" or an Australian rules supporter to define "AFL," the rivalry between the codes would emerge. It seems that somehow each of the codes is defined in opposition to or with some reference to the other codes.

As you may know, the European colonization of Australia was carried out by the British, and along with them came their particular way of doing things, including their schooling system. They have a two-tiered system—private and state. Private schools are often considered elite schools, and state schools are primarily government-funded schools for everyone else. Rugby union was always played in the elite schools and, therefore, was always considered the "gentleman's game." It did not turn professional until the 1990s. Rugby league has always been played in the state schools and has always had a strong connection to the working class.

Rugby was born at the Rugby School in England. There was only "rugby" at this stage. The sport's popularity grew and spread to the general public. Competitions were organized and clubs were created initially by men of the "ruling classes." In the north of England, club membership was open to all classes, and the northern clubs became the strongest in England. However, matches were held on Saturdays, which was problematic for working-class men, who had to work that day. This was especially true for many northern English men who were miners. Players from the upper classes did not have to worry about this restriction.

Many of the clubs lost good men to this restriction, so it was decided that the players could be paid for their time. It was this decision that brought about a split in the code. The Rugby Football Union tried to enforce the nonpayment of players, which meant that working-class men would be excluded from participation, thus keeping rugby the "gentleman's game." This affected the northern rugby clubs more than those in the south, so they broke away, forming their own Northern Rugby Union, which later became known as rugby league.

Australian rules football originated in Victoria, where they wanted to devise a game to help cricketers keep fit during the winter. Even though there is huge support for the Sydney Swans, New South Wales, where Will lives, is still pretty much a league state. Western Australia, South Australia and Victoria are known as Aussie rules states.

I have been told, in no uncertain terms, by many football fanatics that most readers who are interested would simply want to know the mechanics of the game. So for all you lovers of games played with the leather ball, here they are:

Rugby Union

- Aim is to score as many tries as possible.
- 5 points for a try.
- 2 points for a conversion.
- 3 points for a penalty goal.
- Tackles allowed—unlimited. The ball changes only if there has been a mistake/offense or if the ball goes out of play.
- When a tackle occurs, rucks and mauls occur as well. Continuous play with constant competition for the ball.
- Unlimited rucks (when everyone jumps on one another).
- When the ball goes over the sideline into touch, there is a lineout.

Rugby League

- Aim is to score more tries than the opposition.
- 4 points for a try.
- 2 points for a conversion.
- Sets of six tackles, then the other team is given the ball, unless a try has been scored.
- The tackled player "plays the ball" (rolls it under their legs, thus play stops).
- When the ball goes over the sideline into touch, there is no lineout.

AFL

- Field is a circle, not a rectangle.
- Four goalposts rather than two.
- There are no tries, only goals and behinds.
- A "goal" is when a player kicks the ball between the two center posts— 6 points.
- A "behind" is when the ball does not go through the goalposts but goes through the smaller posts on either side of the main goalposts—1 point.
- You are not allowed to throw the ball, you have to "hand the ball," which means resting the ball in one hand and punching it with the other.

Soccer

- You guys know the deal here.

Acknowledgments

To Zac, James and Alex, who were the first young people to meet Will and who continued to offer support throughout the journey.

To the boys from Holy Cross, who either unwittingly provided inspiration or knowingly shared great wisdom—specifically Ben Pullen, Simon Janda, Doug Evans, Andrew Gallagher.

To the OLSH girls, who offered the much-needed girls' perspective: Stephanie, Jamie, Patrice.

To Eva Mills, Zoe Walton, Julia Stiles, Jenny Simons, Helen Young, Tony North, James Worner, Peter Duffy, Bec Smith, Felicity Castagna, Aaron Macdonald, Melina Marchetta, Melissa Williams, Joanna Farrell, Karen Oxley, John Marsden's Tye Estate Writers' Conference, Peter and Lynn and all the folks from Varuna. Thanks for sharing your expertise, skills and time.

To Timothy McGarry, who read every draft and gave invaluable feedback whilst offering unfailing belief and support.

To the Cathedral boys: Victor for his feedback and my current Year 10 and 11 English classes.

To my beautiful family of friends, thank you for your support and love—always.